between

The Spiral Series
Book One

lisa silverthorne

BETWEEN

Book 1: The Spiral Series

Step into the dark and haunting world of the **Between**, where Heather Billot is plunged into a shadowy realm of darkness and despair after committing suicide. In this bleak landscape, soulstalkers roam the skies and Death herself hunts down those who have escaped her grasp. Trapped and alone, Heather must find the strength to navigate this dangerous place and forge a path between life and death.

But when she meets the enigmatic Ross Shepherd, a spark ignites between them and they embark on a journey to escape this forgotten world together. Faced with unimaginable challenges and haunted by their pasts, Heather and Ross must confront their fears and fight to overcome the shadows that threaten to consume them. A gripping tale of love and resilience in the face of overwhelming darkness.

SUICIDE IS PERMANENT

Trigger Warning: This work of fiction is about suicide and its aftermath. Suicide isn't a solution. It won't fix anything.

Suicide is **permanent**. It isn't romantic. It can't be undone. It doesn't resolve your pain. Every person that jumped off the Golden Gate bridge and lived said that they regretted their decision the moment they stepped off the bridge. But it was too late.

- **TEXT or CALL 988** for help
- **TELL** someone
- **ASK** for help
- **REACH OUT** no matter how much it hurts

There are ways to fix what seems unfixable. **You are worth fighting for** no matter how much it hurts or how much you think you don't matter. **You DO matter**. Your light is unique. Without it, the world's entire spectrum darkens.

If you feel suicidal: Text or Call 988
Because You Matter

Novels by Lisa Silverthorne

Standalones:

ISABEL'S TEARS

LANDFALL

PACIFIC BLUE TATTOO

BEAUTY: CAPTURED AND FRAMED

A Game of Lost Souls series:

THE CINDERELLA HOUR

THE PRINCE CHARMING HOUR

THE EVER AFTER HOUR

THE FALLEN HEARTS SEASON

THE RISING SPIRITS SEASON

THE ETERNAL SOULS SEASON

THE ROYAL WEDDING HOUR

THE HEAVENLY HONEYMOON HOUR

THE DIVINE NEWLYWEDS SHOW

THE CELESTIAL COUPLES SHOW

The Spiral series:

BETWEEN

REPRISE

(***releases 7/30/23***)

SHORT STORY COLLECTIONS

THE SOUND OF ANGELS

THE MAGIC OF ORDINARY THINGS

one

. . .

HEATHER BILLOT HUNCHED over her phone, thumbs flying across the screen, saying goodbye to her life.

Instagram—September 8, 2022

"Two years is enough time to get over anything. Any longer and you're an attention whore."

Great quote, Carly! Can't say it to my face, but you have no problem saying it in a sketchy TikTok video for everyone else to see.

Along with these other great Snaps:

"She's too self-absorbed."

"She just brings everyone down."

"I won't hang out with her if she's gonna be all sad and cringe all the time."

"Coz they make pills for that."

We've been friends since second grade. Too bad your maturity level never reached third grade.

Depression is a dirty little secret most of us have to hide. None of my friends want to hear it, but this is my page and my rules. My friend Marta says it makes her uncomfortable. She says I should be stronger. I should stop thinking about it all the time. Think good thoughts. Smile more.

Wow, why didn't I think of that, Marta? Because if I really wanted to, I could just snap out of it. I could just choose not to feel depressed. Like it's a choice I make every morning. Should I wear the red hoodie or my depression today? I'll put on the depression. It looks so much better with my jeans.

Ash and Molly are the last ones listening.

Carly stopped listening a long time ago. She'd rather post rants about me on TikTok from her Stanford dorm than talk to me like the friends we used to be. Or tell me how I'm not the only person who's lost someone close. How she's had a lot of loss in her life, too, so I should think about someone else for a change.

You're right, Carly. Who can forget the agony you suffered when Eric said no to prom—because you asked him the day before. You summoned *amazing* courage ~~Xanax~~ to go with Devon instead. And the horror of that last-minute dress search! It just *had* to match Devon's tux. So much pain and loss! You gave up...your...(bites lip) Dream Dress™. But your strength ~~Valium~~ got you through that horrible, horrible ordeal and made you an expert on loss and grieving.

I just hope that you have better friends around you when you lose a parent. Or the last person in your life that gave a damn about you. So, you never understand what it feels like to be completely alone.

The meds just numbed my brain until I wasn't me anymore.

Senior year was supposed to be the best year of my life.

But I spent it watching my mom, my best friend in the world, shrivel up and blow away from breast cancer.

Prom night? I spent it—and nine hours—in ICU saying goodbye to her. She's been gone two years now and I still feel lost and angry, Carly. So, I stopped taking the meds. There I go being selfish again. But enough about me.

Ash, I've always looked up to you. You always encouraged me and always listened. You stood up for me senior year when those girls shoved me into my locker every afternoon and posted the videos on TikTok. Thanks for seeing the best in me, Ash, especially when I couldn't. I'll miss you most.

The pain has seeped into every corner and crevice until it's smothered the best parts of me. I'm tired of making everyone feel uncomfortable, tired of being dragged for something I can't control. Tired of being alone.

Tired.

Coz I can't just snap out of it or choose to feel better.

I can't just think good thoughts and have it all go away. So, Molly and I are rolling off somewhere new. Going on holiday. And this is the last time you'll hear me. Use the word, depression.

The Seattle waterfront café was quiet except for the whoosh of steamed milk roiling from the nearby espresso machine and soft mumbled conversations filling the small, bright yellow space overlooking Elliott Bay. Warm scent of fresh-brewed coffee mixed with the remnant smell of chocolate from her empty large mocha, whip cream crusting the paper cup's lip. The Orca Café overlooked the steely bay in all its autumn greyness, sunlight absent as she posted her final entry on Instagram.

Her friends and frenemies would find it whenever. Even if they read it now, it wouldn't change anything.

A strange peace fell over her as she stood up, adjusting her white hoodie and olive cargo pants, and dropped her phone into one of the numerous gaping cargo pockets. She picked up her sunset orange backpack, filled with textbooks she no longer needed, and plodded toward the counter.

One last thing to do.

"Hey, Heather," said Jimmy Girard, the tall, lanky café owner who looked tired and stressed in his wrinkled blue jean shirt and faded grey t-shirt that with Orca Café in distressed, blocky white script. "How're classes?"

"Fine, Jimmy," she replied, pulling a worn, black wallet out of her back pocket.

Her silicone pink breast cancer bracelet caught on her hoodie sleeve as she slid out a twenty. It was all she had left after quitting her job at Safeway this morning. She dropped it in the charity box raising money for a no-kill shelter. She didn't need money anymore.

"No blueberry muffin for the road?" he asked.

No, just one good-bye post. She shook her head. "Maybe tomorrow."

There weren't any tomorrows left, but Jimmy didn't know that yet.

At the café, there wasn't anyone—besides Jimmy—that might see her post and try to change her mind.

Or tell her to just smile more and think happy thoughts.

Jimmy squinted at her as she slid her wallet back into her back pocket. His short, brown hair, sprinkled grey at the temples, looked stiff and spiky with gel, lines etched a little deeper in his face today. Like a shadowed charcoal drawing.

"You okay?" he asked, eyebrows pressed into hard lines over his dark blue eyes, offering her a strained smile. "You look kind of down."

Heather shrugged. "I'm good, Jimmy."

She reached into her backpack and slid out a small, white stuffed bear with sparkly fur, a frayed red ribbon around his neck, and black eyes that stared straight ahead. A small, stuffed, red velvet heart dangled from the ribbon. Mom had given her Charles on Valentine's

Day the year before she got sick. The year before everything went to hell.

Heather had been fourteen, ready to take on the world. Until her mom's battle with breast cancer began. For six years, her mom fought it with everything she had, enduring endless rounds of chemo and radiation and surgeries. Heather fought alongside her, crying with her when her hair fell out in clumps, shaving off her own hair to match, and buying wild, brightly colored scarves to cover her mom's balding head.

Celebrating remissions with strawberry banana smoothies, silly music, and get-togethers with Mom's best friends. Lying beside her in the hospice bed, holding her as her last gasping breaths faded into silence.

At twenty, Heather felt shattered. Haunted by the moment when life had left her mom's warm hazel eyes. All that strength and light and love just gone in an instant. Like a switch being thrown. Even now, it was all she saw when she closed her eyes.

Heather's relationship with her dad was little more than a card at Christmas, a card for her birthday, and the occasional phone call. When he was in the mood to talk—a rare event. She hadn't seen him since the funeral. He was too busy with his four-year-old twins and second wife in Boston. She barely remembered him being part of the family. It had been only her and her mom since Heather was six and dad left.

"Jimmy, I need to find a good home for Charles here," she said and set the white bear on the counter beside wrapped slices of hazelnut biscotti, bars of lavender Dagoba chocolate, and half a dozen purple travel mugs with Orca Café printed on them. "I'd like your daughter, Emily to have him."

Jimmy frowned, squinting at her with sudden concern as he picked up the small, white bear. "You sure, Heather? He looks kind of special."

Heather nodded. He'd meant the world to her once, but she couldn't look at him now.

As long as her mother was beating the cancer, he'd had meaning, but now that she was gone, he was just an empty-eyed knickknack that brought back the painful memory of her empty eyes and that horrible hospice bed. Smell of sweat and urine and bleach that she couldn't completely erase.

Charles couldn't bring her back again.

Besides, she was leaving, too. And she couldn't take him with her this time.

"I'm sure," she said, offering Jimmy her best *it's cool* smile.

"Emily will love him, Heather, thanks," said Jimmy, his dark blue eyes studying her a moment or two, like he was trying to see under her thick fall of warm brown hair that covered one eye.

"Thanks," she said and forced a smile, her voice catching in her throat as she stared at the little bear a moment.

Her eyes stung as Charles stared vacantly past her. Like she'd already left. Like she wasn't even there. Like Marta and Carly. Sometimes Ashley.

Goodbye, little guy. Take care of yourself.

"Seeya around, Jimmy."

With a wave, she turned away from Charles and Jimmy. Out into the cool air and sharp wind.

She hefted the worn orange backpack higher onto her shoulder and trudged through the afternoon greyness along Alaskan Way, the air smelling crisp and salty. With shoulders hunched and her gaze on her feet, she plodded onto Colman Dock and into the ferry terminal burgeoning with people and noise and routine.

After buying a walk-on, she waited until the Bainbridge Island ferry began boarding, the *Wenatchee* white and pristine against the steely Puget Sound waters, and drifted into the line of passengers shuffling aboard.

She stood outside, body stiff against the winds buffeting the bow of the ferry as she remembered the island across the bay where she and her mom used to live. Where she'd made the daily crossing over to Seattle to catch the bus up to North Seattle Community College.

When things felt normal. When remission felt possible. When some shred of hope remained like the last thin, warm rays of summer.

She'd wanted to be an EMT once. Maybe a doctor? Until she buried her mother. Nothing seemed important after that. Worth doing.

The *Wenatchee* droned away from the dock, Elliott Bay's deep teal waters churning a frothy glass-green and white as the chilly wind rose sharp around her. She wrapped her arms around her middle, the air growing cold as she thought about Charles, about the Molly in her bag, the Instagram post she'd just made.

Tourists with fanny packs and white sneakers huddled like pigeons outside along the railing, windbreakers fluttering, cameras strung around their necks like scarves as they filmed the Space Needle, the skyline, and each other laughing and posing. Living. Loving. The air smelled almost sweet, tinged with salt.

She remembered happier times on the ferry with Marta and Ash, giggling and goofing off along the decks. Mom, frail and silent, in a booth against the picture windows, tie-dyed scarf around her head, and a forced smile on her face as she tried to hide the chemotherapy's exhaustion. And damage. It went deep, destroying slowly, killing the good along with the bad. More damage than that tie-dyed scarf could ever hide.

In forty-seven minutes, Heather was across the bay and striding through the Bainbridge Island ferry terminal, hurrying around people toward the waterfront. Already, her phone was blowing up in her pocket, vibrating non-stop.

She slid out the phone.

Someone kept calling. Dozens of texts from Ash rolled across the screen.

She dropped the phone back in her pocket. She wouldn't answer or read any of the texts. Not now. Everything had been said already. Nothing in those texts or calls would change anything.

She glanced up at the overcast sky. It would get dark early. Just as well.

Crunching through sea grass and sand, Heather hiked along the shore, gazing at the houses that edged the water. Looking for her old house.

A deep blue craftsman-style house that had been painted a deep somber grey. Like it had been mourning its old family and the life that had lit up its walls with warm gold light. Dark now. Curtains drawn.

She stopped on a little tidal flat near the house and hunched down on the rocky beach below it. When the tide came in, most of this tidal flat would be submerged again.

She checked her digital watch, phone still pulsating—almost like a heartbeat.

Six seventeen. In two hours, it would be dark.

Heather slid onto the pebbled beach and leaned against the rock, phone vibrating desperately as she returned it to her pocket. She hugged her backpack and stared at her black Converse high-tops, waiting for darkness. Waiting for the phone to stop shuddering in her pocket.

Waiting for high tide.

At eight nineteen P.M., the night getting colder, Heather unzipped her backpack and swallowed a big rainbow handful of Molly, washing down the pills with a frosty raspberry wine cooler that she'd saved from a party.

She stretched out in the reedy sea grass surrounding the pebbled beach, whisper of the Puget Sound calling her name. Closing her eyes, she pretended it was Mom's voice in the wind, on the waves.

Waiting for her.

The steady rhythm of the Puget Sound's currents lapped at the shore, intensifying the ecstasy high. It rolled hard through her body now, splinters of joy piercing the consuming darkness, the majestic silence that drew her down toward the earth. She laid her head on her backpack, looking up at the clouds (*was that the face of God?*) and finished the wine cooler.

Waiting for the end.

Time trickled away, her breath ragged against the waves of momentary joy that masked her pain in little icy gasps until finally, the world soon tipped over and set everything off balance.

As the night darkened, she lost consciousness, heart rushing, temperature soaring.

With the continuous flutter and rush of cold sea water comforting her, like the lost sound of her mom's voice, Heather left this world.

two

. . .

HEATHER OPENED HER EYES. In another place.

A strange ashen haze hung over stormy skies. The Puget Sound was gone. She jolted up from tall, billowy grey grasses as a sharp breeze fanned over the ground. Wind whispered across her body as she stared at a forbidding forest of massive, dark, twisted trees all around her. Except for the sea of tall grasses fanning across a windswept prairie behind her.

The cool air smelled like dirty rain in dusk's dull light, fog collecting on the forest floor, hanging like specters. No lights shone in the fading daylight. No sounds of planes overhead or cars rumbling along the interstates. No mournful blast of the ferry's horn. Only the hiss of wind whispered above the rapid hush of her own breath.

Where was this dark place? Was it hell? A crazy Molly-infused hallucination?

Or something much darker?

She'd never been religious and didn't believe in eternal damnation, especially for people in more pain than they could bear. But this place bore little resemblance to the mystical Washington

State forests or bay shores that she knew. Or anything else from the world she'd left behind.

The colors were...wrong. Washed out. Shadowy. Unnatural.

For so many months, her world had squeezed her into ever tighter spaces, growing darker and colder until she couldn't take the strain, couldn't blunt the raw-edged pain any longer. Even now, it gouged her heart, a constant ache that death hadn't soothed.

Right or wrong made no difference now.

She was—here...wherever *here* was. She wasn't sure and it didn't look like anything she'd imagined.

She huddled in the cold grass, shivering as tears threaded down her face. She felt so far away now, more lost than she'd ever felt before. Without even Charles, her little white bear, to comfort her.

And this was so much worse than anything she'd imagined.

Hadn't she just died? Left behind all the bad stuff? Wasn't that what happened when you killed yourself? Wasn't all the bad stuff supposed to stop?

Her head was spinning now. This wasn't what was supposed to happen! Now, she was lost in some surreal landscape, still stuck inside her own head with all the pain and memories she'd tried so hard to escape. Only worse.

How did killing herself make everything worse?

A dark shadow fell across her as some huge, dark creature took flight in the indigo sky, beat of huge feathery black wings like great drums. Its tortured shriek tore across the sky.

Heather rose on her knees and crouched in the grass, cold fear pounding through her body.

What was that thing? What was it looking for?

To her right, tiny amber lights cascaded through massive, towering trees—like redwoods—flickering like fireflies against the grassy grey plains.

Moving toward her, she realized.

Across the swaying, charcoal grey grasses fanning around her, a haunting voice whispered her name and she froze. She didn't recognize the voice. It didn't even sound human.

"Hea–ther," the voice hissed in a taunting, drawn out singsong as the amber lights collected at the forest's edge, the threatening chorus fluttering across the grass. Leering. Mocking.

She started to stand, but froze when the great winged thing beat the air over her head and soared across the sky in a wide arc. The dark thing passed overhead again and her breath caught in her throat.

It had huge, ashen black wings, hawkish yellow eyes, and sharp features like a bird of prey, but it had a vague human form. Two arms and two legs. Like some sort of dark angel.

But the term angel didn't fit. At all. It wasn't protective.

It hunted.

The winged creature ascended into the sky, turning like a vulture in another wide circle above the treetops. Floating on the rush of wind.

A chill brushed her spine. Searching? No, stalking, she realized. Her?

She kept still as it banked over the distant, misty woods and turned back toward the tall smoky grasses.

What was this place between the world she'd left and the silence she craved?

She scanned the horizon and what lay beyond the swaying grey grass. She winced. A darker storm grey sky. More willowy grass billowed against the cool breeze that swept across the hilly landscape. In the distance, large black shapes loomed tall above the grasslands, obscured by a thick leaden haze that clung to the towering things. They looked like some sort of massive plant, tall with long, spindly soot-grey stalks and huge elongated and burgeoning blossoms that were bigger than basketballs. Like massive, unopened frosty grey tulips swaying in the wind. They lined the horizon like clusters of distant smoke stacks, billowing pollen in dusty clouds of smoke.

Was there a city in this place? Gathering places for people like her? What were those menacing plants? Guardians protecting a city or a gathering place?

The sight of the massive plants chilled her blood.

Heather glanced back at the gigantic ancient trees and surrounding forest as tiny amber lights trickled toward her, flowing in a river of light over the churning sea of grass.

Moving toward her.

Fireflies? Embers?

She watched the glow move in a definite path toward her.

Should she trust the lights? She didn't trust the winged creatures or those distant, terrifying plants? Her gut told her not to trust anything in this place.

She held her position as the amber lights danced through the reedy, whip-like grass blades. Some of the lights floated aloft, bobbing in the gritty dusk air and others sparkled along the ashen soil.

There were too many of them. Moving too fast!

Heather scrambled away from the haunting glimmers that pulsed steadily toward her, but her feet tangled in the grass and she fell.

As she rose on her elbows, a ghostly figure hovered above her. A woman. Translucent. Like smoke. With bone-white skin, wide-set pale lavender eyes, and a deadly smile. She was as cold as ice. Like a wraith.

"Who are you?" Heather demanded, skittering backward. "What is this place?"

"This isn't a place," the spirit woman said with a hiss, lights flickering closer. "This is the Between. Where light and dark collide, becoming shadow."

Above them, one of those dark, winged creatures turned another graceful circle as a mournful cry—human—echoed across the plains, sounding far away.

The dark thing shuddered then swerved toward the sound. It hovered above the sea of grass, waiting, listening for the sound again.

Its wings beat the air in a steady staccato rhythm until the cry, sounding weaker, more desperate, pierced the thick silence that hung over the rain-soaked grass. The heavy haze swallowed the sound as the dark winged thing spun in a tight circle and darted toward the noise.

"It's too late for that one," said the spirit woman. "We can't get there in time."

Heather cringed at the awful swooping sound, like a falcon diving for a mouse. In a moment, a shriek of agony like a dying rabbit echoed, and she recoiled, pressing her hands to her ears.

Finally, the dark thing rose into the storm-grey sky, wings beating frantically, heavily, the human silhouette unmistakable in its arms. She couldn't tell if it was a man or woman.

The human cried out again, a desperate, ragged cry that pierced the silence and trailed off into the distance.

"What does that even mean?" Heather demanded.

The spirit woman smiled with a nonchalant shrug at some poor soul just carried off by that monstrous winged thing. Her reaction was more like someone had taken the last bagel from the breakfast buffet than a human life being at stake.

Heather raged. That could have been her.

She scrambled backward from the spirit woman and struggled to her feet. Black Converses finally gained traction and she lurched forward, everything inside her screaming *run!*

Hide! Run from these winged monsters! Into the trees!

"No, wait!" the spirit woman shouted, her voice a harsh whisper as she turned to mist, tangling around Heather in smoky trails. "Soulstalkers hunt here. New arrivals aren't safe."

Tears stung Heather's eyes. She froze, staring out at the endless sea of chalky grass framed by dark woods and those hideous smoke stack-like giant plants. Stench of moldy, dead leaves clung to the cold, gritty wind as her gaze followed the curve of grasslands, trying to see where they stopped. But they went on forever, rolling over hills and valleys, unbroken as they disappeared into the distant haze. Only the dark woods behind her broke up the sea of grass.

If she ran across the unprotected grasslands, she'd be an easy target.

She shuddered. Those winged things would easily snatch her up and carry her off.

To where—to do what exactly? What was this place? Was she prey now?

The life she'd left behind had been so dark and empty, but right now, it was like living in a beachfront Caribbean condo compared to this place of fog and gloam and deadly winged shadows.

But it was too late.

She couldn't take any of it back. She didn't know the way back to her old life. She sighed. There was only this place now. And those awful dark winged creatures hunting people—like her.

Was this—this Between a place of retribution?

Had suicide been a mortal sin after all? The punishment of a vengeful god? Everything she'd ever believed screamed against that possibility.

Religion was only bits and pieces of ancient knowledge broken up and passed across thousands of years, through countless human hands, infinite translations, and endless interpretations. So much of it was cherry-picked to support someone else's current agenda.

But religion or spiritual, nothing she'd ever read or heard described this place.

All she knew for certain was her own heart and the constant need for leaps of faith. Trust. Which she'd done once, long ago. But when Mom died, she gave up on everything, including herself.

She hurt.

Deep, unhealed wounds and despite her efforts to go on alone, those injuries had festered, never fully healing. All the unanswered questions remained while the contradictions and the silence grew. The *whys* and *what ifs* just got too heavy to carry around one more day.

So, she stopped running. Stopped fighting. And gave in.

She gazed up at the sky, not caring if those dark things took her now. She was tired of hurting, tired of feeling, tired of being alone. And not even death had silenced it. She just wanted to sleep. Forever.

The amber lights flowed into a ring in the field of steely grey grass, surrounding her as the spirit woman entwined her smoky form around Heather's body, tendrils of smoke encircling her arms and shoulders.

"We've got to hurry," said the spirit woman above the whisper of wind across the grass. "Before they return to hunt. There are others out here that need to be guided into the woods."

"What are those things?" Heather asked, stepping out of the wispy smoke trails. She gestured at the spirit woman. "And what are you? Why should I care if they take me? Or you?"

"They're soulstalkers!" An angry edge sharpened the spirit woman's voice and angular features. "Controlled by Death, they hunt the lost and despairing in her name. The ones I shelter. These creatures aren't like the pale angels that sometimes fly across the skies, scouting for souls to save. Mostly, it's the soulstalkers."

"What happens to the ones they carry away?" Heather asked, watching the shadows recede on the horizon. "By these—soulstalkers or whatever you call them. Soul stalkers? Seriously?"

She wasn't sure she wanted to know any of this, but she needed to know the score and the sides. Before she was forced to choose one.

"Souls are carried away to the poppy fields," said the spirit woman. "To the final sleep. Forever. While the soulstalkers consume their soul essence to feed Death's power. And feed themselves. They're Death's scouts and hunters."

Heather recoiled. They ate human souls? "Scouts and hunters? Feasting on human souls? Wow…that's—that's monstrous."

A frown creased the spirit woman's smoky brow. "Their silhouettes look the same as the pale angels that sometimes travel these dusky skies and flit along the forest paths, so be careful. Being wrong can cost you eternity."

Heather sighed, pressing her hand to her forehead. Back on

Bainbridge Island, she'd wanted a forever sleep. Here, if she'd stood up sooner from these shadowy grey grasslands, she might have already been there instead of ending up in this painful *between* world.

"A forever sleep doesn't sound so bad," said Heather, her voice sounding small and weary.

Ghostly hands curved around Heather's arms and she felt a strange pressure against her skin. The spirit woman shook her head emphatically.

"To forever dream of what you can never have?" she asked. "To reach out in shadow and touch what might have been or what could be...and have it pass through your fingers? Forever? *That* sounds horrible to me."

Kind of like right now, Heather thought, wincing. That had been her life before she'd taken that ferry to Bainbridge Island one last time.

Mom's life had slipped through her fingers along with a place to live and any sense of security. Without her mom, she was completely alone and after two years of isolation and grief, she only wanted to leave, too. She saw no difference between what she faced now and the solitude of this final sleep.

Maybe these soulstalkers weren't monsters after all? Maybe they were her rescuers?

"Don't you understand?" the spirit woman demanded, her alabaster brow furrowing as a spark gleamed in her dusty blue eyes. "It doesn't have to be like that?"

"Doesn't it?" Heather snapped. "It's exactly what I left behind in Washington State."

"In the Now—perhaps," said the spirit woman with a nod.

Heather frowned. *The now?*

"I'll explain more later," the spirit woman continued. "In the meantime, understand that you're between, not dead. There's still a chance for you. But if you lie down in the fields of grey poppies, all of that hope is lost."

The word *hope* pierced Heather's chest in a raw, burning ache. She'd known as she'd rolled on too much Molly that everything was lost. She couldn't go back and change her mind. She'd accepted it, counted on it, washing down that last bitter pill with the tart taste of raspberries, knowing she couldn't stop it.

Was there a glimmer of hope left in this dark place? Was there a higher power out there? One that had created a place between life and death for the lost like her? Instead of damning them? Giving them—her—a chance to reclaim something, a chance to heal?

"A chance for me?" Heather whispered, her bottom lip quivering as she stared at the spirit woman.

The spirit woman nodded, almost a smile on her powdery lips. "There's always a chance in the Between. It's the battleground between life and death, where night and day become shadow, each one bleeding through the other. While the Human Spiral still spins, there is hope." The spirit woman reached out a feathery hand, smoky fingers like the kiss of wind against Heather's brow. "There's a chance to heal. To go on. But not if you give up...and there are a million ways to do that here. Be warned."

At last, the amber flickers crept out of the trees and into the fluttering grass toward her. Heather smiled. They were lanterns! Carried by people like her—that looked human.

Dressed in dark, billowy clothes, the air smelling like charcoal, the others stepped out of the forest to stand around Heather, glass lanterns held high. They had form and substance like her. She wanted to cry with relief.

Tiny, misty creatures like the spirit woman buzzed and darted around her head, carrying tiny yellow flames in their cupped hands. Almost like fairy lights.

"A new one from the void?" asked a lithe, willowy woman that paced around Heather, her lantern held high.

Her oblong face was sharp, angular, her nose and chin pointed, small brown eyes dull and narrow. She studied Heather. She looked maybe forty, tired face creased. Her long, brown hair was tied at her nape and she wore loose-fitting tan trousers and shadowy, draped fabrics that might have been a blouse.

A young guy moved beside her, dressed in the same shadowy clothes as the woman stepped forward. He didn't look much older than Heather with his ash blond hair, kind oval face, and strong jawline that tapered into the soft curve of his chin. His was tall and lean like a runner. His eyes were a bright hazel-gold despite the dusk, outer corners tilted slightly downward, giving him a sad, vulnerable look. The color almost matched the glow of the winking amber lights in the fields.

She felt her breath catch. He was like a warm summer night, all cicadas, starshine, and heat lightning. Especially when a smile lit his face, eyes turning firefly-bright as he met her curious stare. He nodded, jawline sharpening, laugh lines curving from his eyes and framing his cheeks. In his lingering glance, pain faded those lines. But as he held her gaze, empathy—and something else—smoldered there. Attraction? Connection?

"Lamarr, help me and Barb get her out of this..."

His voice trailed off as he stepped closer, staring into Heather's eyes, at her face. The corners of his mouth lifted into a smile and there was such wonder and mystery in the depth of those hazel-gold eyes.

In that moment, he was the first warmth she'd felt here. He was wool socks against cold tile. A crackling hearth on a cold winter night. Hot chocolate after a snowball fight. He was something she hadn't felt in a long time. If ever.

Was he like her, she wondered, here by his own hands? By suicide? Were the others?

He didn't look away from her as he motioned toward the dark-haired black man beside him. His voice was clear and velvety, like melted butter. It had a soothing resonance. Comforting not commanding.

"Right behind you, Ross," said the man called Lamarr, his voice deep and soothing.

"On it, Ross," Barb replied.

Heather smiled. His name was Ross.

"This place will soon be crawling with soulstalkers," said Ross, pointing toward the stormy sky. "And worse things." He fixed her with his intense gaze again. "I'm Ross Shepherd. What's your name?" His voice was soft and comforting, like a blanket warmed in the dryer.

"Heather Billot," she replied, her voice almost a whisper.

"Pretty name," he said. "Look, I know you're scared and confused, but it's gonna be okay. I promise."

His kind reassurance eased some of her explosive anxiety and fear, bringing it a notch or two underneath completely overwhelmed.

Lamarr was much shorter than Ross, about five foot nine. He was a little older, almost thirty maybe? He had a lean soccer player's build. His coarse black hair was shorn close to his scalp and he spoke with sort of an English accent. With a graceful sweep of his arm, Lamarr lifted his lantern over Heather's head, giving her a better look at everyone. His large, mahogany eyes were soft, framed with thick eyelashes. A smile curved across his dark skin, softening the pain that clung to his long, beautiful face.

He seemed so full of life. A bright light against all the dark and shadows.

Dozens of people and lanterns fanned out across the grasslands, more and more out in the fields as the greyness darkened.

"Worse things?" Heather asked Ross, still holding his gaze with her pleading green eyes. "What's worse than those soul-eating, flying soulstalkers?"

A deep sadness darkened Ross' large hazel-gold eyes. His ash blond hair looked washed out against his haunting, vibrant eyes. Like Lamarr, he seemed too full of life to be in this place.

"Avana's right," said Ross, laying his hand against Heather's arm. The deep heat of his touch startled her, sending warmth into the darkest corners. "This place is a battlefield. From the Heavens to the Nethercore, they fight for souls. Pale angels, soulstalkers.

Even Death walks these hills and woods. She commands the soulstalkers."

Heather frowned, shaking her head. "Why here and not the physical world?"

Ross sighed, brushing ash blond bangs out of his eyes. "If you're here, then you've cheated Death. She's relentless to escaped prey. Sends her soulstalkers after us." He glanced up at the sky and over his shoulder at the growing crowd of people and lanterns. "If they fail, she joins the hunt." He pointed at the black-winged things circling above the grasslands. As you can see, there's lots of prey. We need to get to safety. Now."

Avana, the spirit woman, slid between them, her smoky form tracing white, misty rings around Ross as she turned in a pirouette and encircled Lamarr.

"None of these humans are safe, Ross," said Avana in a loud voice above the rush of wind and rustle of grass. "Even you." She cleared her throat and turned to the growing crowd of people. "All of you, back to the woods! To the great tree! Hurry!"

Ross and Lamarr motioned Heather to follow them, lanterns held high. "You heard Avana," said Lamarr, his voice barely above a whisper.

Ross pointed to the path of flattened grass that disappeared into the woods. "This way," he motioned. "Everyone, stay close until we've reached the trees. We'll be on safer ground there—out of Death's sight."

Heather took a step toward Ross then stopped, frowning. "Please...tell me this place is just a bad dream." she said, almost pleading. "That I'm imagining all of this."

She hoped this was all a terrible dream and that any moment, she'd wake up back in the Orca Café, posting to Instagram on her phone, mocha in hand, Charles with his sparkling white fur beside her.

"I told you, Heather—it's the Between." Avana chanted as she spun into the air, smoke rings floating behind her. She twisted her hazy form around Ross again and then flitted into the air. "They're so slow at first, not understanding. Tell her again if you have to, but get her into the woods. Now!"

"You took your own life," said Ross. "This is where you go after that." He didn't look away from her face, his expression changing. Softening. Relaxing, she realized, even though they were in danger. "Wish it was a bad dream and you could just wake up." His voice was husky, distracted, but he didn't look away from her. "I'll—uh, make sure you're uh, safe though. We...just need to—to hurry."

She nodded.

He gently gripped her sleeve, tugging her toward him. "Heather, right?"

His kind eyes and warm cinnamon voice comforted her, made her feel safe. The warmth of his hand burned deep across her skin, deep in her chest, jumbling up all the fear and chaos swirling inside her. She felt a bond with him. Trusted him. Like she'd known him through a hundred lifetimes.

This time, she followed. Lamarr hurried beside her on the left.

"Another lost one to deal with," said an older Latino man walking behind them. "There are more arriving every day."

"You got here just like I did," Heather snapped. "Sorry, that was ungrateful. Thank you for helping me."

The man nodded. "It's okay. I felt the same way when I got here. But there are so many now—I fear for all of us."

"We're all lost," Ross said over his shoulder. He reached out and squeezed Heather's hand and she wanted to melt into the heat of his fingers. "This way," he said in a velvety tone, motioning her forward with his lantern.

Wings beat the air nearby. Swooping low across the meadows.

Everyone dropped to the ground, arms over their heads, hunkering low in the grass.

"They can sense our despair, our hopelessness," Ross said in half-whisper. "They hunt the ones that have given up...but they'll grab any of us if they can."

Wind rolled across the plains. Grasses swished. Distant beat of wings resonated through the darkening sky.

Heather knelt in the half-light, waiting for the flutter of wings to dissipate.

Only when silence returned to the sloping meadow did the others rise from the cold, misty grass. Heather followed.

"More will hunt with the dark," said Ross, leaning close to her. "We've got to hurry before we're swarmed."

Her body went cold and she froze. Swarmed?

"What about the others?" Heather asked. "Others that just got here like me?"

Ross sighed. "We'll pick up the search when it gets lighter. It's too dangerous until then. It's all we can do."

"There are pockets of forest like this one all through the Between," said Lamarr, still beside her. "Other groups like ours outside the Red City. They'll shelter new arrivals."

"The Red City?" she replied. There was a city here?

"The ones that survive the soulstalkers and don't stay in the woods end up in the Red City." Barb. From behind her.

"Why doesn't everyone live in this city?" she asked, turning to face them.

Lamarr and Barb laughed in that knowing way that made Heather feel naïve. Dumb. And annoyed.

"The Red City's controlled mostly by demons," said Ross. "There are some pale angels there too, but it's too crowded and dangerous for my taste."

Lamarr nodded, leaning closer. "I hear it's a big, dangerous cesspool. Four quarters and a no man's land in the center."

Barb poked Ross' back. "Ross has been there. Tell us about the Red City, Ross!"

Lamarr's mahogany eyes grew wide. "You've been there?"

Ross nodded. A haunted look touched his eyes as he stared into the growing dark, his face pinched. The memory looked painful. "Once. While looking for Jessie."

"What's it like?" Lamarr demanded, shaking Ross' shoulder.

Ross shrugged, staring down at his hands. "Pale Quarter's small but safe, run by pale angels. Void Quarter is a battlefield. Shadow Quarter's where Death has reach. Where her highest order soulstalkers gather, not the field feeders like here. Red Quarter's controlled by demons. And all of them battle for souls. Like they're poker chips."

Heather shook her head, recoiling. Red City sounded terrifying. Like the worst crime-ridden city she could image. Times one hundred. Where souls were constantly hunted. This place in the woods didn't sound much better though.

Ross offered her a reassuring smile. "But in the city center, there's a sizeable circle of no man's land. Protected. They call it Amity. People like us are in charge. They're trying to make it into a real haven—as much as any place in the Between can be. Getting there is too dangerous though. Have to cross soulstalker warrens and hunting grounds." He sucked in a pained breath, sighing. "And the poppy fields."

"These pale angels," said Heather. "Why do they call them that?"

His smile became a smirk. "Because they don't have halos like other angels, so they're literally a pale light against regular angels. Not sure if they lost their halos or just never had them. One of the great unsolved mysteries of our woodland refuge."

"Seeing a pale angel is so rare, Ross," said Barb. "Afraid that mystery will never be solved."

"Heaven doesn't care enough about suicides to send real angels," Lamarr said in a quiet voice. "Our souls are just shadows compared to everyone else's souls."

Ross tugged on Heather's sleeve. "Let's move faster," he said.

She lurched forward, hurrying beside him as he led the way into the woods. She watched the sky for those hideous winged things as the haze of amber lights trickled toward the woods ahead.

Thick, gnarled tree trunks spiraled on the horizon, towering high into the charcoal sky, branches forming canopies in the ashen half-dark. Unlike the soulstalkers that cast only darkness, the branches cast no shadows. There was no sun, just an eerie half-light, almost an afterglow. Like the last thin, gleaming flicker of a burned-out light bulb. The massive trees glowed from within, thick swaths of amber light pouring through the dark forest. As she got closer, she realized that the light came from windows and doors built into the tree trunks. Inside them.

A refuge to escape from all this darkness.

The air smelled warmer now, like the scent of a roaring campfire. Almost savory with tomatoes and garlic. Heather almost expected to see a writhing bonfire with burning wood and a sputtering stew pot, but only trees and that strange wash of amber light penetrated the blanket of nightfall. But not its silence. No crickets chirped or cicadas chirred. No bird trills. No sounds of airplanes or cars. Just heavy, uninterrupted silence. And wind hissing through branches.

Still, this little clearing felt safe. Insulated from the terrors roaming the quiet and the dark. The clearing felt more alive somehow, reedy glow like firefly beacons, guiding the lost back to camp for the night. Away from the soulstalkers. She shuddered.

And those poppy fields.

Heather leaned close to Ross. "Don't the soulstalkers see your lights?" she whispered.

He shook his head. "They hunt our despair, not our lights. That's what they feed on. Usually anyway. The lights, our chatter—it means nothing to them. They hunt the ones that have given up. But if they're hungry enough, they wouldn't hesitate to pluck people from ours and other groups. Despair's a beacon, so be careful with your thoughts."

Dark and bare, the gnarled tree branches clacked in the breeze, the wind a lament as it swirled past. Avana rushed ahead of them toward another clearing with a ring of massive trees, larger than any trees Heather had ever seen, including redwoods.

Lights rushed ahead, illuminating tree trunks as the grey skies darkened. Was it nightfall?

Heather shivered. It was so dark and cold here, so much darker and colder than she'd ever imagined possible. What had she done? How would she get out of here? Was there anything beyond this cold, desolate place? She felt so far away from anything familiar and safe.

Maybe she should have let those winged things carry her off?

"Does it ever get light here?" Heather asked.

The corners of Ross' mouth lifted, quirking into a brief smile. He nodded. "Morning will come. It's mostly dusk—and night—in the Between, but there is a morning." He sighed and stared at the horizon for a moment. "It's hard to take at first."

Barb, the brown-haired woman with angular features moved toward a massive tree that seemed as wide as a city block and several stories tall. Its trunk towered into the darkening sky, black leafy branches splayed in the deepening indigo. No stars sprinkled the sky. No moon lit the way.

Lights flickered from windows carved into the great trunk as Barb pressed her hand against the bark. A door popped open and she ducked inside, others following behind her. As the little fairy lights fluttered inside, Ross cupped his hand ever so lightly around Heather's elbow.

"We're safe in here," he said in a reassuring tone. "With the smoke people—that's what us humans call them. They're the tiny lights you see—and Avana. They can change their size at will and go from solid to smoke in moments. They live in these forests and from what I can tell, the soulstalkers keep their distance from them. As does Death. Usually. Not sure why."

He held open the door in one hand, standing just over six feet tall to Heather's five feet six frame. She hadn't realized he was that tall until now. He motioned her inside and she ducked under his arm as Avana swept past her, growing solid as she passed.

"Lamarr, make sure tonight's watch is covered," said Ross.

"Taken care of," said Lamarr. "Barb's up first. Then Javier."

Heather took a few steps into the great tree and stopped, staring at dozens of humans dressed like Ross who stood beside her now. He wore folds of feathery fabric draped in muted greys and charcoals over loose dark pants. She glanced at her own clothes. They had changed in the dusk, becoming draped folds of dark grey fabric over loose charcoal pants. But her familiar, black Converse high-tops made her smile. Probably an illusion, but they were a small comfort here.

Ahead, two sets of wooden stairs wound up into the huge tree. The air smelled like fresh-cut wood and sweet grass as she took tentative steps into the structure. Polished dark woods formed banisters and floorboards, a fireplace carved into the far wall, trickling fragrant cedar smoke into the perpetual dusk outside.

People milled about, looking dazed as they went about day-to-day activities: cooking, sweeping, and other chores. Things they did when they were still alive. Some of them weren't human. They were the smoke people like Avana, some appearing in ghostly form and others taking on a more solid, almost human-like form. The rest seemed as real and as human as Heather.

"Why are they pretending to eat and drink? And clean?" Heather asked Ross, shaking her head. "It makes no sense."

Ross nodded. "It won't for some time. We do a lot of things here that have no purpose, just small comforts. Familiar routines. There isn't any hunger or need for sleep. It's all kind of frozen here. But some create routines for themselves—to keep from losing their minds." He sighed. "If I'd known about this place, I'd have kept my hand off that trigger."

Heather turned to stare at him. "You killed yourself?"

She sighed, wanting to kick herself. A stupid question. Of course, he had! Every human in this place killed themselves.

He nodded. "We all did," he said. "Like you. That's what got us here." His gaze fell to the floor, the hollow glow of the fireplace dancing across the shiny floorboards. "Even now, the pain haunts me," he said, his voice almost cracking. "But it's better than the alternative, I guess. A good reminder."

"Is it?" Heather asked. "If you're still in pain, then what's the point? Eternal torment? Minus the flames?"

Ross made a sour face. "There's no such thing as a place of eternal torment that I've seen or heard mentioned. Except for right here." He pressed two fingers against his forehead. "This is your eternal torment. Spending forever inside your own head with no hope of climbing out again."

He was right. She'd spent the last years of her life trapped in that dark place and now, the rest would be spent here.

Just how long was forever anyway?

Heather motioned toward the door. "Then why not just let those soulstalkers take you?"

Ross shook his head. "Because of the Spiral," he said, his voice softer now, warm hazel-gold eyes sparking.

She felt so drawn to him. If she'd met him in Seattle, on the pier, on a ferry, she would have gone out of her way to meet him. Talk to him. Did he feel the same attraction she felt? It made her chest ache. Maybe if she'd met him before, she wouldn't be here now? For two years, she'd felt disconnected from everyone and everything. That one, single link might have been the lifeline that saved her.

"What's the Spiral?" she asked.

Avana was beside her now, her smoky form becoming opaque and pale as she studied Heather with unblinking eyes. Diaphanous white fabric draped Avana's thin body like swaths of silk.

"Yes, tell her about the Spiral, Ross," said Avana in an acerbic tone, grinning at him.

Ross and Barb glared at Avana along with the handful of other lost souls wandering the tree's main floor.

"You mock me as usual, Avana," Ross said, glaring at the spirit woman.

"What's the Spiral?" Heather asked again, her gaze flicking from Ross to Avana as they scowled at each other almost in challenge.

"The Spiral of Life," said Ross, at last returning his gaze to Heather. "It's how we move in and out of the human void." He bowed his head, sighing. "The Spiral touches everything—especially the Between. The transition. We're between life and death now, fair game for any creatures to claim—even demons. Our only hope is to find the Spiral and return to the cycle."

"Dear, dear, Ross," Avana chided, her tone a mix of mocking and taunting as she turned misty and coiled around him. "Don't give this young woman false hope when it's obvious that none of you has any hope." Avana chuckled. "Or courage either." She waved her arm toward the humans huddled in small groups throughout the room. "If you did, you'd all leave this safe little tree and go search for the Spiral. None of them have ever bothered to even look." A cruel grin appeared on her face, mocking Ross. "And don't pretend to be so gallant, Ross. You're no different than the rest."

Ross' brow furrowed as he continued to glower at Avana until the spirit woman looked away. Only then did he turn back to Heather.

"That's because these—smoke people refuse to help us," he said, his tone sharper. "They only give us a place to rest our heads because sheltering humans protects their forests. And it keeps the battles off their doorstep. But they don't actually want us to find the Spiral."

"So sad," said Avana with a cold stare. "Blaming your cowardice on us."

"Cowardice?" Ross gritted his teeth, eyes narrowing. "Every day, several of us go out and brave soulstalkers and the dark to help the newly arrived find safety."

"Only the ones closest to the great tree, isn't that right, Ross?" Avana's tone was caustic.

Ross turned away from Avana as she dissipated into a cloud of mist.

"And without those newly lost and despondent souls, the Between would cease to exist," Ross fired back at her. "And your great tree would be overrun by soulstalkers."

"There are hundreds of you arriving here every day," Avana crowed as trails of smoke wound around Ross' head. "More than enough to never run out of souls here. Ever!" Avana cackled, smoky trails looping and swirling around Ross. "And the soulstalkers have no use for my people. Only yours."

Ross looked fearful and ashamed, but anger darkened his eyes.

"Every time one of us is taken by the soulstalkers, part of the Between crumbles," Ross insisted, his eyes wide, his mouth flattening into an angry line. "It gets a little smaller. So, Avana gives us shelter and tries to keep us right here. To save herself. But never kid yourself into believing the smoke people care about your existence, Heather. Because they don't."

Heather recoiled from Avana as the woman slithered around Ross in a half-smoky form, arms crossed, her condescending laugh echoing through the room.

"Poor, pathetic Ross," said Avana in a sharp tone. "He desperately wants to be incorporeal like us, so he can stand outside his own human suffering." She laughed, the sound like the snap of brittle twigs. "In all the time he's been here, he's never once tried to find the Spiral. So, he must want to be one of my people. He wants to make the great tree his home."

Ross bowed his head, looking embarrassed, pain rising in his warm hazel eyes. Heather winced. No, it was defeat.

"Alone, I'd never reach the Spiral and you know it, Avana." His voice was soft. Tired. Lost.

Avana leaned toward him, chuckling. "They're only poppies, Ross."

Wincing, he turned toward Heather, face flushed. He looked broken. That comment hurt. Cut him deep.

"It's dangerous out there, Heather, so don't go out alone to find anything. Unless you want to finish the job you started." He cast a forlorn look at Avana. "Unfortunately, your courage is the first thing to go here. Excuse me."

Ross pressed past Avana, moving toward a winding wooden staircase to the right.

"Ross, wait!" Heather started to follow, but Avana touched her shoulder and she turned.

"Let him go," she said as Ross disappeared up the stairs. She looked disgusted. "Ross talks big, but does nothing. Like the others.

You'll find that the norm here. In time, you won't know the difference and you'll become just like them. All of you do."

Heather's gaze narrowed. Something about Ross felt familiar, something she connected with, understood at a deep level in her heart. She looked into the cavernous well of Avana's dusty-blue eyes, like a mountain lake, and knew she'd only find bottom in them.

"He had courage once," said Heather. "We all did. Otherwise, he wouldn't have survived as long as he has here. You're just selling him short. And your contempt is pissing me off."

Avana laughed, her tone caustic. "Is it romantic, this act of suicide? Heroic? Brave? No. Courage is about overcoming the void, surviving it. Not succumbing to it. He was weak. All of you were weak and that's why you're here. If I'd designed the world, I'd have eliminated this Between and sent all of you cowards into oblivion. At least fight for yourselves!"

"You don't know a damned thing about what any of us went through!" Heather glared, gritting her teeth, wanting to hit this smoke woman. "Ross is right. You exist because of our pain and I'm going to prove you wrong about a lot of it." She propped her hands on her hips, against the shadowy fabric draping her body. "It's easy to look at death from a safe, immortal distance, isn't it, Avana?"

Avana smiled as Heather ran toward the staircase.

She pounded up the stairs. She needed to find Ross, convince him to leave this creepy place. Besides, he'd taken up for her against Avana and let this bitch emasculate him for his trouble. No one else had bothered.

With every level she ascended, Heather found shadowy corners of life within the great tree. Little fabrications of the only life, the only world any of them had ever known. Every level had a series of little nooks and rooms, a narrow hallway winding through them. Where people created small studios and private spaces. Each room seemed like a tiny time capsule, furnishings from times and places Heather could only imagine.

One nook looked like an old English cottage with thatched roof and rough-hewn furniture. Another space looked Japanese with bamboo and red rice paper walls, bamboo mats, and green pillows. Across from it, another nook looked Victorian with heavy, mahogany furniture, velvet wallpaper in burgundy and green, and a grandfather clocked that ticked steadily yet its hands never moved.

How did these things exist here? How were they made? Maybe they weren't even real and she was imagining all of it?

Voices whispered past as she walked up another flight of carved, wooden stairs. Soft murmurs and muffled voices filled the expanse, punctuated by an occasional sob or sniffle.

By the time she reached the top, she felt exhausted and she didn't even know why. In one of the spaces, she found Ross lying on a twin bed. The walls were white plaster and the floor old oak hardwood, reminding Heather of her grandparents' old farmhouse. Ross stared out a big, square window into the dark forest below. Two blue table lamps cast pallid yellow light through the room, shadows pooling in the corners. A cold fire twitched in the small, brick fireplace. The flicker of firelight was soft against his oval face, turning his hazel eyes to embers.

"Hey," she called from the nook's threshold. "Mind if I come in?"

"Not at all," he said, motioning her inside.

He propped his elbow on his knee. The pain had lightened a little in his eyes, almost a smile touching his face as she sat down on the bed. It creaked, blue blanket rustling.

"Sorry to run out on you like that," said Ross, sighing. "Avana's attitude is hard to take sometimes."

"How long have you been here?" she asked.

A haunted smile rose on his face. "I don't really know. There's no sense of time here. No change of seasons. Just slivers of morning and night and this constant dusk. It doesn't take long to forget things here, to lose track."

"Do you remember the year you died?" she asked.

"It was just after Thanksgiving," he said. "It was 1961, I think. In a little town in Indiana. Called Flora. Must have been big news in that small town."

Heather shuddered, wanting to cry, wanting to scream. He'd been here for over sixty years. Regardless, they looked about the same age.

Her hands shook as she stared out at the darkening forest. Everything was so strange and cold, so dark and foreboding. Nothing familiar or safe anywhere. The endless, shadowed landscape made her edgy, made her crave bright sunlight and neon. Anything to lighten the hard-edged corners. And the overwhelming panic rising inside her.

"It's hard at first," he said, sympathy lighting his eyes again. "The whole shock of waking up is jarring, especially after fighting that well of despair for so long. Even worse when you realize that committing suicide changed nothing. And then you deal with creatures like Avana."

"I don't understand any of this," she said with a sigh. "I'm supposed to be dead. I mean, shouldn't I know nothing right now? The dead know nothing and all that. I'm not religious, so I never believed in hell or an afterlife."

He shook his head, making Heather even more confused. "I was raised in the Bible Belt's rusty buckle, so I thought suicide was the end, too. We all did. If I'd known it was just a transition to something worse than I'd left behind...I would've held on longer."

A transition?

She covered her eyes, trying to rub away the dryness. She'd never thought for a moment it would be something temporary. Like a redirect page on the web.

He sighed. "When Jessie got sick, I stopped believing in anything. But something deep inside tells me that this Spiral exists. I can't find it alone and no one wants to leave the safety of the tree to find it."

She smiled. She did. Anything was better than these illusions of despair.

"This Spiral...is it another chance? Really another chance?"

Ross shrugged and stared past her at the window. "It's a chance at something else. If you're expecting to return to the moment you took your life, forget it." His warm hazel eyes hardened, anger like a knife blade. "You can't go back to your old life or those challenges. All of that's done now."

Her heart sank a little as she lay back against the smooth wooden walls. She watched the lamplight flutter across his face.

"Then why bother finding it?" she asked.

At last, fire rose in his eyes, a spark of life and purpose that she hadn't seen in anyone else's eyes or in their faces. It was little more than a pale flicker, but it was hope.

"The Spiral is a chance to try again. Another life, another time— same lessons. I'd be willing to give it all another try."

Another life? Another try? Would she even want another chance? Right now, that terrified her.

"How did you end up here?" Heather asked, changing the subject.

Ross ran his fingers through his bangs, a faraway look in his eyes as he stared past her again.

"My girlfriend and I planned it when we found out she was terminal. They gave her a year at most. So, one night, we closed the garage door and turned on the car motor. We climbed into the Bonneville's backseat and I held her in my arms, knowing—" A heavy sigh shuddered through him, his eyes glassy. "Knowing there had to be something better. We were so sure!" He bowed his head, his teeth gritted, hands balled into fists. "We were so wrong, Heather. So wrong!"

Heather frowned. On the surface, it sounded so tragically romantic, but now, she knew better. Knew it was just tragic. It was just more death.

"You said something about a gun."

He nodded. "Her parents found us. Jessie was almost gone and I wasn't far behind. She lay in the hospital three months in a coma before finally going on." Anger rose in his face as he struck the floor with his fist. "But me? I survived. And they blamed me for Jessica's death. On the one-year anniversary of her death, I bought a bottle of Jack and some hollow points. Did the job right."

He wiped his eyes, turning away from her.

Stunned, Heather could only stare at him. How could he fire a gun at himself like that? She reached out and laid her hand on his arm. The contact sent sparks through her fingers. Electric. Raw.

He looked up, wincing, as if he didn't deserve her comfort, but he didn't pull away. He stroked his fingers across hers, the heat like a brushfire. It softened the sharp ache in her chest.

"Is your girlfriend here with you?" she asked, glancing around, but the hurt in his eyes burned through her and she knew he'd endured something awful after arriving in the Between.

Something she couldn't imagine yet.

"She was," he said, his voice breaking, "before I got here—to the Between, but she didn't last long." He brushed the back of his hand over his eyes and looked up, his watery gaze meeting her eyes. "Javier and Ester said the soulstalkers carried her into the field of poppies within days of her arrival. Days...is there even such a thing anymore?" He shook his head. "I've tried to find her several times, to try and rescue her, but—I can't bring myself to enter the poppy fields. They're so dangerous. Alone would be another suicide." He sighed, shaking his head. "Isn't that ironic?"

"You mean those hazy smoke stack things in the distance?"

He nodded. "It looks like a city on the horizon, but it's not. Far from it. Those billows of smoke are rising from huge grey poppies that choke the air with some sort of pollen that puts you to sleep. Forever, if you stay too long."

The poppy fields reminded her of the huge factories near her grandmother's house outside Chicago, sprawled across the landscape, belching thick streams of dark smoke into an overcast sky. She wanted to stay far away from these poppy fields.

"Maybe I should go there?" Ross replied, sounding weary, a hand against his forehead. "End this for good."

"What? Ross, no!"

"That's what she and I both wanted. To go to sleep and not wake up again." His hands shook. "So why can't I bring myself to enter those fields and join her?" He dropped his head into his hands. "Why am I still here—in this wasteland—fighting a losing battle? She must wonder why I wasn't here when she arrived. Maybe she thinks I betrayed her?" He sucked in a breath. "Let her die alone. Avana's right. I am a coward."

Heather winced. Like Ross, she felt that spark of something flutter inside her. Something that made her want to fight instead of sleep.

She grabbed hold of his arms, shaking him.

"Ross, no! She has to know how much you loved her," said Heather. "If she didn't have the strength to go on, she'd want you to find your strength and fight back. For you and her. To live a life she couldn't. You're no coward. You've been fighting back, Ross. You just need someone else to fight beside you."

Then it hit her like a freight train. The remorse. The guilt. The shame. Her mom had expected her to fight, too. To fight through the grief and loss and go on when she couldn't. To make a life that mattered, a full one, not one cut short like hers. She didn't even fight for herself.

Her voice grew small and clamped. "Someone like me."

His head snapped up and that spark inside him lit his whole face. "Someone like you?"

She nodded. "I just gave up and let it all win. A quiet little death with only seagulls and Molly to see me off."

"There's nothing little or quiet about death," said Ross, frowning.

"Maybe not, but I failed myself and I'm ready to fight back, Ross. I'll help you find the Spiral. And take out some of those soulstalkers, too."

She was already tired of dulled sensations, everything except pain. And this place of illusions and ignoring what had happened to them. What they'd done made her sick to her stomach. Just as strongly as it had on the Bainbridge Island beach—where she'd left her body behind.

Like an old coat. Left it there like it didn't matter. Like she didn't matter.

It seemed so strange now. Had she even cut herself off from ever seeing her mom again? Who'd gone someplace far from this Between, this transition state. Had she trapped herself in this place between living and dying? Forever?

A piercing scream vibrated through the entire great tree. From outside.

Ross jolted off the bed, eyes wide, moving toward the stairs.

"What is it?" Heather cried.

"That was Barb's voice. She was on watch."

His voice was grim, determined as he surged down the steps, scattering dozens of smoke people into swirls and rings, shoving past listless humans and empty faces. Heather barreled down the stairs behind him.

He rushed toward the heavy, dark walnut door, leaping for its hefty brass handle. He shoved it open into the thick darkness, hinges groaning, and plunged forward. Without a moment's hesitation, Ross threw himself into the chaos near the doorway.

Soulstalkers!

Heather clamored out behind him, passing through Avana who dissipated into a hazy mist, and launched herself into a tangle of wings and shouts. Fists raised.

three

. . .

WINGS POUNDED the night as Barb screamed again. Soulstalkers swarmed her, dragging her across the clearing, her feet clawing deep ruts into the ashen soil. Lifting her into the air.

Barb flailed.

"Let her go!" Ross shouted.

He shot forward, feet rasping against the ash and damp black leaves as he tackled a soulstalker that clawed at Barb with taloned hands and feet.

It turned and hissed at him. Mouth gaping. Needle-sharp teeth glinting. Dark eyes wild.

It looked feral, inhuman, harpy-like. It shrieked, the high-pitched tone raking Heather's spine, turning her skin to gooseflesh.

"Leave her alone!" Ross shouted, pounding one outstretched wing with his fists, beating the soulstalker back to the ground.

The second one wheeled around, wings furling, grabbing hold of Ross. Scratching his face. Trying to hit him in the eyes.

The third soulstalker wrapped both spindly, bone-white arms around Barb and stretched its wings wide, legs bending to propel it into the sky.

And carry off Barb forever.

"No!" Heather shouted and launched herself at the soulstalker.

The three of them tumbled to the ground, the sound blunted by the ash and powder covering the thick forest floor.

Heather grabbed a handful of feathers and ripped them out with a sharp snap of her fist.

The soulstalker raged, a hawk-like screech echoing against the trees, the sound bouncing along the ground and ringing in her ears.

But it didn't let go of Barb.

Heather slammed the heel of her hand upward, catching the soulstalker's sharp, beak-like nose, hitting it hard enough to break it. Its spongy nose shifted, a shrill scream piercing the silence. Assuring her that blow had hurt. A lot.

Talons sliced through the air. Raking her sleeve. Like the burn of acid.

Heather pushed the pain away and grabbed another handful of feathers, tearing them off the edge of its other ashen wing. She kicked the bend of its legs. Hard. And punched its face with her fist.

This time, the hideous winged thing let go of Barb. She fell from its thin arms and tumbled to the ground as the soulstalker leaped into the air to escape Heather's next blow.

She turned.

Ross had one soulstalker on the ground, dark feathers scattered everywhere as the second soulstalker grabbed him around the neck, dragging him off the first one.

His face had a long gash down one cheek that dripped blood as he slammed his fists against the reedy arms clutching his neck.

The first soulstalker scrambled up from the ground, lunging at Ross, talons raised.

Heather threw herself onto its back and bit down hard on its neck. The skin was rubbery, tougher than she'd expected, but she punctured its skin. Inky black blood streamed down its neck as it screamed and flailed, trying to dislodge her.

Ross flipped the second soulstalker over his shoulder and

slammed it hard into the ground, rolling to his feet. He threw both arms around it and body-slammed it to the ground. Grabbing its wispy black hair in both fists, he beat its head against the forest floor until inky blackness pooled in the ash.

Only when it stopped convulsing did Ross get to his feet.

The first soulstalker beat its wings and flexed its talons, trying to dislodge Heather from its back. It whipped around in circles, slammed against tree trunks, but she held fast to it with a headlock. She had to keep it away from Ross, so he could defeat the other one.

But he was up and running at the first one, grabbing it by both wings. Heather let go as Ross smashed it face-first into a nearby tree.

It crumpled, wings folding against its back, talons curling up, legs quivering.

Screeching, it shuffled behind a tree and gathered enough energy to throw itself into the air, wings frantically flapping as it caught an updraft and soared up and over Ross.

Into the night.

Leaving Heather and Ross panting and leaning against the nearby trees.

Blood dripped down his cheek, chest heaving as Barb crawled toward the doorway and collapsed inside the great tree.

Heather struggled for breath as she patted Barb on the shoulder and moved over to Ross. He laid his head back against the thick trunk, breath heaving, face bruised, and dripping blood.

"That looks bad, Ross," she said, dropping down beside him.

She reached up and smoothed ash blond bangs out of his eyes. He nodded, looking drained as the adrenaline left him. He looked dazed, chest heaving as he held his left shoulder at a funny angle, arm dangling.

He grinned, staring at her. "That felt good."

"I can tell," Heather said with a chuckle as she blotted the cut on his cheek with a fold of his shirt fabric.

The blood was a faded red, not bright like normal human blood. But at least it wasn't black like those soulstalkers.

"Nice to make them bleed for a change," said Barb from the great tree's doorway. She wiped her forehead with the back of her hand, ash clinging to her chin and cheeks. "Thanks, Ross. Heather." She sighed. "Thought I was a goner. Didn't expect anyone from inside to come and help me either. Figured they'd all just watch from the windows while those monsters carried me off."

"Not a chance," Ross said, pain in his voice as he reached out to Heather and laid a dusty hand against her face.

His touch was radiator-hot and she wanted to lose herself in it.

"You saved me," he said in a half-whisper, sounding almost surprised.

Heather shook her head. "No, I didn't. Just gave those jerks some of what they gave us."

"Us? I like that." He cupped her cheek. Stroking with his strong, squared fingers. He seemed lost in her eyes a moment, the gold in his gaze lighting up his whole face as he smiled.

She hadn't meant it like that, but hearing him say it made her feel warm all over.

"But yes," he said, still out of breath. "You saved me. Twice."

Her face scrunched with confusion as she leaned into his hand, nuzzling, desperate to hold onto the heat of human touch.

"When?" she asked.

"First time on the stairs when you had my back, gave me hope when you said you'd help me reach the Spiral." He grimaced, reaching up to caress her face. Cradle it. Stroke it.

"And the second?" she asked in almost a whisper.

"When you hammered that first soulstalker and put it on the ground. That was damned amazing, Heather. Thank you."

She returned his smile, reaching up to grip his hands, wanting to feel that spark of life still fluttering through him.

"Returning the favor," she said in a quiet voice, leaning toward him. "You saved me first, remember? When I got here. And again, when you told me about the Spiral. First hope I've felt in two years, Ross."

He pulled her close and wrapped her in his arms, holding her against his chest, the heat of his body pressing through the folds of her clothes. She closed her eyes, reveling in his touch. Like flame consuming firewood.

"Me, too," he whispered, his lips brushing against her ear.

It sent chills through her body. She slid her arms around him. He felt so familiar, smelling like rain and woodsmoke. Like she'd known him all her life. He fit in her arms just right, like he was meant to be there. Like she was meant to be there.

"God, I needed that," he said, still holding her close.

She nodded against his right shoulder. "So did I," she whispered against his ear.

"Barb! Ross! You two okay?"

Lamarr was standing in the great tree's doorway, a terrified look on his face. He bent down to Barb who leaned against the tree's trunk, still shaking.

"We're okay, Lamarr," she said in a tired voice. "Thanks to Ross and Heather there."

Lamarr stood up and rushed over to Ross, but stopped. "You, two all right?" he asked in a quizzical voice.

"More than all right, I think," said Barb with a chuckle.

Heather felt Ross' hesitation, his arms still around her. Finally, he sighed, the sound vibrating through her chest as he slid his arms free and suddenly, she felt cold as he struggled to his feet. But he held out his hand to her and she grabbed hold, letting him help her to her feet. He stared at Lamar, his left shoulder hanging much lower than his right one.

He wouldn't let on how much pain he felt, but she already saw it narrowing his eyes and flattening his mouth into a grimace.

"Ross, you're hurt!"

Lamar reached toward him, but Ross held up his right hand, waving him off.

"Soulstalker got me in the shoulder as it tried to remove my left arm from its socket. Thought being dead would exempt me from injuries, but apparently, we can be hurt and we can bleed here. A new experience for me after all these years."

"Wow, Heather," said Lamarr, turning toward her. "You haven't even been here a day and you've already saved Barb and Ross and shaken up the entire great tree." He grinned, that smooth South African accent like silk. "And kicked three soulstalker's arses. What'd we ever do without you?"

Ross nodded. He turned, reaching out with his good hand to cup her face and brush her warm brown hair out of her eyes.

"What did I ever do without you, Heather Billot?" his voice burned through her, his eyes smoldering.

Why was she so drawn to this guy? And why did he feel so damned familiar? The attraction had been intense. And instant.

"Knowing you, Ross Shepherd, might have kept me alive in Seattle," she said, reaching out to gently squeeze his left hand.

He shook his head. "And if you hadn't shown up here, I'd have never met you. The only good thing to come out of the Between."

His comment startled her. But it was true.

Ross had lived and died before even her mom was born. There weren't even seatbelts in cars when he died. Her cell phone and the internet would have blown his mind. Their worlds were so different, but that no longer mattered here. Right now, their world was this dark, forbidding landscape filled with soulstalkers and lost souls.

Maybe the Spiral could bring them together on equal footing? In the same time?

"Ross," said Lamarr, "why don't you let me treat your shoulder? You can't walk around like that?"

Ross gripped his shoulder with his right hand, wincing. "Not sure there's anything you can do, but thanks just the same."

Lamarr crossed his arms. "I was a medic in the South African Defense Force for four years." He reached out and with gentle pressure, he examined it. "It's dislocated. I can get it back in the socket at least and get you into a sling."

Heather reached out and brushed a lock of hair out of Ross' eyes.

"Let Lamarr treat your shoulder, Ross," she said and stroked his cheek. "I can distract you with questions about the Spiral."

"The Spiral?" Lamarr replied, glancing from Heather to Ross and back again. "What are you, two planning? You know how dangerous some of those paths are, Ross. And even if you find it, no one even knows how the Spiral works." He sighed and uncrossed his arms. "Might be a wasted trip."

"Or the trip of a lifetime," Ross said in husky voice as he took Heather's hand in his.

She squeezed his hand. "Tell me more."

Lamarr stepped between them and took Ross by the right arm. "Not until I've got this arm back in socket and in a sling," he said, steering Ross toward the great tree. "Then you can ask him anything you want about the Spiral."

Heather laughed, nodding as she followed them inside. Ross reached out and blocked Lamarr from closing the door.

"First, get Javier Jimenez out there on watch with Barb Galki again."

"Why?" Lamarr asked.

"So, the soulstalkers will think twice about attacking two of us on watch."

Lamarr nodded. "Deal. Then we fix your shoulder."

"Agreed," said Ross with a sigh and closed the door.

Lamarr stopped a stocky, brown-skinned man with short, clippered black hair and spoke in a low voice. Heather heard Lamarr mention Javier as he pointed over his shoulder at the front door.

Avana appeared in a translucent smoky haze as Heather followed Ross toward the stairs. She paused beside the smoke woman.

"Hey, Avana," Heather called. "Just watched Ross Shepherd attack two soulstalkers at once as they tried to carry off Barb." She glared at Avana. "Coward my ass."

Avana was silent, looking annoyed as Heather followed Ross and Lamarr up the winding wooden stairs to Ross' space with its twin bed, blue blanket, and picture window.

Ross glanced at Heather over his right shoulder.

"Coward my ass?" he said with a chuckle. "That made my day."

She just shrugged, smiling as Lamarr led him into the cozy blue room, sitting him down on the twin bed.

"Now you can distract him while I work, Heather," said Lamarr as he searched for a suitable sling.

"Done," said Heather, plopping down in front of him on the bed.

She crossed her long legs and studied his tired face and pained expression. And the drooping left shoulder.

"Okay, tell me about this Spiral, Ross," she said.

"Like I said, it's a way out of this place. A chance to try again, Heather."

Another chance to be brave? Something she couldn't be the evening that she ended her life. She'd let the weariness take her. Why couldn't she fight for herself? She'd let the world reassure her that she didn't matter. She'd believed it, not hesitating to swallow all those pills.

"A chance to know we matter," she said in a half-whisper as she laid her hand on Ross' arm.

He choked up, nodding. "Yeah," he said in a thin voice. "Something I've never felt before."

"I did once," said Heather, staring out at the thick darkness swirling through the forest, wind screeching past the window. "Maybe I can again? Through the Spiral."

He nodded, laying his hand on hers. Heather felt her numbness ebbing.

"What is the Spiral?" Heather asked.

Lamarr gripped Ross' left shoulder in one hand and his upper arm in the other, manipulating it.

Ross winced, a cry of pain escaping through his gritted teeth. He sucked in a breath as Lamarr moved the injured arm with gentle but firm pressure.

"It's a myth," Lamarr snapped as Ross swallowed a gasp. "He knows no one's ever found it either. Not even in the Red City." Ross glared at him and Lamarr rolled his eyes. "Yes, I've spoken to others in the wooded camps all over the grasslands' edges. No one's ever found it. And survived. They say Death walks that path like a bloodhound, refusing to let us cheaters near it."

"Why?" Heather asked, frowning as Ross cried out.

"Because we'd cheat Death twice," said Lamarr with a grunt, applying more pressure as he moved Ross' arm. "This arm doesn't want to cooperate," he said with a hiss of breath.

"The Spiral—touches...everything, Heather," Ross said, struggling through the pain.

"Easy, mate," said Lamarr. "Almost got it...bear with me now."

Ross nodded, eyes smashed closed as he sucked in a tortured breath.

"There's a path like no other, almost hidden—" He yelped, the sound of bone grinding. "In the Place of Paths, deep in the forest. Leads—to—to...Spiral. The way—out."

A loud pop echoed through the space.

"Got it!" Lamarr cried, stepping back from Ross. "Shoulder feel better?"

Ross nodded, unable to talk for a moment. Heather reached out and rubbed his right arm until the pain dissipated from his eyes.

Lamarr tied a grey cloth at two corners and slipped it over Ross' head. With slow, careful movements, he slid Ross' left arm into the sling. "Now, wear that for a couple days and you'll be golden, mate."

At last, Ross smiled. "Thanks, Lamarr. I owe you one."

Lamarr waved him off. "Saving Barb and not letting those things into the tree...I'd say we're even." He pointed a finger at Ross. "But not if you and Heather run off to that hidden clearing and let Death get you. Waste my fine medic skills."

"We're going to find it, Lamarr," Ross said, his voice quiet and focused. "It's our best shot of getting out of here," he said, turning his hopeful gaze to Heather. "Besides, we have nothing left to lose."

She felt fear rise in her throat. But they did. They had so much to lose. The Spiral was their last chance.

"We have everything to lose, Ross," she said in a quiet voice. "That's our last chance out there. Our only chance."

He glanced out the window and then back at her again, nodding finally. A hint of fear glimmered in his eyes. He felt that finality, too.

"And we'll have to battle hordes of soulstalkers, probably demons, and maybe even Death to reach it."

His voice hung in the silence that built through the space. Lamarr patted his sleeve and then squeezed Heather's shoulder as he left them alone.

The silence built. Until Ross pulled her close with his right arm, his embrace comforting. They huddled together in the top of the great tree as winds raked the window, whistling like banshees.

Heather knew that she and Ross had to get this last one right. Or disappear forever.

four

. . .

IN THE BETWEEN, there was no night and day.

Only a sameness separated by a greying lightness at the windows that told Heather something had changed. She had no idea how much time had passed, but she noticed the fade from dark to almost dark several times from the great tree's windows. Most people pretended to sleep and wake because they didn't know what else to do. Heather understood at first, but slowly, she realized that for every sort of hour people slept (there was no time either), they faded a little more from existence.

Their inaction made her crazy. She wanted to run through the forests, searching for the Spiral. Or set out to find this distant Red City somewhere out there beyond these towering great trees and all these lost souls in denial. How long before she joined them?

The people who only went through the physical motions of their former lives also turned hazy and misty, but the ones that kept trying —kept fighting—appeared solid. Like Ross, who always appeared sharp and in focus to her. Everyone else was in some stage of giving up. Of letting go.

Obsessed with their past. And their deaths.

Like Lamarr who so seemed faded around the edges, flattened somehow—fading. That loss of opacity terrified her, so she stayed away from Lamarr, Barb, and Javier who milled about on the lower floors of the great tree, huddling together and whispering about where they came from. About lives already lost. Javier's soft brown eyes and long face always looked desperate and haunted.

Yet they did nothing to change things.

Heather passed their little nook at the top of the second floor as she headed upstairs to find Ross. Polished light maple wood, spongy green cushions, and a small stone fireplace adorned their simple space. Like pictures in Mom's photo album from 1972.

Half a dozen glass lanterns guttered, lining a shelf that curved around the tree walls below a large, round window. The smell of warm lamp oil and cedar warmed the small half-moon space. Oil lamps? Were they from Javier's memories?

At the sound of their muffled voices, she stopped on the stairs.

"Stop talking about it so much," Barb said in a half-whisper, whipping her brown ponytail off her shoulder. "It'll just hurt more." She leaned against the paneled wall beside a small, crackling fireplace.

Everyone huddled near lights throughout the great tree. Heather understood. The warm glow and brightness were the only comfort from the persistent dark and grey. And they didn't require reaching out to someone else. Fear of rejection was almost as painful as the isolation, but the risk of reaching out was so much greater. The fall-from height so much more terrifying.

Even she couldn't gather the courage to reach out to them, to tell them that she cared. That they mattered. Like she had Ross.

She felt a lightness inside whenever she thought of him. He was familiar somehow in a way she still didn't understand. She felt an odd sense of connection even though they'd just met. And she sensed that he felt a similar comfort around her. Granted, she'd only been here a short time. Days? Was that even a measurement now? Regardless, he seemed taken with her. Searching for closeness. Like what he'd lost? Like she felt a similar need?

Lamarr sighed, his dark skin looking blurred, mahogany eyes downcast as he leaned his head against a tan plastered wall. He sat with arms propped on long, lanky legs that folded into bony knees. He hadn't smiled since the night (day?) she arrived.

"I know," said Lamarr. "I can't help it."

Javier nodded, struggling to his feet. He was a chunky, short man with thick black hair and a kind face.

"But don't you understand?" Javier almost pleaded, his Puerto Rican accent heavy and excited. He splayed his hands, staring at Barb and Lamarr still seated on the floor. "If I stop talking about my life, about why I'm here, then—"

His bottom lip quivered and he was shaking now, the emotions pumping through his short frame. His voice became so quiet that Heather could barely hear him.

"Then I'm afraid I won't exist anymore."

Barb snorted, slapping her leg with her hand. She already looked shadowy against the wall, like an out-of-focus picture, a graphical blur applied to her body and face.

"Isn't that why you...you know—killed yourself?"

The muscles in Javier's jaw tightened, grief contorting his face. He threw his arm over his eyes, dropping to the floor. He slid toward the fireplace, holding out his hands to warm them in the heatless flames.

"It was," he said, teeth chattering, body shaking. "Until I woke up here. Now that I've had lifetimes to think about it...since 1872 anyway... I don't want to lose who I was. Who I am." He sighed, rubbing his forehead. "Or be carried off by one of those soulstalkers."

Heather stepped into the nook, drawn by their sincerity. It was the first conversation she'd heard in the tree that wasn't feeding illusions and pretending to be somewhere else.

"I hate the bitch I used to be," Barb replied, crossing her arms against her thick middle. "Didn't give a damn about anyone but me.

Did what I wanted, took whatever I could get hold of, and didn't care who I hurt."

At last, the anger slipped away. She stared at the two men, both younger than her and her brown eyes softened, thin mouth twitching.

"Now, every day I'm here, she comes back to hurt me," Barb said, bowing her head, like she couldn't look anyone in the eye now. "To remind me of how terrible I was. I thought that killing her was the kindest thing I could do. I guess it serves me right for having to live with her every day. Forever."

"I hated where I came from," said Lamarr, his voice so soft and fluid with his South African accent. "Cape Town was so violent, so scary. I did things during Apartheid I would have never done otherwise. To fight back, to not let them destroy us. That seems like a lifetime ago now, but I couldn't outrun my own conscience. I tried to shut it up. Waking up here brings it back to me every day. I wish I could have left South Africa before the violence, before I...before I let them make me into a monster."

Heather ached at their stories, wanting to say something to comfort them, but there was nothing she could say or do. Especially here. Regret was a powerful emotion. So was giving up. She'd carried around both like these people for a long time. But seeing the flatness of their outlines, the fuzziness that was sapping away who they'd wanted to be, tried to be, Heather knew it would take something huge to change them. And herself.

"What about you?" said Barb, staring at Heather. "New girl? What's your story?"

"Heather, isn't it?" Lamarr replied.

They stared at her now and Heather felt uncomfortable with the sudden attention.

She felt embarrassed as she tried to put into words what led her to end her life. It sounded so rash and foolish. So small compared to what they had gone through.

"I lost my mom to cancer two years ago. I was eighteen. I struggled to deal with the loss, but her absence got larger and darker until I felt like I was drowning in it. She was my only family. None of my friends understood. Then one day, I just gave up. And woke up here." She bowed her head. "Saying it out loud makes me sound so whiny and weak."

She felt a hand on her shoulder and looked up. Lamarr was beside her, his eyes filled with kindness not judgment.

"We've all been there, Heather," he said, his voice deep and clear. "A place none of us ever expected to land, on the other side of it, reflecting back."

Barb snorted. "Tell me about it. I've been here since 1983 avoiding that look back. At the horrible person I was. So, I volunteered to go to Vietnam. Worst nurse ever."

"What do you mean?" Heather asked, squinting at Barb.

"I was with 71st Evac in Pleiku," said Barb, her voice cold and clinical, her gaze staring past Heather. "So many wounded. Some days, over a thousand at a time. I was fresh out of nursing school and so arrogant. Doing triage. On kids! Eighteen—nineteen-year-old kids...messed up, mutilated. And I decided who lived or died. Me, fresh out of school!" Her eyes were glassy now. "I kept it all inside. Couldn't let anyone see me cry."

"How long were you there?" Heather asked.

She knelt beside Barb. Reaching out and touching Barb's shoulder. Barb flinched, pulling away.

"Two years. Came home in 1970, two weeks before Christmas. They told us not to talk about our service in public, not to wear our uniforms."

"Why?" Heather asked. "Why should you have to hide saving lives?"

Barb shrugged. "Too many people pissed off about the war, I guess. They said it was to protect us from protestors. So, I put mine away and went back to Pennsylvania." She laughed, the sound caustic. "Stayed away from everyone. Anyone. By New Year's Day, the dreams and flashbacks started. The faces of the kids I'd marked as unsalvageable. Me, right out of school. Deciding who lives and dies."

Heather couldn't imagine having to make those decisions. Especially at a warfront.

"Thought I knew everything," Barb continued, "but I didn't know squat. After that, I just went through the motions. For more than a decade. Finally, on the next Christmas Eve, I couldn't block the pleading, desperate faces anymore, so I put a gun in my mouth. I was thirty-eight. And here I am."

Barb looked away now, her arms slipping around her knees as she rocked back and forth.

Horrified, Heather couldn't look away. Barb had gone through so much, thought she was a horrible person. She'd saved so many lives, but all she could see were the deaths. Heather felt bad for giving up so easily compared to what Barb went through back then.

She glanced at Barb who stared down at her faded hands. Heather couldn't help herself. She threw her arms around Barb and hugged her tight.

"I wish you knew how many people you probably saved," she said.

Barb struggled against the hug, but Heather's persistence won her over and Barb put her arms around Heather in a listless embrace that quickly turned into a death grip.

"It took a strong person to do what you did over there, Barb," said Heather. "To make those decisions. I wish you could see that." She glanced at Lamarr and Javier. "I wish we all could."

Barb let her go, but when Heather got to her feet, she noticed that Barb's features were sharper. For a moment, she saw peace in Barb's expression. Heather smiled, understanding a simple truth about Barb, about her own life. And death. Like Barb, her focus had been wrong. She'd never looked at the road ahead, only the one behind. And not once did she try to look past the wreckage to see what had survived. She only saw what had failed.

Until it became her prison. And her death sentence. That truth stung. Made her uncomfortable.

One of the smoke people fluttered past, floating through the room and out again, toward the stairs. Heather backed away, relieved at the distraction, and followed the spirit up to the top level to find Ross. And put this despair out of her mind.

Ross met her at the top of the great tree's stairs and showed her where several empty rooms looked out on the dark forest.

"Feel free to claim a space for yourself," said Ross, motioning toward the empty spaces. "The nooks mold themselves to how you view them. Your emotions change them." He shook his head. "I don't know exactly how it all works, but it just does. Avana wouldn't answer when I asked."

Heather walked into one of the empty spaces. "And no one else questions it?"

Ross' face brightened. "I never thought to ask anyone else."

"I'll ask Avana later," said Heather, turning her gaze toward the walls.

She closed her eyes and imagined her space. White woodwork. Pale green walls. Bamboo floors. A fireplace in the corner. Nice soft bed with lavender sheets and a thick down, mint green comforter. Wispy lavender curtains. A puffy, green reading chair with an ottoman. Charles the bear. Stars painted on the ceiling. The whisper of the sea.

The sound of the ocean made her breath catch. She opened her eyes to pale mint walls and bright white woodwork. Light bamboo flooring covered the uneven space, lavender curtains fluttering at the window. She turned toward the bed that stood against the far wall, green puffy chair and ottoman in the other corner. She glanced up at the ceiling, seeing little blue and white lights sprinkled across it. Everything was there!

But her heart sank when she didn't find Charles the bear.

"Where's my bear?" she cried, turning to Ross.

He shook his head. "I like what you've done, but I don't see a bear. A cherished possession?"

Heather nodded.

"Sorry, I should have told you that. You can't bring across personal possessions. Not even a copy of them."

"Why?" she asked as she sat down on the bed.

He stepped toward it and sat down beside her, sliding his arm around her shoulders.

"Nothing meaningful from our old life can cross over. Only memories. I don't know why, maybe because that life no longer exists, but I've never been able to put out family photos or bring pets into my space. It's probably good that we can't. It'd be too painful."

"You're probably right. So, you can see my space, too?"

Ross nodded. "Everything you've projected appears in the great tree."

Heather reached out and slipped her hand into his. "Will you show me the rest of the place?"

"Of course," he said with a smile and pulled her to her feet.

They went down all the levels. Ross showed her throngs of people who never left their nooks, feigning life as usual despite being dead. Not dead—between. She had to keep reminding herself of this difference.

It was the only thing that kept her going.

Throughout the great, gnarled tree, people slept and cooked meals even though there was no hunger or need to sleep here. She smelled the scent of bacon in some places, curry in some, others smelling of grilled onions and barbeque. Some scents she didn't recognize. If she smelled something unpleasant, she just ignored it and that erased it from her experience. Which came in handy whenever she passed spaces where someone had bathed in a favorite cologne.

Heather still didn't understand the cooking and chores. Was it to pass time? Convince each other that they somehow still lived?

Avana and the other smoke people seemed to keep the human

illusions well-stocked. But many illusions seemed to stock themselves. And permitting these unnecessary routines kept the peace.

Going through the motions of living let them fool each other into believing they were still alive somehow, even if they were now chained to the drudgery they'd tried to escape.

She glanced at the endless array of nooks throughout the great tree with their different lights and colors and furniture.

But Heather didn't want to go through those motions. She didn't know what she wanted, except an end to her pain. She was no different than the others. Had they all been like her in the beginning? Doing all those same, awful routines only reminded her of her past—and the pain-over and over.

"Do you pretend like this?" Heather asked Ross as he paused on the winding wood staircase.

"No," he said, shaking his head. "Not anymore. At first, I did, because I didn't know what else to do. When I found out about the Spiral, everything changed."

"For you or this place?" Heather asked.

He shrugged. "Both, I guess. I started spending my time trying to convince others about the Spiral. They know it exists, but they're too afraid to try and find it. Afraid of the soulstalkers, the Demon Veils to the east—but mostly of Death."

How ironic that the thing they'd all craved so much as human beings was the one they feared most here? Wouldn't it be easier to just seek out Death and end this? Heather sighed. But that would feel like committing suicide all over again. She understood what was at stake now. What she had to lose.

"What do you do now?" Heather asked, studying his face.

Ross thought a moment, his brow furrowing. He was handsome in a boyish kind of way. Not too thin or thick, way above average. He had those honest nice guy looks. If she'd seen him on the street, she'd have checked him out. And that smile? It would have melted her right there on the street. And she felt safe around him.

"I just try to forget all the stuff I used to do," he said with a sigh, "And all the creatures and places out there. Especially the poppies because then I think of Jessie. And I feel sick inside all over again."

He hadn't given up like Barb and Lamarr. And his Jessie.

Heather shrugged and started down the staircase. Ross followed.

"What's the difference between sleep and death here," Heather asked. "It's all the same, isn't it?"

Ross shook his head, but kept quiet as two smoke people, a man and a woman, sauntered past on the stairs, their pale skin and powdery grey eyes like Avana's. She felt their sharp indifference radiate as they passed Ross in solid form. Heather knew they could instantly shift into smoke, so she kept away from them.

Grabbing hold of Heather's arm, Ross pulled her close as they walked down the circular stairs away from the smoke people. To the first level.

"They'd have you believe there's no difference," said Ross, his voice low and intense, "but they're just as afraid of Death as we are. They say the poppy fields' sleep is a long but painless way of reaching Death." His gaze flicked from Heather's face to the ascending smoke people. "To me, it's anything but painless."

"Why are these smoke people afraid of Death?" Heather asked, staring at him with wide eyes. "I thought they were immortal."

"Very long-lived, but not immortal," Ross replied. "They're prey for soulstalkers and demons, too," Ross replied. "There's some strange game they all play here in the between, some weird game of survival. But Death holds all the cards. Death has power that the others envy. Whenever she takes a soul from this plane, it somehow damages the between, making it crumble a little bit more."

"What do you mean, crumble?"

"Once, this place was as opaque as the world we left behind," said Ross, motioning toward a dark window. "The skies were pale blue, the grass muted greens. The air smelled soft, almost fragrant. And all of the forest paths led somewhere. Now, everything is just darkness and shadows."

Heather stopped at the bottom of the stairs. "The skies were once blue here?" She longed to see a blue sky again.

Ross nodded. "According to Ester anyway. Back then, soulstalkers were a rare sighting. Avana says that too many of us are showing up here before our time, damaging the structure that was never meant to hold so many people. For so long. So, every time someone arrives, the between becomes darker, blurrier, more transparent."

"Like a shadow," said Heather.

"Exactly," Ross replied. "Now, hordes of soulstalkers hunt here daily, the demon population climbs, and the poppy fields have taken over the landscape. They're everywhere. It's overcrowded. Too much chaos."

Heather imagined great swaths of powder-grey soil sprouting massive grey poppies, the fields covering the landscape like smoke-spewing factories.

"And don't even get me started on the Red City," said Ross with a sigh. "I've heard the gates to the city have entirely closed."

"What? Closed?" Heather wanted to go there.

"Avana says that if something doesn't change, the between will become more nightmare than shadow. Until it all fades to dark."

Like too much contrast on an image. The thought of this place in unending, pitch darkness with those hideous soulstalkers hunting in packs made her skin crawl. Was it too late? Could the darkness be reversed? Or at least paused?

"Is there any way we can stop it? Reverse the damage?"

Ross shrugged. "No one I've asked knows the answer to that. But I have a theory," he said, his gaze sharpening.

"A way to fix it?" Heather asked.

He seemed pleased by her attention.

"My theory is that none of us was meant to stay this long, to lose ourselves in these mind tricks and traps. That's why the Spiral's out there. For us to discover it and move on."

So, maybe there was a chance to change this place? And themselves. At least some hope that maybe this wasn't forever.

Heather moved toward the fireplace on the main floor. The tree's dark, polished wood glistened against the guttering flames. The warmth looked inviting, familiar, and she couldn't help but move toward it. She sat close, holding her palms toward the crackling flames, and Ross sat beside her.

The lack of heat was disturbing. She felt cold inside.

"Why do the smoke people act like we're a burden?" Heather asked, watching Ross' expression, but it didn't change. "Didn't they need us as much as we needed them?"

Their attitude annoyed her.

"Makes them feel important," said Ross, "like they have power over everything, but they're as powerless as we are."

He poked a thick log with the toe of his boot, shoving it farther into the pop and crackle of flames.

The conversation fell away to the encroaching silence that filled the great tree. So many people inside, yet the interior was so silent. Filled with whispers and denial. It made Heather uneasy. She wanted to talk to fill the expanse.

"How much of this place belongs to the smoke people?" she asked. "What are they, anyway? Ghosts?"

"As far as I know, these small forest oases belong to these smoke people. But the forests shrink every day." He nodded at a smoke person's wispy vapor as it twined its way down the stairs. "And I don't really know what they are," he said, lowering his voice. "Every time I've asked, Avana launches into one of her shrill tirades, so I stopped asking. They're different than the soulstalkers and some of the other creatures."

Heather let out a hiss of breath. "Other creatures?"

Ross nodded. "I've seen others...moving in the gloom. Most keep to themselves. Avana's people seem curious, but neutral. And most avoid the Convergence. Where the Endless Paths meet."

"Why? That's the way out."

He sat up, leaning forward, excitement in his eyes. "Yes, exactly. Where all the paths begin. I'd like to take you there."

Heather glanced out the window at the darkening landscape. "Is it safe?" she whispered.

Ross nodded. "Safe as the dark," he said with a wry smile. "It's dangerous, but so is everything here. Death doesn't usually hang out at the Convergence unless there's big game for her scythe. The soulstalkers avoid the forests, but they hunt around the edges. If we stay out of the deeper grasses and keep to the woods, we'll be safe enough."

The thought of sitting around this tree forever made her shudder. She had no idea how much time had already passed, but she'd spent enough time in here, creating a space upstairs that she didn't want to become too comfortable.

How long had she fed her own shellshocked reaction to waking up after so much Molly? Days? Months? Years?

That possibility terrified her.

"Let's go," said Heather. "Anything to move around again." To feel like she was doing something that mattered.

Grinning, Ross pulled her to her feet and they moved toward the door.

Ross took hold of Heather's hand, squeezing, his hazel eyes wild now. His touch sent a jolt of excitement through her, something she hadn't felt in a long, long time.

"Will you still help me look, Heather? And follow the paths with me? Together, we can find the Spiral. And lead the others to it. Give us all a second chance."

"As much as I'd like to settle into this lodge of denial, let's go. Where do we start?" she asked.

Ross pulled her toward the door. "I'll show you the Convergence. Where all the paths begin. It's the best place to start searching."

"Lead the way," said Heather.

five

· · ·

ROSS OPENED the door and Heather stepped out behind him into perpetual twilight, sky a pale, washed out grey, thick stands of trees muted blurs of grey-green, black, and yellow. The ground looked almost ashen. Was this morning in the Between?

In the shadows ahead, pale lights flickered like fireflies as Ross weaved his way around the massive trees toward a narrow path that led deep into shadowy darkness. An unsettling silence hung over the forest. No birds. No distant sound of airplanes. Not even a whisper of wind against tree limbs that moved like specters above them. Like something unseen had passed over them.

Heather's heart raced, the memory of the soulstalkers returning.

Were they already out here? Watching? Hunting? Waiting for someone to venture too far from safety—like a rabbit caught out of its warren?

She followed Ross closer.

The massive great trees towered above them, some tall and spindly like river birch with creamy white trunks and others squat and thick like giant gnarled oak trees. She expected to smell the cool scent of damp leaves that clung to the trail, but all she smelled was dirty rain.

Sometimes, if she turned her head just right or thought back to the world she'd left behind, she'd catch the scent of something familiar.

Like the cool scent of pine or the thick smell of loamy soil that mounded around the trees. Or a hint of woodsmoke, husky in the cool air, but none of those comforting scents carried over to the Between.

It all had a musty, dirty smell to it. Like a hot Detroit rain, aged vinyl, old rubber tires. Or spring thaw in Toledo, smelling like asphalt and urine. Cleveland two days after a heavy snow, smelling like old, hot motor oil. Things she remembered from visits to her grandparents' houses, one in Ohio and one in Michigan.

But all of those cities were still so vivid in her mind. Not like the Between's constant grey sky, muted colors, and blunted smells. A shadow of the former world. She saw that now.

Ahead rose another ring of trees, smaller than the redwood-like giants with rough, charcoal trunks where the great tree stood. Ross ran into a small clearing and stopped beside a nexus where seven trails branched out from the clearing in all directions. The ashen trail softened his footsteps to whispers. He moved toward a winding trail that coiled off to the far left.

To the right, another trail ambled beside it that led straight into the woods and abruptly jutted into a sharp angle to the left. Beside that, five other trails trickled into the forest, each a different direction. One ambled straight ahead and the other four twisted off to the right. Disappearing into silent gloom and still trees.

"One of these leads to the poppy fields," said Ross, standing on a dusty trail that looked like cold campfire cinders. "It's this one, I think. The trail of ashes."

"What about the other trails?" Heather asked, walking past the edges of the other five. "Where do they lead?"

Some paths looked greyer than others, but all of them had that same powdery, ashen texture to the soil.

"One leads to the Demon Veils," he replied. "Not sure which one. Another one leads to the soulstalkers' lairs." He stepped across the paths, moving toward the farthest one on the right. "And one leads to the Spiral."

He halted in front of the last two paths. One had soil that looked like a mix of salt and ash and the other path looked like red clay. "One of these leads to Death's scythe. I don't know which one, but this one leads to the Red City. It's a dangerous path."

The distant sound of a blade's singsong echoed in the hushed forest.

Ross froze, his gaze lurching toward the sound. A cold chill fluttered down Heather's spine. They knew where two of the paths led. But who knew what stood at the end of these other five trails.

"More dangerous than the others?" she asked.

He shrugged, glancing into the distance. "It's surrounded by... barbed wire and this weird red haze. You can't see the city until you're on top of it, so anything could lurk along the path. End you before you reach the gates."

"Creatures?" Heather asked.

Ross shook his head. "No, souls like us." He sighed and ran his fingers through his sandy blond hair. "It's like they're trying to hide the way into the Red City."

Heather moved toward him, arms crossed, feeling like a target out in these woods.

"Why would they do that?"

"Too many souls, I guess," he said with a shrug."

Living inside these trees felt so strange to her and unsafe. She wondered why anyone would remain in them instead of trying to find this city.

"I'd prefer a city to these isolated—and vulnerable—trees," she said, motioning behind her toward the great tree.

"Same," said Ross. "It feels more normal and alive than cowering inside these tree camps. Each quarter has its own architecture and personality, but most of the humans end up in Amity at the city center. Where humans run things."

"You said you were there once," Heather replied, studying the path as it disappeared into the forest's deep shadows. "Why'd you leave?"

Ross nodded. "Took me a while to find my way inside. Unfortunately, I got in through the Void Quarter. Almost got carried off by demons, soulstalkers, and one of the rogue bands of humans. There are many ways to cease existing here, Heather. But even when I got out of the quarters and into Amity, it was a constant fight for power and freedom. And I got tired of the fighting. So, I came back here. To this great tree."

A chill shuddered through her. "Many ways to die or disappear here...what does that mean? Like by Death's scythe? Or something else?"

He shook his head and stuffed his hands into his pockets. "It's unending war in the Void Quarter. Everything fighting everything. You can bleed and die in the Between, but by the next morning, you're back in this place. Ready to fight and die all over again. I never made it past the Void Quarter. And the Shadow Quarter is walled off from the other quarters." He turned away, bowing his head. "You can hear gunshots, swords clashing, and explosions from a good distance down this path. And so many shadows everywhere. Most of the soulstalkers won't even fly over the Red City—much less hunt there."

Not even the soulstalkers hunted there? Too dangerous—or too hopeless? Was it worse than a place called Demon Veils?

"Maybe they disguise the path...to keep everyone out," Heather offered. "Or to throw off Death?"

A peculiar look touched his face. "I never thought about that," he said, his voice barely above a whisper. "Maybe."

Six ways led to ruin and only one even hinted at the hope of a second chance. And those were just the largest trails. Maybe one of the multitudes of smaller trails was the only path to the Spiral? There was no guarantee that they'd ever catch sight of the Spiral. Much less reach it. These paths might lead them right to demons or those fields of grey poppies—and ceaseless sleep.

Ross caught her gaze and held it. A shimmer of fear fluttered in his warm hazel eyes as he cupped her dark hair in his hand with its bright coppery highlights.

"You're so different than Jessie. Or any other woman I've known. Jessie was the sweetest person I've ever met, but she was so timid, always looking for approval. Her parents went to this crazy fundamentalist church, wouldn't let her read certain books, play cards, or even dance. They made her terrified of the world. Of everything."

He reached out and ran his fingers over a copper lock that highlighted her dark brown hair, tucking it behind her ear, his fingers scorching her skin. He touched her right ear, sending shivers down her neck as his fingers brushed across the diamond stud earring Mom had given her, tracing the small silver swirl and finally the small gold hoops.

"She'd have been too afraid to change her hair like this. Or pierce her ears so many times—even once because her parents said everything was a sin. She always talked about piercing her ears, but she was too afraid of what people might think. "

Heather laughed. "It was just something to do."

"But you weren't afraid, Heather. You did it because it pleased you, not everyone around you."

She shrugged. "Maybe things were different in your time? Harder for women to speak their minds."

"Maybe you're right? I loved Jessie and I know how hard she struggled against her parents' expectations. They suffocated her and she just wanted to escape. She never got to step out from under their control and become her own person. That's what hurts the most. She might have been like you. Bold. Outspoken."

Heather studied him a moment. He thought she was bold and outspoken? She'd never thought of herself like that.

"You think I'm bold?" she said.

"You just, I don't know, think differently," he said. "You have a viewpoint on things that I've never considered before." He smiled. "It's nice."

He turned away, returning his gaze to the trails, and scanned the surrounding trees and mist. Looking for soulstalkers and other dangers? Something else?

Heather followed, walking across the clearing as she examined each of the seven paths again.

"You have no idea which one leads to the Spiral?" Heather asked. "Not even a clue?"

He shook his head. "Only guesses. I only know for certain that the white and grey ashen path leads to the poppy fields and the red clay path leads to Red City."

Sighing, Heather moved beside him. He had probably walked that trail to the poppy fields a million times, trying to gather the courage to go in after his girlfriend. Still, the only way to know where the paths led was to follow each one and see where it ended. But no one had found the courage to do that, no one still at the great tree, at any rate.

It was too dangerous and they had everything to lose. If they encountered Death on the way, their journey would end—forever.

Forever. It still hadn't quite sunk in that she was dead.

Not forever dead yet, though. Was their such a thing? But here, there was nothing like human sleep and no dreams.

Without dreams, was there still hope?

She didn't know anymore. Did the souls in the poppy fields still dream? Or had their being gone dark, waiting for their souls to turn to dust? Like coma patients with only autonomic functions waiting for their bodies to wear out and shut down?

A horrible thought and she couldn't imagine being trapped in her body like that, waiting to die? Maybe that had happened to her on Bainbridge Island? Maybe her body lay in some hospital, autonomic functions churning on while her brain had gone dark?

A terrifying shade of grey that she hadn't considered. An

outcoming she'd never considered when she'd swallowed all that Molly.

She'd expected a binary result and never considered anything else.

Like her world, the Between wasn't a black and white reality. It was endless shades of grey and as humans, they named things after their past experiences. Humans and smoke people called it sleep, but Heather knew it wasn't sleep. It was a sluggish, numb death.

Besides, there was no time here. She had to remind herself of that. No days, no needs, and no wants—other than escape. It was truly between life and death. And she was fair game for whatever entity wanted to claim her. Before, she couldn't understand how short two years was and how, with time, she might have hung on longer.

If she'd just reached out to someone besides Molly.

"What if we fail?" she asked, gripping Ross' arm. "What if the path we take leads right to Death?"

He sighed, not turning around as he stared off into the forest. "When we took our lives, we assumed that path led to certain death. But we were wrong. Isn't the risk worth one more roll of the dice?"

Her only answer was yes. She missed her mom so much that even now, it ached through her, even here. Never had she felt so far away from her than right now.

Ross was right.

"Maybe I could even see my mom again?" she said.

He turned around. An ache burned in his eyes, a dejected look shadowing his handsome face. He looked past her, eyes narrowing as he scanned the trees again.

"Ross?"

He took a few steps away from the paths, hands on his hips and then turned his back to her.

She cringed, at last understanding.

The one person he wanted to see was forever lost to him. Sleeping for eternity in the poppy fields, forever out of his reach.

"I'm so sorry," she said finally. "I'd...I'd forgotten."

He sighed and finally turned to face her, eyes hollow, lips pressed into a grimace. "About Jessica?" He nodded. "Sometimes, I do, too. And that scares me. It's almost worse than the pain, isn't it? Forgetting them?"

Heather wanted to ease the deep ache inside him. Of all the people she'd encountered here, he was the only one that felt real. His eyes were a little cloudy as he stared into the trees again, biting his lip.

She moved toward him and gently gripped his arm, turning him to face her. The pain in his glassy eyes sharpened as he met her gaze.

"You haven't forgotten," said Heather, shaking her head. "Her loss resonates in your eyes, on your face. In everything you say. I understand a little about how that feels. I lost my mom two years ago. She was all I had and everything just sort of fell apart from there. That's why I'm here. Like you."

He nodded, his gaze falling to the ground.

"I understand. Jessie was all I had." He winced, rubbing his forehead. "Never really knew my folks. Dad died in the war and mom was never the same after that. Left me with relatives until I turned eighteen. When Jessie got sick, we both went crazy."

"Sick?"

He nodded. "It was something in her blood, something making her sick all the time, so sick that she didn't care what happened. Doctors said there was no cure, that it'd kill her. Cancer of the blood or something. That's when we decided to leave—together."

Heather put her arms around him, holding him close. "Ross...I'm so sorry."

He felt solid and real as her arms pressed against him and that connection gave her the only comfort she'd felt since waking up in the Between.

She wanted to cry. Rage. But never let go.

His arms enfolded her, tightening, and she felt his tears warm against her face.

"Thank you," he whispered in a shaky voice.

He didn't have to explain. He was moved by her proximity, by her touch, by the feel of another warm body against his, and for a long time, they held one another in the ashen silence until finally, he let go, holding her out at arm's length. This time, a faint smile rose on his face, lighting it with an almost inner glow that she hadn't seen there until now.

He let her go and rushed toward the paths. Holding out his arms, he turned in a circle.

"Choose a path, Heather," he said with a curt bow and motioned toward the paths. "The white ash path leads to the field of poppies and the red clay path leads to the Red City, but the others...I haven't a clue. One of them leads to the Spiral."

She hesitated a moment, but moved toward him and the paths. She walked in a circle around the clearing, examining each path again, whether it curved or cut straight through the forest. She studied the soil, whether it was dark or light, had a distinct texture or color—was wide or narrow.

But the one path that stood out to her, that she kept going back to was the far-left path. Its soil was sandy and ashen, reminding her a little of the trails through the beach grass along Bainbridge Island. She walked toward it with measured steps. The beach-like path led out toward the edge of the fluttering grasslands, snaking around the forest's edge, and disappearing from view.

A risky path. It cut through the grasslands, making it easy for soulstalkers—and anything else hunting them—to swoop down and carry them off.

She glanced at the center path with its deep, charcoal black soil that disappeared abruptly into the forest's deep, cool shadows. Looked like the safest path, concealed from anything hunting them, but she had no idea what lurked beyond those shadows.

In the Between, what looked the safest was probably the worst choice.

"The sand and ash path," she said finally, pointing toward it.

"Why that one?" he asked, a surprised look on his face.

"It doesn't seem like the easiest one to follow—for us or the soulstalkers. So maybe it's the safest?"

His gaze flicked toward it, tracing it with his gaze into the distance. Finally, he nodded.

"I'm intrigued by your choice," he said, the corners of his mouth quirking into a smile. "The grasslands path it is. We'll try the hardest path first and see where it leads us. But be wary. And be prepared to fight."

"Agreed. You watch behind and I'll watch in front. We both watch the sides."

He smiled, his expression brightening. "Point and flank. I like it. I'll go first then—on point. Ready?"

Heather took a deep breath and nodded.

Ross stepped onto the path and Heather hurried after him. The wind whipped around them, rustling the folds of their grey clothing. She felt anxious, her body tense as she kept her gaze moving left to right and then over her shoulder. Ross' gaze shifted across the landscape ahead, his posture stiff as he moved ahead. Together, their footfalls made only a slight whisper in the silence.

"So, you've never been down this one before?" she asked in a quiet tone, her black, Converse high-tops scattering dust clouds with every step.

"Only to the edge of the forest. Never beyond that." His sentences were short, all his attention focused ahead and around them and she felt his unease. "Only saw grasslands and poppy fields in the distance." His gaze swiveled left and right, his pace increasing. "Not a soulstalker in sight. Terrified me."

The path crisscrossed through the grasses and then veered back toward the forest's edge. Wind rose, grass swishing against her legs as she listened for the beat of wings on the horizon. Hiss of movement. Rustle of vegetation around them.

The forest grew distant as they moved deeper into the endless sea of tall grasses. Her anxiety climbed.

So vulnerable. Out in the open. Nowhere to hide if soulstalkers swooped out of the sky.

They traveled for what felt like miles until the path veered off deeper into the tall feathery reeds of grass, like cornstalks, leaving the forest behind. Ahead, a wide expanse of windy hills rose out of the grasses, rolling toward a distant grey haze that went on forever.

Fear hung cold and heavy in her stomach at the growing openness that surrounded them. They were easy prey for the soulstalkers here.

A rasp of grass whispered behind her.

She turned. Crouching. Expecting wings to rush at her.

But only the sound of the wind moaned.

Her heart raced as she whirled back around. Ross had continued on ahead. When he realized she wasn't beside him, he stopped and turned around.

"Heather? What is it?"

She cast an uncertain gaze behind her and then toward the sky.

"Thought I heard soulstalkers."

The muscles in his jaw twitched as he cast a look toward the sky and scanned the horizon left and right.

"We have to keep watch. They hunt continuously for lost ones, even when it isn't night. They feed on despair, so do your best to focus on the Spiral." He gave her a reassuring smile, but it faded quickly. "It's all we can do."

"What if they come after us?" she asked, heart racing, expecting shadows to pass overhead at any moment. "We have nowhere to hide out here."

He gritted his teeth, balling his right hand into a fist. "Fight them. Fight them for all you're worth. With everything you've got. And don't stop until they let go. Together, we can defeat them."

He meant that. Heather was sure that the image of those things carrying off his girlfriend must still haunt him. She couldn't get that image out of her own head. It must torture Ross every single day.

"What if this path leads right to their camps? Dens? Burrows?

Wherever they live." Heather had no idea if they lived like humans or animals. Did they live in caves? Holes? Cities? Or where they shadow things that materialized out of the air?

"We run like hell back down this path, toward the forest," said Ross, his tone clipped. "They can't fly well in cramped places, so they'd abandon any chase into the woods. But on open ground... they're on familiar terrain. Just be careful and keep an eye on the sky."

Nodding, she started toward him again. "I'll keep a close watch then," she said as she followed Ross through the sprawling sea of grey-green grass. "Those things look like a cross between a human and a raptor. Are there truly angels here? Angels of light or good or something?" She whirled around and shouted at the sky. "Angels! We need your help!"

Her voice echoed across the grasses, the sound hollow, rising in layers until it dissipated.

Ross was beside her, grabbing hold of her and yanking her down into the grass.

"Ssssh! You wanna call down a whole wing of soulstalkers on us?"

They huddled, unmoving in the grass together, listening for the sounds of wings beating the air.

But only silence greeted them. The same response she'd gotten for calling out to angels. Guess Heaven didn't care about souls that had given up like they had?

Was Avana and the smoke people the only helpful creatures in this place? Everything else seemed hellbent on consuming them. And she was about as helpful as a tanning bed in a burn ward.

Ross pushed his bangs out of his eyes. "I've never seen anyone—including the smoke people—fight soulstalkers or anything else." He chuckled. "Until you arrived, Heather."

"I used to be a fighter," she said. "Somewhere along the way, I got beaten down so many times that I gave up. And decided not to get up again. It's a little late now, but I'm gonna get up from that mat and fight these things." She reached up and squeezed Ross' shoulder. "Will you help me fight them?"

Ross nodded, those hazel gold eyes burning. "That year without Jessie was a gut punch that dropped me to the mat. A knockout and I never got up again." He reached out and gripped Heather's hand. "Never wanted to until now. Let's fight for ourselves, Heather."

Heather at last felt the fire in him, ready to set this sea of grass ablaze. "Time to rise," she said, lacing her fingers in his, feeling the burn against her palm as it raced up her arm into her chest. "Let's change the landscape, leave our mark—light a blazing trail to the Spiral and empty the great tree."

Ross nodded and together, they got to their feet and returned to the path.

His steps quickened along the winding path and Heather matched his pace, watching behind them and around them as they headed deeper into the sea of grass.

The sky lightened to a pale, dove grey as they followed the endless bends and curves of the path, wide enough now for two people to walk side-by-side. They walked for what felt like miles, not a treetop in sight.

Only this endless sea of grass.

As the pathway turned into a sharp left, serpentine curve, a stand of grass rustled.

She grabbed Ross' arm and they crouched low. Freezing position.

Her gaze darted toward the movement, at the glint of something warm. A flash of rich orange. Two somethings.

That's when she realized they were eyes. She held her breath, shaking, as two large, round eyes peered through the thick stands of grass surrounding them. Deep pumpkin-orange, the color so vivid that it startled her.

Heather couldn't look away. "Ross?" she said finally in a half-whisper.

Ross glanced left and right, swiveling his body to scan the grasslands behind them.

Didn't he see the eyes? Was a massive creature with huge teeth about to leap out of the grass and devour them?

She shook his arm and pointed ahead at the eyes.

"What is it?" he asked, frowning, hazel eyes intense as he scanned left and right for movement.

Heather pointed again as the eyes blinked. "Right there," she said in a quiet voice. "See! Eyes!"

If it had been a predator, they'd have already been devoured or carried off. No, whatever it was, it was curious, watching them from a distance. The eyes looked timid, uncertain—kind—and just as fascinated by her presence.

Ross squinted at the creature, stumbling back as it slid out of the swaying grasses. Wings unfurling around it.

"Holy hell!" Ross cried. "What is that?"

"Soulstalker!" Heather shouted, stumbling back.

Ross stepped in front of her, fists raised, eyes narrowed.

Heather stood her ground behind him. She couldn't wait to rub this in Avana's pasty white face.

"Show yourself!" Ross demanded.

The creature rose to Ross' full height and stared at him unblinking. But it wasn't a creature. It was a he and he had human form.

She gasped at the soft pearlescent sheen of his pale skin. Like those shimmery face powders that reflected light. His wavy walnut brown hair hung soft around his face, harvest moon eyes gentle. He had creamy taupe wings the color of a sparrow's underbelly that twitched and fluttered at his shoulders as he glanced from Heather to Ross. He wore loose-fitting tan trousers, a blowsy flowing ivory duster, and a diaphanous shirt that draped in ivory folds across his chest like layers of mist.

"It's definitely not a soulstalker," said Ross, his eyes wide as he stared at the winged man. "Coloring's wrong."

The winged man's form was solid, not the brilliant, ethereal angel form that she'd expected. He was all mist and smoke and light like

Avana and the smoke people but floatier (was that a word?) somehow. And he had physical form. She could reach out and touch him. She sighed. Last time she believed anything from Wikipedia. Of course, everything here was like a bad Wikipedia article.

"Soulstalker?" the winged man snapped, eyes narrowing. He crossed his arms, sparks lighting his pumpkin-orange eyes. "You insult me. They are nothing more than winged vermin. None of the realms would ever claim them."

"Why?" Heather asked.

She took a step toward the strange angel-like man as Ross lowered his fists.

The winged man's jaw sharpened as his mouth pressed into an angry line. "Why? Well, everybody knows they are just shades of unions between the fallen, the pure, and the naive. And shadows. Taught to hate and fear the light. And follow only the basest of instincts."

"How are the pale ones—like you—different?" Heather touched the gentle curve of his wing, surprised at how soft it felt against her fingertips.

"That tickles," he said with a chuckle, but his eyes turned sad. "But now, you shame me." The winged man sighed, arms falling to his sides as he stared at the ground. "Forgive me. I forget that so much of human knowledge cycles up and down through the ages, lost and found and reshaped again. Pale angels descend from these same unions, it's true, but we turned away from the hatred and the shadows. We focus on what light remains, hoping that one day, we will be welcomed in the other realms. For now, we are here."

Offspring of angels and fallen angels? Demons? That was creepy. And it was beyond anything she'd ever heard of or read. Like some crazy Greek mythology gone all wrong.

"Wow, part demon, part angel, part human, part shadow...I didn't even know that was a thing," said Heather.

"Me neither," said Ross, face scrunching in confusion as he glanced at Heather. "So...what are you—exactly?"

The winged man looked calm as he faced Ross, but then his gaze settled on Heather again. "A creature of light," he answered, holding his head high. His voice was comforting, the tone bright like sunlight on water. Heather felt drawn to him. "Angels—and demons sadly—are like humans. We choose whether we rise or fall."

"Avana called your kind pale angels," said Ross. "I've only seen one since I came here. It flew overhead when I first arrived."

The pale angel nodded. "That was me, Ross. I try to protect the new arrivals whenever possible."

Ross' eyes widened. "Why are you here now?"

"Surveying," the pale angel answered, lifting a hand toward the grasses. "With so many soulstalkers here, I thought perhaps I might..." His voice trailed off, sadness in his round, pumpkin eyes. "I know that look," he said with a sigh. He laid a hand on Ross' shoulder. "It's not within my power to carry you beyond the Between."

"Why not?" Heather asked, stepping toward him. She tugged on his sleeve. "You're not confined here, too, are you?"

He shook his head. "Not entirely, no, but I am limited by my station." His voice turned sharp. "By my birthright. Pale is light in its most diluted form and that closes many a door between realms to us. There are many of us here, but we're outnumbered by the soulstalkers because your kind, the lost, have crowned them king."

"How?" Ross snapped. "We have no power to change anything here. Those things were everywhere when I got here! Way too many to fight."

The pale angel shook his head. "Another illusion you keep alive. By ignoring why you're here, by just accepting it and going about your earthly routines, you make this place darker. By giving up, you seed more poppy fields. And more shadow creatures come to hunt."

Heather felt a chill rush across her spine. By doing nothing, the lost souls like her had created an uninterrupted stream of soulstalkers. Somehow, she had to figure out how to break this cycle.

"I can't change what is and yes, the soulstalkers outnumber us, but we're not powerless. Not by any means." His hand pressed against her shoulder, the faint rustle of wings unnerving. "There's still light left here, Heather," he said in a soft voice, gently squeezing her shoulder. "I just hope it's enough."

She sighed. She hoped so, too.

"What lies ahead on this path?" Ross asked, pointing toward the trail that disappeared into darker grasslands.

The pale angel flapped his wings, rising into the air until he hovered above the grasses that swayed in the constant breeze.

"Soulstalkers," he said without emotion. "Droves of their hovels nestle among the grasses on the hillside ahead."

Heather felt her breath quicken at the memory of those shadowy things swooping out of the sky like falcons. It filled her with dread. They were, by far, the creepiest thing she'd encountered here.

"And what's beyond the soulstalkers' hovels?" Ross asked, his face taut. He looked apprehensive, his gaze darting from the pale angel to the trail ahead.

"Poppies," said the pale angel. "More of them spring up with every turn of dusk."

Another field of ceaseless sleep. She shuddered, fear cold against her fingertips.

"Ross, we've got to turn back," she said, gripping his hand.

Ross stared out at the horizon, ignoring her plea. He seemed a million miles away, lost in a memory that pinched his face and wrinkled his brow. She could almost see the turn of days—of years— flash past his eyes. Was he still trying to find a way into the poppy fields? Or to forget that Jessie was out there somewhere, sleeping away the days as she pulled farther and farther away from him? And rescue.

The pale angel squinted at Ross. "What is it that you seek?"

"The Spiral," Heather replied.

The pale angel's face brightened. "At last!"

A fierce screech echoed across the grasslands. Heather jumped at the sound and whirled around, shaking as brush rustled nearby. She turned toward the movement.

Two soulstalkers rose into the air in a blur of grey, careening toward them.

The movement shook Ross out of his trance.

"Run!" he shouted, barreling toward the clearing.

Heather bolted into the tall grasses after him.

Brush whipped against her legs, a shadow passing overhead. She gasped, running harder.

The rush of wings hissed against her face.

Heather swerved right then left, weaving through the grass, trying her best to confuse the things chasing her.

Arms snapped around her middle!

She shouted as something jerked her off her feet. Into the air.

"Heather!" Ross shouted. "No! Let her go!"

She struggled, gasping, as the ground sank away, air turning cold as Ross followed below, running through the grass beneath the soulstalker.

Wings popped around her head, the feel of cold, leathery flesh pressing against her body. The creature reeked, smelling like a wet dog that had rolled in garbage.

A rock hissed past the soulstalker's head, Ross' aim just a little wide.

Heather swiveled in the soulstalker's grasp, trying to break free of the thin, clay-like fingers gouging her stomach and arm.

Trembling, she looked into its face and tried to free a hand to gouge its hard, black eyes leering at her from beneath a shock of soot-black hair.

She fought against the grey, plaster-like skin molded around its long, lean limbs and leaned forward, trying to bite it, but she couldn't twist into position.

Wild-eyed, it mumbled something in a strange, velvety tongue she didn't recognize, its mouth gaping with sharp, pointed teeth.

Massive, ashen—almost black—wings stretched to their full length, spanning at least six feet as they furiously beat the air.

"Heather! Fight back!" Rose shouted from somewhere below.

Another rock whizzed past, nicking its wing. It bobbled, righting itself.

At last, she twisted her right arm free. She grabbed a handful of stiff feathers. Tearing them away.

The soulstalker screeched.

Gritting her teeth, she ripped more feathers out of the creature's wings.

The soulstalker howled, halting in mid-air, its grip on her loosening.

Heather grabbed at the other wing, yanking out another fistful of feathers until the soulstalker's talon-like grasp released her to protect its wings.

And she was falling! Dropping like a stone toward the grey-green grass below.

Air whistled past, a long moment of quiet calm until the ground interrupted it, smashing into her body.

For a moment, she couldn't move, the pain too intense. She was already dead. Why did it hurt so much?

Suddenly, Ross was beside her, covering her body with his as he shielded her in the tall grasses, another rock in his fist.

"Stay still," he hissed.

A shadow fell over them, wings thumping the air.

Heather's gaze snapped toward the shadow. And the flash of pumpkin-orange eyes.

The pale angel!

She wanted to shout in relief.

Two soulstalkers rushed toward them, but the pale angel beat his wings in a furious staccato, keeping them back as he hovered over her and Ross.

Two more times, they circled above, diving toward the grass, but both times, the pale angel fought them off.

With a defeated shriek, the soulstalkers surged away across the grasslands, disappearing on the horizon. Moments later, they returned, two shadows hanging at the edge of the grasslands.

Waiting.

The pale angel landed in the grass beside Heather and Ross.

"C'mon," he said, dropping onto one knee, wings curving around her and Ross. "I'll escort you back to the woods. But stay right under my wings where they cannot reach you. Do you understand?"

Ross nodded as he slid his arms underneath Heather and helped her to her feet. She was still a little stunned from the fall. Gently, Ross held her up as she regained her balance, the comforting feel of his arm still around her waist.

Still stunned, her body barely reacted. She concentrated, forcing her left foot forward and then her right. Again. Left then right. Again.

Ross was beside her, his shoulder pressed against hers as she moved through the grass beneath the pale angel's wing shadows.

The soulstalkers followed at a distance, but the pale angel's steady presence hovered beside her and Ross as they followed the long path back toward the distant trees.

The pale angel stayed close until finally the two soulstalkers stopped pursuing them, lagging farther behind as the forest rose ahead.

"We're almost there, Heather," said Ross. "Hang on, okay?"

She nodded, trying to speak, but only air rushed out of her lungs. Why? She was dead. Was this just her own projection, imagining that the air had been knocked out of her?

After what seemed like forever, the path wound back toward the forest.

When Heather finally stepped underneath the familiar canopies of dark river birch and oak trees, a sense of relief washed over her.

Ross still had his arm around her waist as he led her into the clearing. Only when she was surrounded by trees, their branches obscuring the grey sky, did she collapse to her knees against the forest floor. The pale angel fluttered beside her, his steady gaze tracking across the tree line and behind them.

"That was too close," said the pale angel. "Glad I was there."

"Me, too," said Ross, a hand on Heather's shoulder. "You okay, Heather?"

She nodded. "Just got the wind knocked out of me," she said in a thin voice. "I'll be okay."

She had no idea how someone who was dead could have the wind knocked out of her lungs. Yet here she was, gasping for breath when hers had expired some time ago. She stretched out in the grass, staring up at the deepening grey sky.

"Thank you," she said to the pale angel. "So...what do we call you?"

"I'm called Zakhart," he replied.

"Zakhart, what do you know about these other paths?" Ross asked, motioning toward the other trails leading through the forest.

Zakhart shrugged, only the hint of a shadow furrowing his brow. His wings twitched as he scanned the horizon. "Not much. I know I followed one of them from the Spiral to get here."

Heather bolted up from the ground, her eyes wide as she stared at Ross, who was grinning now.

"You came from the Spiral?" Heather cried.

Zakhart laughed, the sound lyrical against the heavy silence. "We all come from the Spiral." He motioned over one shoulder toward the soulstalker hovels. "Even them. Even the fallen. We all start from there, at any rate."

Heather gripped Zakhart's ivory sleeve. "Please, will you take us to the Spiral?"

Zakhart gazed from Heather to Ross. Desperation burned in Ross' eyes, his muscles corded as he waited for the pale angel to respond.

"Why do you seek it?" Zakhart asked.

She couldn't stop the caustic laugh from escaping through her gritted teeth. "Isn't it obvious? Hello?" She held out her hands. "We made a mistake, an awful, horrible mistake. And if we could just return to the Spiral..."

Her voice trailed off as the pale angel shook his head, sadness glazing his pumpkin-orange eyes.

"It's not that simple, Heather," said Zakhart, wincing. "You can't just follow a path to the Spiral and step into it."

Ross lurched forward, fear sparkling in his eyes, mixing with a look of shock. He gripped Zakhart's robes with both hands.

"Why not? What does that mean?" Ross demanded. "All the stories, the whispers about the Spiral. Just find it and it'll fix everything. Everything!"

Zakhart looked frightened. He stepped out of Ross' grasp as his wings unfurled to their full height. He seemed ready to take flight and desert them now, leave them to the emptiness of the Between after snatching away their last thread of hope.

"I'm sorry," said Zakhart, bowing his head. "It doesn't work that way."

Ross let out a scream of rage as he sank down in the grass.

Heather turned away, tears stinging her eyes.

And just how did it work? Were all the cautionary tales right after all? Get it right in this life with all its ambiguities and contradictions and confusions. With no clear instructions and no consistent rules.

Get it right the first time or you'll be damned for eternity.

Heather sat down beside one of the trees and covered her face as the hot tears burned her eyes. She couldn't even get being damned right.

six

. . .

"ROSS, LISTEN TO ME," said Zakhart, bending to grip Ross' forearms. "It's not hopeless, but it isn't as simple as just walking into the Spiral. You need to understand that."

Zakhart crouched in the grass, wings folding around his shoulders as he studied Ross then Heather, but his expression was blank.

What was he thinking? What judgments were passing across those warm coppery eyes?

"But we don't understand that!" Heather pulled her hands away from her face, glaring at the pale angel with his sparrow-like wings. "Why isn't it that simple? Isn't it about repentance? Learning what you did wrong and fixing it? Isn't it about love? The Golden Rule and all that? Taking another leap of faith." She shook her head. "To your death. But all of it's just more noise, isn't it, Zakhart?"

"Heather—careful," Ross said in a quiet voice. "We're in enough trouble just being here."

The pale angel remained quiet still no emotion on his face.

"But none of that stuff matters, does it, Zakhart?" Heather couldn't help but laugh, it was so absurd. She scrambled to her feet and turned in a circle, arms spread, high-tops kicking up a cloud of dust as she shouted at the sky. "It's about plain old punishment after all?"

Ross looked stricken, but she saw agreement burning in his eyes. He felt the same way.

She glared at the pale angel. "So, it's all obey or be smited! Obey rules written by a zillion men and translated a bazillion times without any historical context anymore! A million languages. A gazillion versions. Disagree with a jumble of things with no context, things that make no sense anymore, and get sent to Hell?"

"Heather, stop," Ross said with a hiss.

Heather snapped her hands to her hips and scowled at Zakhart. "Well, I don't believe in Hell! And I want no part of some higher power that rules by fear and demands my obedience to obscurities while they remain perpetually silent." Some of the fire burned out of her voice. "Whatever truth that may have existed has been lost for centuries. And now, people cherry-pick from it to spread hate and segregate anybody that's different. If that's the truth, then please —smite me!"

The corners of Zakhart's thin mouth quirked into a slight smile. But Ross just looked confused. And fearful. She couldn't tell if he was embarrassed or angry about what she'd said, but something smoldered beneath his eyes. Awakening.

He moved over beside her, cringing like he expected retribution at any moment.

"Smite me, too," he said finally. "Because I agree with every word." He stood up straighter.

Heather couldn't help but grin. She reached out and rubbed his arm a moment. He was standing by her even if it meant being struck dead.

"Ross, if you're expecting a bolt of lightning to strike you and Heather dead again, it's not going to happen." Zakhart's voice was buttery and soft, a brightness in his tone that surprised Heather. "The universe isn't interested in punishment. Just progress."

"Progress?" Ross raised an eyebrow and cast a confused look at Heather.

Zakhart nodded. "Sometimes, humans mystify me. Those words were never meant to be worshipped or used as punishment. They were a gateway. And now, the universe lies empty because your kind is too busy killing each other to prove who's more righteous. Ignoring the future to fight over the past."

Heather moved toward Zakhart, intrigued by his words. She glanced at Ross. He was watching her, his expression filled with surprise, but respect lit his hazel eyes. She smiled. For her.

"Ignoring the value of people—and their stories—to worship a book is just sad," said Zakhart. "Each of you leaves your imprint on the world as you live a life. A story." He motioned from Ross to Heather, wings rustling. "Every interaction, every success. Every missed moment, every intention crafts your story. And that story remains, imprinted on the landscape and on others when you pass from the world. In every human heart and mind, story after story remains. Life stories that capture hopes and dreams, failures and successes—even lies and truths. The universe reads all of these stories, Heather. They're the only books it cares about."

"Even when the story just suddenly stops?" Heather asked. "When it has no ending?"

Zakhart's expression softened. "Especially those stories. Because they weren't finished yet. They fell into those dark crevices between story and page. So many lost pages of chasing dreams and living lives." He motioned toward the paths. "Found here. Between. This is where you'll find the lost pages of your story. Where you can pick up the spine's unraveled threads and sew it all back together into a book when it's complete. Turn it into a finished story."

Heather bowed her head. "I don't know how to change what I did."

"None of us does," said Ross, sliding his arm around her shoulders and holding her close.

The pale angel reached out a feather-soft hand and lifted her chin. She met his warm gaze.

"It can't be changed, Heather. That act is long past, the page long turned. You've got to understand that you're no longer connected to that world, that life. All of that's fallen away. But just because that life is over doesn't mean your story has ended. What matters now is what happens next. You need to finish your story, Heather. You, too, Ross."

"But nothing ever happens here," Ross snapped through gritted teeth and let go of Heather.

Zakhart looked surprised, but he remained quiet, letting Ross vent.

Ross paced around her, hands balled into fists. "Every moment is the same as the last one and the last one and the last one until—" He gazed at Heather and his face brightened. "Until Heather appeared in the grasslands."

Zakhart smiled. "Something *did* happen. Don't you see? You distanced yourselves from everyone around you until you decided to take that final step and disconnect from life. Both of you had given up. But here, you finally found kindred with another soul. A small change in the void. But it needs to be bigger."

"How?" Heather asked.

Zakhart pointed across the field. "Back in the smoke people's refuge there are others like you. Find them. Seek them out."

Heather frowned. Most of those people in the great tree never even spoke. How could she find people who didn't want to be found?

Zakhart turned toward the clearing, pointing to the farthest path on the right.

"On that far path lies the Demon Veils. Many of your kind have already gone into those Veils. And they've lost sight of the return path." He motioned at Heather and Ross. "Find the others. Reach them like you've reached each other."

"We can't save everyone," Heather said with a groan.

"No," said the pale angel. "But why not try anyway?"

"What about the poppy fields?" Ross asked. "Can we still reach them? The ones who've fallen under the poppies' spell?"

Zakhart bowed his head. "There's always a thin chance of reaching past the sleep of hopelessness. Or Death. For most of them, it's already too late." He pointed toward the three paths to the right. "The path of red clay leads to the Red City. One of the other paths leads to the Spiral. The other leads to Death. She walks among the Veils and the poppy fields, bringing the final death to the truly lost."

"What exactly is the Red City?" Heather asked. "Ross was there. It...it sounds terrifying. Like another battleground."

Zakhart's jaw tightened, his deep orange eyes narrowing. His wings twitched, his body stiffening as he gazed across the clearing.

"For some humans, it wasn't enough to just take their own lives. For those who committed atrocities before ending their lives, there is another place for them to sort out their natures—far from here."

"Like Hitler?" Ross asked.

The pale angel nodded. "Yes, like Hitler. The humans within the Red City are a dangerous lot. Some don't even realize they're dead. Others can't let go of their rage. And some can't let go of their hatreds. Much of that plays out in the city streets, over and over in an endless unbroken cycle."

"Are they trapped there?" Heather asked.

"Trapped by their own natures," said Zakhart, nodding. "But not by walls or fences. I'd avoid the Red City and the traps of the Demon Veils. Stick to those in the great trees."

Ross' eyes burned with determination, his hands relaxing at his sides. He got to his feet, turning to stare at the two paths Zakhart had pointed out.

"What about the poppy fields?" Ross asked, his voice barely above a whisper. "Like my Jessie?"

"As I said, Ross, there's a chance. But the longer they sleep, the faster they fade away. And only if Death hasn't already found them. Be warned though, if Death finds you, she will cut you down, too. Her scythe rarely misses, so be careful."

Heather rolled her eyes. "A scythe? Really? I thought that was a cliché."

Zakhart sat down in the grass and stretched out, his wings folded behind him.

"Death appears as the Between expects," he said, thrusting his hands behind his head. "Don't like her image? Then change it."

Change it? Heather frowned. How would she do that? Not everything Zakhart said made sense.

"So, you're saying if we connect with enough people in the great trees, we'll just magically find this Spiral?" Heather asked.

Heather dropped down in the grass beside the pale angel. Ross moved beside her, kneeling on one knee, but he kept his gaze on the horizon. Watching for soulstalkers, she realized.

Zakhart laid his head back and stared up at the sky. The smirk on his pearlescent face made her want to slap him, like he knew the answers but wouldn't offer them until she asked the right question. He seemed callous, heartless, dangling this trinket in front of them with no real way to reach it.

"Yes, in a way," said the pale angel. "When you've figured it all out—why you're here and what matters, for starters—the Spiral will call to you. When you hear it, it will lead you to the right path. Without that understanding, you could follow every one of these paths and never find the Spiral."

Heather bristled. "Why are *we* responsible for saving everyone here? None of them lifted a finger to help me when I arrived here."

"Didn't they?" Zakhart asked in a knowing voice.

He was so irritating! She glared at Zakhart. He was treating her like a child and she resented it.

"Think back, Heather. What was the first thing you saw?"

"Grass," she snapped. "An endless sea of grass. Grey skies. And lights—"

Her words caught in her throat, her face burning with embarrassment.

Dozens and dozens of lantern lights had filtered out from the forest's half-dark to lead her out of the sea of grass, away from the clutches of the soulstalkers. They led her safely to the great tree. Smoke people led the way, but a lot of souls just like her had come out to shepherd her into the great tree's safety. They could have just ignored her, let the soulstalkers take her, but they didn't.

She choked up. They didn't even know her, yet they'd saved her from the soulstalkers.

"It was such a simple act, but with great impact, wouldn't you say?" Zakhart said, wings fluttering.

She nodded. "You're right. I might have ended up in the poppy fields if they hadn't come out with their lanterns." Her gaze fell onto Ross. "But you reached out the most. Why?" She turned toward him and stroked her fingers down his arm. "After all the people you'd ushered to safety, people who had no interest in the Spiral, you still reached out one more time. To me. Why?"

Ross smoothed her hair with a stroke of his hand. "I've thought back to that moment a lot, Heather. There you were, lying in the grass, huddled in the cold wind, fear shining in your soft green eyes. Those streaks of copper and burgundy so bright in your hair. Something about you seemed to defy this place somehow. Seemed to fight against it." He grinned. "Like you were ready to stand up and duke it out with every last soulstalker. I just wanted to drop down beside you and fight back. For the first time in a long, long while."

"That's how you saw me?" Heather asked, shaking her head. She'd never inspired anyone. Ever. Most people barely noticed her.

He twirled a strand of copper and burgundy hair around his index finger. The soft caress lasted only an instant and then his hand fell away.

"You made me feel something for the first time since I got here."

His voice was warm and intense, rushing over her like a car heater in winter.

Heather slid her hand into his and entwined his fingers with hers. His hand felt solid. Warm. Strong. Not smoky or faded like everything else in the Between. She felt kindred with him, a connection back to something. Something she hadn't felt since her mother passed away.

"It's all anybody ever wants, isn't it?" Ross asked Zakhart who was grinning now, those pumpkin-orange eyes lit with satisfaction. "To feel connected."

"It's all a Spiral," said Zakhart. "Nothing is an isolated event because it all flows together. Every moment affects another."

For a brief second, something whispered to Heather across the landscape. A distant voice. It spoke her name only once and the moment she heard the word, it faded into the hush of wind that whispered, rustling the trees for a moment until it softened into the greyness.

That voice was unmistakable. It was her mom!

Heather turned her head toward the sound, her lips parting to answer the voice she hadn't heard for so long. The sound ached through her.

I'm here, Mom, she wanted to shout. For an instant, the world tilted, making her dizzy, and then righted itself.

Zakhart sat up and folded his legs underneath his billowy duster. He propped his elbows on his knees, studying Heather's face. He didn't seem so smug now. He seemed...happy. "It called to you just now, didn't it?"

Heather frowned. She shook her head. "No," she said. "It was my mom calling to me."

She'd felt a moment of spin, of momentum, as if the world had ticked forward a click or two then slowed to a stop again. Had she finally done something right?

Ross shook his head, his eyelids hooded as he squinted at Heather then Zakhart.

"I heard that voice, too," said Ross, shaking his head. "But it was my dad's voice." Memories lit his eyes. "It's been a lifetime since I've heard his deep, rumbling voice."

"No way," Heather snapped, crossing her arms. "That voice was totally female. It was my mom."

Ross laughed. "Female? Not a chance! Unless she's got a beard and smokes cigars."

Zakhart held up his hands, wings unfurling as he rose to his feet and stepped between them. "You each heard the voice of someone you loved, didn't you?"

Again with that smug look! Like he knew everything she was about to say before she said it. Were all angels this arrogant and smug?

"Someone close to you who died?" Zakhart continued.

Heather glanced over her shoulder and nodded.

"Yes," said Ross. "My dad. He died before I killed myself."

"Don't you understand?" Zakhart replied. "You both heard the Spiral. That's the only way you could have heard their voices. It's the one thing that connects everything."

Heather gasped, a chill fluttering through her chest. Ross looked stunned. He drew his hand to his mouth and stared at Zakhart.

"Then that was really my mom?" she replied, her voice breaking.

She bit her lip, fighting back tears as she began to shake. It had been so long since she'd talked to her mom, heard her voice fill the house, felt her soothing presence in the next room.

"I kept all her messages in my voice mail. I was so terrified that I'd forget the sound of her voice, so I replayed them. Over and over. And broke into a million pieces every time." She sucked in a breath as tears welled in her eyes.

Ross slid his arms around her and pulled her into a tight hug, one hand stroking her hair. She started to pull away, but the warmth of his body and the depth of his concern eased the horrible ache in her chest. She wrapped her arms around him and pressed her face against his shoulder, losing herself in his proximity, in the heat of his body against hers.

Every time he held her, she felt that connection and the memory of warmth returned her for a little while.

"Thank you," she whispered in Ross' ear.

"For what?" he asked, his voice soft.

"For this. After Mom died, everyone treated me like great grandma's vase."

"A vase? What does that mean?" Ross asked as Heather lifted her face from his shoulder.

"You know, that vase everybody hands down through the family," said Heather. "The one no one wants on their coffee table because it's awkward and out of place no matter where you put it. It doesn't go with anything in the house, but no one wants to insult the family tree by giving it to Goodwill. So, they just tuck it into the back of a cabinet somewhere and forget about it."

"You're much more important than some hand-me-down vase, Heather," said Ross, his voice sharpening. "Never forget that."

"So are you, Ross," Heather said against his ear. She turned toward Zakhart again. "C'mon, let's go back to the tree," she said to Ross. "Try to rouse the others." Heather winked at Ross. "Put this vase out on the table."

Ross laughed. "Okay, we'll put out all the vases then," he said and pulled her toward the path that led back to the great tree.

"Thanks, Zakhart," Heather called to the pale angel. "Will we find you here again?"

"Just call for me and I'll find you," he replied and took to the air, circling above them.

Heather watched him rise into the greyness until he was a speck on the horizon. Grass swished against her legs as she turned toward Ross who ran through the grass. She struggled to keep up.

"Demon Veils or poppy fields?" she asked.

He stopped in mid-stride and stared at her a moment, the smile fading from his face. Replaced by brooding.

"What if I can save her?" he replied. "What if there's a chance for her and me again?" At last, the smile lit his eyes.

"I'll help you," said Heather, squeezing his hand. "If there's a chance, we'll find it, okay?"

The thought of losing Ross stung, but she'd help him no matter what.

"I've never met anyone like you before, Heather Billot," he said in a soft voice. "You're the first person here that ever wanted to help me find the Spiral."

"Have you ever seen it?" she asked as he laid his hand on the door handle. "I mean, do you even know what it looks like? What to look for—beyond what Zakhart told us?"

Ross was quiet for a moment. Finally, he shook his head.

"No, but I've heard stories about others who've followed the path. Unfortunately, no one knows if those people ever reached the Spiral." He shrugged. "No one's ever returned to the great tree after finding it. Maybe it's too difficult to come back? Or too far?"

A fire burned in his sunny hazel eyes as he stared into her eyes. She smiled. He had such nice eyes. Like maple leaves in autumn. The sky at sunset. Glow of driftwood embers at a beach bonfire.

"This is gonna sound weird," he said in a quiet voice, "but I'm really glad you're here." He reached out and brushed a lock of coppery brown hair out of her eyes.

"Why's that?" she asked, her voice almost a whisper.

His smile lit the hollows of his face. "You're the first person in a long time who's listened," he said, his fingers lingering against her hair a moment. "Just listened. And you want to fix things. Gives me hope."

"I'm glad you're here, too," said Heather. She brushed her fingers across the top of his hand that felt warm to her touch. "I'd feel lost and freaked out without you here."

Nodding, he studied her face a moment or two. "Let's go back—before we run into soulstalkers."

Ross grabbed her hand, tugging her toward the clearing and the massive trees. Abruptly, the forest rose ahead in the sea of grass, tiny flickers of light in the deepening greyness.

"Let's get some of the others to help us," said Ross. "Back at the tree. We're safer in groups."

Heather   stiffened,   remembering   Avana's   condescension, especially toward Ross. She'd mock him if he talked about saving anyone from the poppy fields, but Heather didn't care.

She wasn't sure why Avana treated lost souls like she did, but she wouldn't let her demean Ross. The guy had done nothing but try to help her and the others. Somehow, she'd make Avana see that. And the others. She'd do her best to get through to them.

No, it was more than that. They had to reconnect somehow. She had to figure out a way to get them to understand. Otherwise, they were all stuck here.

———

Dusk had darkened to indigo by the time she and Ross returned to the great tree. Inside, everything seemed just as they'd left it. How much time had passed? Minutes? Hours?

The silence inside the tree was claustrophobic. It made her skin crawl!

She glanced over her shoulder at the throngs of people filing in and out of the first level. In silence. In denial. Serpentine coils of smoke floated through the room, winding around dozens and dozens of humans standing like statues, sitting motionless on chairs and sofas, all of them staring out the dark windows. The silence was like a heavy wool blanket on a hot summer night.

It was suffocating.

"The others look lost in their own worlds," she said in a half-whisper. "Ross...I don't want to become like that. I'd rather sleep in the poppy fields."

Ross was already nodding. "Me, too. But I still think I can help them. *We* can help them. It's not too late. If we find the Spiral and come back here, we can tell the others what we've seen. Maybe then they'll want to save themselves?"

Heather shook her head. "They don't seem to care what happens. Even when you send them out in pairs on patrol, Ross."

The smile slid from his face as he cast a forlorn look around the room, at the huddled groups of people.

"You're right. Even the patrols don't seem focused on keeping our little corner of the forest safe. They don't even seem interested in finding and protecting new people who arrive in the Between anymore." He shook his head, his eyes sparking. "Most of these people were here when I got here. I've got to at least try and help them. No one else has ever tried before."

Heather frowned at all the people sitting around the room. Like some mountain lodge for freaks. She sighed. And she was the newest club member.

People of all nationalities, teenagers to geriatrics, but all of them had one thing in common. Apathy.

Glazed, faraway expressions. They didn't seem to care where they were. They looked almost drugged. Like they had no understanding of what they'd done or why they were here.

Heather knew exactly what she'd done and she'd accepted the consequences. But…if there was a chance to change things, to somehow leave this place, then she had to try.

They seemed like fixtures in the main gathering room, growing out of focus and less opaque with every change of the light. Almost like furniture against the pale maple-like wood that covered walls, floors, and ceilings. People sprawled across the large burgundy rug that covered the shiny floors and crowded onto a big U-shaped burgundy sectional that stood in front of the fireplace. Wooden benches curved around the circumference of the room, filled with more lost people. The benches perched under windows that looked out into the forest, but everyone sat with their backs to the windows as flameless lanterns flickered in each window. They gave off no heat —like the people around them. She expected the scents of fresh-cut wood and warm wool, but the air just smelled stale.

Around the large gathering space, people huddled together in silence. Some stared at the floor. Others sat around the fireplace. Only one or two talked softly to themselves or each other. Heather winced. They seemed perfectly content here and it sent a chill of fear through her.

What if she became like them? Content in this place of emptiness. Where there was no time and nothing changed. Forgetting what she'd done and why.

Forever.

She wanted to forget what she'd done, but something down deep kept her fighting against that easy path now. Maybe that was the point of this place? To remember. To understand. To change it.

"Do they even remember that they killed themselves?" Heather asked, pointing at an old couple curled up on the closest end of the sectional.

Ross shrugged. "Some do. Some have tricked themselves into believing they're away from home, on vacation." He nodded toward the old couple. "Avana says those two were among the first lost ones in this place."

"And they're still here?" she cried.

Heather hurried across the room to stand in front of the old couple. Ross rushed after her.

"Heather, don't," he said in a soft voice.

"Hi there," said Heather, offering the couple a warm smile. "I'm Heather Billot."

The bronze-skinned old woman with hawkish features, brown eyes, and greying dark hair braided and piled on top of her head turned and smiled at Heather.

"Hello, Heather, I'm Ester," she said, laying her hand against her ivory drape of clothing. She gestured at the square-jawed old man sitting beside her, his hair thick and white, his aquiline nose prominent, brown eyes sad. "And this is my husband, Matthew."

"Why did you both come here?" Heather asked, motioning at the gathering room.

Ester turned to stare at her husband, a grimace bowing her mouth. He shook his head, looking confused.

"I—I don't know," she said finally.

"I tried to tell you," Ross said in her ear. "Most people here block out what happened to them. What they did to themselves."

Heather turned to Ross. "Then how do you expect them to look for this Spiral if they refuse to even acknowledge that they killed themselves? Why would they even care about it?"

Ester gasped, her hand flying to her mouth as she stared at her husband in horror. His face twisted into a grimace as he shook his head.

"It's true, you know," said Heather, turning back to them. "That's why we're all here. Because we took our own lives."

"No," Ester snapped, her brow wrinkling, her brown eyes sparking with anger. "No, that's not true."

"Isn't it?" Heather asked. "Why can't you admit it to yourself now, after it's already done?"

Avana glided down the stairs, wearing an arctic-white dress, a pale blue sheen clinging to the silky fabric.

"Why not, Ester? Matthew?" Avana's tone was sharp and mocking. "Why don't you answer the young lady?"

A cruel smile touched Avana's smooth face. She seemed to delight in their confusion.

The old woman shook her head and lay her head against her husband's shoulder.

"We're on holiday," she said in an angry voice. "That's why we're here."

"You see, Heather. I tried to warn you about them." Avana's hard, judgmental gaze fell on Ross. "All of them. But you'll have to learn that for yourself. Until you become just like them. All of you do."

Heather moved toward Avana and grabbed her forearm. A look of surprise washed across Avana's pale face.

"Maybe you know the others," she said, motioning over her shoulder at the old couple. "But you're wrong about Ross. And me."

Avana tilted her head back and laughed, the sound rasping against Heather's ears.

"Am I now? You've known Ross only a short while. How can you have that much perspective on anything, little human?"

"Because I see hope in his eyes," said Heather. She laid her hand against Ross' chest. "And I feel it here. In his heart."

Ross laid his hand on top of hers and squeezed.

"Apparently, you're not familiar with human facial expressions either. Like the poker face."

"The what?" Avana replied, her face scrunching in confusion.

"Never mind," Heather snapped, rolling her eyes as Ross began laughing.

His eyes burned like embers, his whole body burning bright against the faded, muted souls filling the great tree.

Avana glanced at Ross one more time, the hint of surprise in her icy eyes. With the flip of her hair, she dissolved into smoke and flitted around the room. She was translucent as she passed through Ester and Matthew, four men playing cards, a group of women huddled by the fireplace, and finally Ross. She hovered beside Heather now, her form turning solid again as she stared.

"There's nothing to read, my dear. Nothing in this room but emptiness and denial. Can't you see it?"

Heather smirked at Avana, pointing at Ross' animated expression and then her own face. "That's why they call it a poker face, Avana. So, the other players can't see by your expression that you have a great hand. The beauty of humans is that we're like the elements. Enduring like earth and changeable like the wind. When we find the courage to change directions, we don't always show it on our faces. Or give away our intentions."

Avana laughed. "Courage? You all gave up. I'd call that cowardice."

Heather felt the burn in her cheeks. She glared at Avana.

"What do you know about courage? Until you've felt pain so deep that you'd choose oblivion at your own hand over feeling anything for one more minute, then you don't know shit."

Avana fell silent, an expression Heather couldn't read replacing her condemnation. Poker face? Or stunned silent?

Heather motioned at Ester. "She's terrified because she knows what she's done, but she can't face it. Why? I don't know yet. Maybe because there's no way out? Why live with that torture when you can block it out? It's how people survive."

If she could call this place surviving. It wasn't even existing. It was the remains of a failed attempt to suffocate their own awareness. Okay, maybe it hadn't been courageous, taking her own life, but it took a lot of guts and a lot of despair.

She sighed. Maybe Avana was right?

The thought of trying a second time made her shudder. And it didn't make her feel brave.

That's why Ross' story amazed and horrified her. He'd had the guts to make that second attempt. Still, she saw the courage underneath his pain, courage that kept him moving here. She hoped it would save him and not destroy him.

Ross stared at her a moment or two then smiled. "She's right, Avana. If they believed that the Spiral existed, they'd see a way out. Maybe then they'd do more than pretend they were on holiday?"

Avana tossed her head back again, her ghostly white locks floating around her, and laughed. "It'll never happen, but I might just enjoy watching the two of you try." She sighed. "I'd enjoy watching someone with courage for a change."

Then her gaze was on Heather. There was no mockery in her face now.

"You have more than I've seen in a long time here, Heather. I hope you find a way out of the Between." She held out her arms. "I hope you show the others a way out, too."

Rising toward the ceiling, Avana floated away toward the stairs, disappearing as Ester and Matthew laughed and cuddled like they might have done in better times.

For a few moments, Heather watched them, almost forgetting.

That same smell of dirty rain filled the air, a washed-out hint of woodsmoke from the fireplace that crackled above the murmurs and whispers. Was that scent from her imagination?

"I almost expected something to be different, too," he said in a quiet voice, gently squeezing her shoulder. "But understand that *we* are what's different."

Heather gazed at Ross a moment. He was right. She'd already seen the change in his eyes. A look of strength there. Determination.

Gone was that almost wild-eyed desperation she'd seen in his eyes a few times. The same desperation that she must have mirrored back to him when she arrived. But she also saw something else that remained, something that made her smile.

Hope.

He was thinking about his Jessie. Heather could almost see the images flutter across his face. For the first time since he'd arrived here, he had a chance to save her. And he was making plans. He was thinking!

Still, she couldn't help but feel that she was losing him at the same time.

"How do we change them?" she asked, motioning toward Ester. "Convince them to trust something they can't see?"

"By getting past these illusions," he said.

Ross moved over to an empty couch near Ester and Matthew and sat down, facing them. They stared at each other, not even acknowledging his presence.

Heather followed, sitting beside Ross. She drew her long legs underneath her and faced Ester.

"How is your holiday going, Matthew?" Ross asked.

The old man sat up, looking confused—almost dazed—as he stared at Ross, his liver-spotted hand shaking as he clutched Ester's aged but smooth hand. Matthew was tall, but a bit thick around the waist, hollowed dark eyes bright against his straight, white hair. Ester had a willowy shape, tall and lean, almost bony, her steely grey hair coarse and wavy.

Heather had never seen either of them leave that sofa.

"Ester, where are you from?" she asked.

"The Empire," she answered.

Heather frowned. "Where?"

"Well, Rome, of course," she said, almost indignant.

"When did you leave?"

"Just after Caesar was murdered and Augustus became Emperor," she replied. "We haven't been back since."

She heard traces of an accent in Ester's voice, nothing like any Italian accent she'd ever heard. Their words sort of bent as they spoke, like they were changing into something that Heather understood. Had Ester really come from ancient Rome? If she had, then why did she have a name like Ester? Or Matthew? Those names didn't sound right.

"Ester's not a Roman name, is it?"

Ester's face darkened, fear touching her brown eyes. "We took Christian names after Caesar's threat had passed. If only we'd known that there were darker days still ahead." She pressed her hand to her mouth, clutching Matthew's hand tighter.

"Ester, what is it?" Matthew asked, turning toward her. She was trembling, her eyes wide. Like she was seeing something horrible.

Finally, whatever she remembered seemed to fade and her smile returned. An oblivious smile, like she'd just hit a switch and turned something off. She cuddled closer to her husband.

"It's nothing, my love," she said, laying her head on his shoulder. She brushed long, thin fingers through his hair. "Nothing at all. We're safe now. Safe."

Ester had been through something terrible before taking her life. Heather wondered if it was worth making the old woman relive it again, but the longer Ester pretended none of it had happened, the longer everyone stayed trapped in the Between. Reliving what happened would make Ester acknowledge and face what she'd done. And it would bring her one step closer to escaping those memories forever.

Heather rose from the couch and sat down on the couch arm

beside Ester. She slid her arm around the old woman's shoulders and Ester turned toward her.

"What's the matter, child?" Ester asked in a soft voice, looking concerned like her mother used to when she came home from a bad day at school.

There'd been a lot of those. Bullies never seemed to take sick days or stay home much, always making time to push around people with the most to lose.

"Just that we're not safe here," said Heather. "It feels safe, but the longer we stay, the more dangerous it becomes."

"Nonsense!"

"Heather's right, Ester. Listen to her," Ross replied.

Ester's jaw tightened, but she didn't turn away. Instead, her grip on her husband's hand grew stronger, as if she thought that Heather might try to pull her away. His tawny skin was darker than Ester's, making her taut hands look almost ghostly.

"I don't know what you mean," said Ester, her tone flat.

"You and Matthew never dreamed of this place," said Heather. "Neither did I. It was the absolute last thing I expected when I opened my eyes...afterward."

Ester pressed her mouth into a tight line, her eyes misting, her grip on Matthew's hand tightening.

Heather looked down at her hands a moment. "See, I took my own life. Just like you and—"

Ester chuckled and cast an amused look at Matthew who laughed along with her.

"We did no such thing," said Ester, her chin raised. "Suicide is the unforgivable sin. It's punishable by the abyss." She gestured toward the fireplace's warm glow. "As you can see, we're nowhere near an abyss, child. You've just had a bad dream. That's all. Why don't you go have some supper? You must be starving."

Heather shook her head. The dead didn't eat and when they slept, it was forever. No dreams. No consciousness. That's the place they all edged closer to with every dusk.

A step closer to those fields of grey poppies. Or Death herself.

"No, Ester, listen to me—"

Ester brushed her hand across Heather's forehead. "You look exhausted, child. Some hot soup and some sleep will do you wonders."

Sighing, Heather rose from the couch and walked away toward the fireplace. It was impossible. Ester and Matthew wouldn't listen. They wanted to remain in their own limbo for eternity and there was nothing she could do to stop it.

Zakhart insisted there were others like her and Ross here, people who wanted to change what they did, but all Heather saw were people trapped so deeply in their own illusions and fears that they had no desire to leave them.

How long until she joined them?

"It's not easy to get through," said Ross from somewhere behind her.

She didn't even turn around as she slumped against the wall and held her hands to the fire. It wasn't real, she told herself and stuck her hand into the flames. Fire licked at her hand, down her arm, but she felt no heat. And no pain.

She wasn't flesh and blood anymore, so there was nothing to burn.

"Heather, don't!" Ross pulled her arm back.

She got to her feet and turned to stare at him. "Why? It's not real." She motioned around the room. "None of it's real! Because I'm dead, Ross!" She spun around, the stoic faces rushing past, their expressions unchanged. "We're all dead and this place is just some wild illusion pulsing through my brain as it dies. I'm still lying on that Bainbridge Island beach, aren't I? Waiting for everything to shut down."

She gripped her head in her hands. But her brain wasn't turning off. It was torturing her slowly. This place, these people were conjured out of bits of her dying mind as the oxygen stopped flowing and her heart stopped beating.

Why wasn't all of this fading away and leaving her in peace? Like she'd expected. Like she'd planned.

She balled her hands into fists, shaking. "Why won't it turn off, Ross? Why? I did everything right! I took enough Molly. Timed it so no one would find me until morning. Even left a note on my Instagram page. So why does it just go on and on like this?"

Ross slid his arms around her as she sank to her knees, cold tears against her cheeks. But she didn't put her arms around him. She didn't want to feel his warmth and comfort. Didn't want to feel attracted to him. Didn't want to feel anything. Still, that bit of warmth, that hint of connection pushed through anyway.

And she needed to feel it. To touch him.

She gripped Ross' arms and squeezed her eyes closed as her heart began to hurt. It felt so good to feel someone's arms around her—to feel something good—even for a few moments. That need ached through her now.

"I don't understand either, Heather," said Ross softly, his hand against her hair, stroking gently. "And I've spent far too much time trying to drag the others out of their memories. So much so that I've even given up on mine."

"I just want to go to sleep," Heather whispered in his ear and he held her tighter.

"No!" Ross shook her. "Don't say that. You're the first one who's even tried to fight back, Heather. The first! You even found a pale angel. You heard the Spiral call to you. Don't let them win. Don't become like them. Please, Heather—I need you." His voice was strained and tight now. "Don't let go...you're the only reason I'm still here."

She pulled away from him. "But we need them, too, Ross. Can't you see that? Without them, we'll never escape either."

She dropped back to the floor and wrapped her arms around her knees, resting her head against her arms.

"I'm so tired, Ross," Heather said with a groan. "Ashamed and tired."

"So am I," said Matthew, rising from the sofa.

"Matthew, no!"

With eyes wide and mouth agape, Ester grabbed hold of his arm, but the old man moved away from her. Ester reached her hand out to him, but he moved out of her reach.

Heather's eyes widened as she watched him walk across the room toward her.

Matthew stood there a moment, glancing back at Ester, but then he crouched beside Heather. He studied her with his intense brown eyes, then Ross, and then gave her forearm a reassuring squeeze.

Heather held her breath, afraid to say anything and risk sending him back into his own fragile illusion.

With stiff movements, Matthew knelt on both knees beside her. And took her hand in his. It felt warm and firm.

Ross sank down beside him and Heather.

"How did you end your life?" Heather asked, unable to stand the silence any longer.

Matthew cast a painful gaze at his wife who stared out the window, lost in her own little world, and finally bowed his head.

"We were to be fed to the lions," said Matthew, folding his tall, bulky frame into a sitting position by the fire. "Interrupted by Caesar's most timely demise, but we were still in prison, Ester and I. Augustus saved Rome, but not those already grievously injured by Caesar's wrath. We remained there in prison, ignored by Augustus until we could stand it no longer. We found a sympathetic guard who brought us poison. Only then did we escape for good."

Matthew pointed at his wife who hummed to herself as she began dusting the tables around the sofa with a faded white handkerchief.

"Ester refuses to remember," he said with a sigh and his eyes turned glassy. "But with good reason."

Heather shook her head, studying his thin, lined face and dark eyes. "Why won't she remember?"

"Our daughter," he said, choking up. "Our daughter went to—to the lions two days before Caesar was killed. Our son was to go next, but he—" Tears rushed down the old man's face. "He threw himself on a Centurion's sword. After killing six guards. He was with us here, in the great tree, for a long time until he set out alone. On one of the paths."

Matthew struggled up from the floor. He crossed his arms and paced, trembling now.

"Said he'd found a way out. Past the soulstalkers. Said there were other creatures that would help him. They dwelled far away in the marshlands beyond the forest. Demons. Thraecius said they would help him escape and he returned here each time before darkness covered the dusk. Trying to get us to follow him. And once—"

His voice hitched in his throat and he sucked in a breath.

"Once, he said Juliana came to him in the marshlands, eager to lead him out."

Heather rose to her feet, a chill washing over her, and moved toward Matthew. "But wasn't Juliana killed by lions?"

Matthew nodded, hands pressed against his face.

"She couldn't be in the Between then, Matthew," said Ross. "Didn't your son understand that?"

"He did, at first," said Matthew, continuing to pace again. "But after a while, everything becomes clouded. And you forget what is real and what is imagined. That gets worse the longer you're here."

Heather shuddered. She was already questioning her memory.

"The demons," said Matthew, "they made him believe she'd come here to search for us. To find him. That's when Thraecius seemed to go mad. He was completely unreachable. He left for the clearing and never returned to the great tree. That's when Ester withdrew completely from all of it. And slowly, I have, too, I suppose. It hasn't mattered, you see."

"Maybe it does now?" said Heather, feeling encouraged. One of them had listened. If she and Ross could bring back Thraecius, then maybe the others here would listen, too. "Maybe we can find

Thraecius and bring him back from the Veils? If we can bring him back here to you, will you and Ester help us find the Spiral?"

A smile warmed Matthew's face as he turned around to face Heather.

"You could bring him back? From the demons? I–I didn't think that was even possible. How would you even find him?"

Heather felt the fear tremble through her. She had no idea whether they could even reach these Demon Veils, much less find Thraecius inside them. Maybe Zakhart understood this place after all? Nevertheless, she would at least try to save Thraecius. And anyone else she found behind these Veils. She despised Avana and the smoke people, but they had to be better company than demons. Well, maybe not, but they were definitely safer.

"Ross?" she replied, moving toward the quiet young man. She took hold of his hand and squeezed. "Will you help me find the Demon Veils? And help convince Thraecius to return here?"

He nodded. "I've never been that far from the great tree, but I'm willing to try and rescue him. If it'll get us more help to find the Spiral. And the poppy fields."

Excited, Matthew's steps lightened as he rushed over to Ester. He took her in his arms, forcing her to look into his eyes.

"Ester! Listen to me, love. They're trying to bring Thraecius back from the marshlands!"

The distracted smile faded from her face, her expression serious as she turned her gaze toward Heather and Ross.

"Thraecius?" she said. "Have you seen my Thraecius?"

Heather moved toward Ester and patted the old woman's hand. "No, but we're going into the marshlands to search for him. We'll do our best to bring him home to you, Ester. I promise."

Ester let go of Matthew and pulled Heather into a tight hug.

"My Thraecius...coming home after so long. Is it even possible?"

She looked around the room as if she'd never seen it before, the understanding at last flickering there. Heather saw the cloudiness in her brown eyes fade. In the old woman's face, she saw understanding.

Ester understood where she was, what she'd done, and what might have already happened to her son, Thraecius.

"I hope we aren't too late," said Heather in a hushed voice.

"So do I," Ester said in a half-whisper. "His rage weakens him. Lets them control him. He loved his little sister more than his own life. Maybe that will save him?"

Ester let go, her gaze drifting off to the darkening windows, that singsong hum returning to her lips. An ancient song Heather didn't recognize.

Matthew patted Heather's shoulder and then returned to Ester's side on the couch.

"Thraecius was distraught when they took Juliana to the lions," said Matthew. "He'd plotted violence against the soldiers and did many of them great harm before he took his own life. That anger fuels him here, too."

Heather felt sick, unable to comprehend the horrors these people had endured. But she also knew that anger was as dangerous as despair here. The darkness and the dusk creatures fed on it, thrived on it.

Did the demons feed on that rage, too? Would they hunt for it? Were they drawn to anyone holding onto so much rage?

Thraecius probably stood out like a fast-food sign on a dark country road. Even if they did find him, Heather didn't know how she'd get him to come back. If she could convince him that the only way to see his sister again was through the Spiral, maybe he'd follow them back to the great tree?

But how could she convince him of anything when she had just as many doubts? She didn't know who to trust. The flying things looked so much alike from a distance. And the voice in the forest—had that really been her mom? Maybe it was some dark thing taunting her?

A soulstalker? Demons? Death?

Maybe Zakhart was really a demon trying to lure her to the

Demon Veils? Maybe the stories about this Spiral were more cruel jokes that the universe was playing on her?

Turning around, Heather ran into Avana as she moved toward the door, the firelight's flicker casting thin shadows through the great tree.

"I wouldn't go out there, Heather," said Avana, staring at her, looking almost sad. "Darkness brings out packs of soulstalkers to hunt."

Heather's eyes narrowed. She glared at Avana, floating there in her translucence. So condescending. So unaffected by everything. Why couldn't she understand the pain that led people to end their lives?

Avana didn't want to understand. What was she? What were these smoky spirit people? All of them floated through the great tree in silence, more oblivious than the human souls. Like they were alone here. Avana only cared about protecting the great tree. As long as the Between remained intact, she didn't have to care about any of them. Or anything.

"I'll take my chances," said Heather. "I'm tired of being trapped in here. Tired of being safe! Tired of all these people who don't give a shit about finding their way out! At least searching for Thraecius is doing something!"

Heather flung open the door but she didn't turn around.

"Ross, are you coming with me?"

"Heather...not when it's dark," Ross said from somewhere behind her and it made her ache all over.

His voice sounded heavy. Defeated? A chill brushed her spine. He hadn't given up, too, had he? She couldn't take it if he had.

"We'll be safe enough," she said and turned around.

"Avana's right," said Ross, moving closer to her. "They flock like starlings out there when it's dark. We'll wind up in the poppy fields."

Was it true? He said he'd help her find Thraecius. Now, even he was hesitating? It made her ache all over. Had she lost him to the great trees apathy?

"Better there than deluding myself in here," she snapped, crossing her arms. "What if there's no Spiral, Ross? What if it's just more tricks? What if we were really, finally dead the moment we killed ourselves? And this place is just our brain's way of letting us down easy."

Ross took a step toward her and she backed away, wind rushing past the open door. At last, something familiar moved out here. Something she recognized from her world. A strong wind.

"Think about poor Thraecius, Ross," she said, cringing at how he had left the world. It haunted her. "All he did was kill the monsters who fed his sister to the lions. Then himself. Look where he ended up. It's not right!" She motioned toward the burgundy sectional by the window. "Look at his parents. They killed themselves to escape prison and being fed to lions. And they're punished for eternity? No. I refuse to accept this eternal torment bullshit!"

Several of the people within the tree had come down the stairs, gathering around the fireplace, standing behind Ross to stare at her. With empty eyes and blank faces. Even the smoke people stopped their regular routes up and down the stairs, watching her with unaffected stares.

That hollow pain rushed back. Like a knife blade slowly cutting her chest, the past rushing back again.

Like the blank looks her friends had given her when she told them she was falling apart a year after her mother's death. Then two. Like the unapologetic bank officer selling off the Bainbridge Island house to pay bills owed by Mom's estate, giving her two weeks to leave. Sorry, kid. It's just business. Nothing personal, all right? Like the apartment complex manager who'd stared right through her when she explained she'd be late on rent because she'd been kicked out of the only home she'd ever known. Helpless as they sold off the pieces of her life, one torchiere lamp and one bean bag chair at a time.

All of those people had stared right through her—like these lost souls surrounding her. Sorry, no exceptions. Life was nothing but a series of exceptions! Some happy, some not so happy—some even excuses—but they gave life texture as her mom used to say. Substance.

Heather looked at Ross and winced, feeling distance between them for the first time. The fire had cooled in his eyes. How long before he had that look everyone gave her a few months after Mom died. That *why can't you get over it and be like the rest of us* look. That *why can't you fix it with a pill and stop making me feel uncomfortable* look. Smile more. Get over it.

She glanced at Avana and the smoke people trailing up the stairs in wispy coils of smoke. That's when she saw it. That's when she finally understood what was happening here. She backed away toward the door.

Avana. The smoke people. They'd all been human once.

With every passing dusk, they'd given up a little bit more and a little bit more until they finally gave in and faded away. To these husks—wisps of smoke—all of their humanity gone. These smoke people that wandered the stairs and ignored everything around them.

And this was her future if she stayed here.

Now, she understood the imbalance that Zakhart had hinted at, that even Ross had sensed but couldn't fight. Too many of these hopeless spirits crowded the Between, bringing hordes of soulstalkers and other dark things to hunt them.

The Between was overcrowded. And it was crumbling.

The silence in the room was cloying. The vacant looks suffocating. If she stayed here, she'd become just like them. Like Ester and Matthew—even Ross—who hung onto solid form by a thread. They were one step away from becoming a smoky zombie that floated through this place.

Forever.

"It's so too late for you people," she said with a snarl, tears welling in her eyes.

She flung out her arms in frustration, heart racing as she motioned at the trails of smoke filling the room. The sickly yellow flicker of the cold hearth fire casting thin shadows of people pretending to eat and sleep against the great tree's dark windows. She had to get out of here.

"Go back to your illusions! Keep playing these little games with yourself. Keep telling yourself you're still alive and go through the days like everything was still the same."

Like all the pieces were back in place again. Like nothing had ever happened.

Heather slapped her arms against her side. "We killed ourselves! It's our fault we're here. Stop pretending it's someone else's fault and do something about it!" She pointed at a trail of smoke floating past her face. "When you become like this, it's too late."

The only sound in the room was the rush of wind past the windows, branches clacking and scratching against the panes.

Heather turned and ran out into the indigo darkness, wind swirling around her, rustling the silky fabric of her clothes. Her Converses pounded the footpath as she rushed away from the great tree and into the dark woods, toward the clearing with the seven pathways.

If she couldn't find Thraecius or the Veils, she had a fifty-fifty shot at finding the path that led straight to Death. She'd found it once. How hard could it be to find it a second time?

seven

. . .

"HEATHER, WAIT!"

Ross' voice echoed in the distance behind her, carried along on the wind, but she kept running. Past the rustle of trees, the beating of wings.

Shadows fluttered along the edge of her vision, hovering at the tree line and the swaying trees along the path.

She didn't care anymore. She didn't want to connect with anyone. Didn't want to try and help people who didn't want help. Besides, she couldn't even help herself. She only wanted all of this to end, along with the pain in her chest.

All of it.

She ran down a pathway that curved away from the trees, winding through the sea of grass that fluttered in the wind.

A dark wing dipped toward her from the indigo sky, arms outstretched. She veered right.

"Hea—ther," it taunted, its singsong voice echoing above the swaying grass. "Come out and play."

Arms grabbed her around the waist. She stumbled, losing her balance.

Soulstalkers!

She screamed, falling against the forest floor. Damp leaves and twigs clung to her hands and face as she struggled to free herself.

"Heather, stop it! It's me, Ross!"

He rolled her over, grabbing her flailing arms as she screamed and swung out at him. The determination in his gaze wilted her anger and she stopped struggling. Sadness welled in her chest, bubbling into her voice.

"Let me go!" she shouted, but the anger had left her. "Let me go," she said, sounding defeated. "I'm tired, Ross. Just let me go, okay?"

"No!" he shouted through gritted teeth, still gripping her arms. "I won't let you give up now. Not when there's a chance to change everything." He sighed, motioning behind him. "Your anger woke me up again, Heather. It woke up a lot of others, too."

She sagged in his grasp and closed her eyes. "But if they won't do anything about it, it doesn't change anything. Look at Lamarr. And Barb. Look at Ester and Matthew. Even Thraecius. Think about how long they've been there." She shook her head, her eyes brimming with tears. "What chance do we have?"

"A slim one," Ross said in a quiet voice and held her tight.

Wind rushed through her hair above the distant flutter of wings across the grasslands. She longed to feel his heart beating against hers, feel the rise and fall of his chest against hers. Comforts she'd taken for granted until now.

"But if you give up on me now, Heather Billot, there won't be any chance."

And she'd never see her mom again.

Nodding, she let the sorrow burn her throat as the tears trickled down her cheeks. Ross pulled her closer, cradling her as he stroked her hair. She nuzzled her face against his neck, arms enfolding him. For a moment, she lost herself in his touch. Lost herself in the feel of his hands against her face and shoulders. The brush of his lips against her neck. It was a contact she craved. She hadn't felt another body against hers for a long time.

Soulstalkers fluttered through the sea of frosty green grasses, calling to her, taunting her as they floated nearby.

"Come out and play, Heather," one of them called again, leering as he motioned to her with his index finger.

It hovered close, shaking its shaggy, dark hair that framed its thin, angular face. Dark grey wings beat the air, flexing against its muscular shoulders and lean body. It grinned, pointy teeth glistening as it reached out with long, gangly arms and taloned fingers.

Ross let her go as he picked up a rock. He flung it as hard as he could, hitting the soulstalker in the face. It screeched, grabbing its nose with both hands and sank into the grass with a thump.

Heather laughed when the soulstalker hit the ground.

"Too rough for you?" Ross shouted.

In a moment, the soulstalker rose into the air, spitting, and cursing at him which made Ross laugh.

"How 'bout this?" He threw another rock that slammed into the soulstalker's throat.

It let out a muffled screech and rose higher on the wind, soaring away from the trees.

Heather grabbed a rock and heaved it at another soulstalker lurking near the clearing. It thunked against the creature's chest. With a shriek, the soulstalker flapped away.

"Man, that felt good," said Heather, grinning.

"You okay, now?" Ross asked, taking her face in his hands as he studied her, a soft expression in his eyes. Something she couldn't quite read.

She nodded. "Thanks for getting me to keep fighting back," she said. She reached up and brushed the hair out of his eyes.

"Let's get out of here until it's safer, okay? When it's lighter, we'll follow the path to the Demon Veils."

"I-I can't go back to the tree yet, Ross. Not until I've talked to Thraecius. I have to know what keeps him among the demons." Why would he want to stay there when his parents were at the great tree?

Ross sighed, glancing at the ground a moment. He let go of her face and took hold of her right hand, gripping it tightly in both his hands.

"There are too many soulstalkers prowling," he said, his voice calm, but his eyes betrayed him, the fear glinting like a sharp blade. "They nearly carried you away just now."

"But what if there are other pale angels out there, Ross? Like Zakhart. Angels that would help us?"

Ross shook his head. "Zakhart's the first one I've ever seen, Heather."

Raising her hands to her mouth, Heather shouted, "Zakhart! Where are you?"

Ross slid his arm around her shoulders as she scanned the trees for a glimmer of sparrow's wings, a hint of pumpkin-colored eyes.

Only the rustle of leaves and beat of shadow wings touched the quiet.

"He won't come out alone, Heather," said Ross, a hand on her shoulder. "It's too dangerous."

Heather called for the pale angel again, but when only the whistle of wind answered back, she turned toward the woods, arms crossed against her chest. Ross was right. They should wait for the skies' greyness to lighten before they set out for the Veils. Or the poppy fields.

She cringed, knowing she'd have to go back and face everyone, but she doubted any of them were lucid enough to even remember her tirade. They'd all probably gone back to their tidy, little routines by now, forgetting what she'd even said and what they'd done.

"Heather?" A voice echoed somewhere above her, the flutter of wings close. "Are you all right?"

She looked up as Zakhart landed beside her. In another moment, two more pale angels hung above the treetops, descending in a slow freefall to the forest floor. Both were women, each with those warm coppery eyes like Zakhart.

Heather grinned, rushing to take hold of Zakhart's hands.

"I knew you'd come," she said, smiling at him.

He stood up straighter, his chest thrust out. "You said you needed me. How could I not answer that call?"

The female angels set down beside Zakhart. Long and sinewy, their taupe-colored, gracefully curved wings fluttered and then folded against their backs. They were tall and beautiful, one with tawny brown hair, the other with wheaten hair like Zakhart. Both pale angels had intense, copper eyes, but the color seemed lighter than Zakhart's eyes.

"You've brought reinforcements," said Ross, nodding at the other angels. "I didn't know pale angels even existed. But why show yourselves now? I've walked these paths for...for as long as I can remember. Why haven't you ever helped me? Or the others?"

Zakhart grinned. "You never asked."

Ross shifted beside Heather. "I never even thought to ask. Boy, do I feel stupid now." He sighed and looked away.

"Sadly, no one at the great tree ever sought help like Heather." Zakhart continued. "She searched the grasslands for a way out and she called out for help. She was the first human I've ever seen up close before. She even asked my name." He shrugged, poking the ground with his toe. "She was the first one I thought I could save here. And now, I see she's found others who want that help." He turned, smiling, toward Heather. "What can I do to help, Heather?"

"Zakhart, we need your help to reach the Demon Veils," she asked.

The female pale angels stared at one another, fear in their gazes as they shook their heads.

"Not the Veils!" they said in unison. The brown-haired angel stepped forward, laying a hand on Heather's arm. "You don't want to go there, little human."

"Halea's right," said Zakhart. "If the dusk creatures don't get you, the demons will. Why would you want to go there? It's the saddest place in the Between."

Sad? Why was it sad? She had no idea what this place was, but his comment sent a chill through her. "We need to bring someone back," she said in a quiet voice.

"Someone who needs our help," Ross added.

"No, absolutely not," Zakhart cried, crossing his arms. His eyes glistened in the dark clearing. "It's too dangerous."

"But you told us we had to reconnect with the others," said Ross, his voice sharp. "We already know that every connection's a risk."

"Those you're still able to reach," said Zakhart, turning toward Ross.

"The demons' hold is so strong," said Halea. "Besides them, you risk getting trapped among the Veils."

"Razasha, tell her!" Zakhart said, looking flustered.

The other pale angel called Razasha stepped toward Heather, hand outstretched. Her hair rippled into long, wheaten waves as her wings unfurled with a rush of air. She laid her hand against Heather's shoulder.

"Not trapped against your will, of course," said Razasha. "Nothing here is against your will."

"Isn't it?" Heather replied, pulling away. "I can't leave this place."

"At your own doing, Heather," said Zakhart, his face shadowed with a frown, voice calmer now. "You chose to come here, remember?"

Heather nodded and bowed her head. He was right. It was her fault. And every day she remained here.

"What if the demons trap us, too?" Ross asked, squinting at the wavy-haired angel.

Razasha shook her head. "Demons are more subtle than that." Her voice was soprano-clear like the singsong of water against crystal. "They aren't very fierce, but they thrive on deception. They're actually quite weak by nature, but here, they're very dangerous." She stepped back beside Halea.

"They'll deceive you," said Zakhart. "They'll trick you with your own weaknesses. Your own hopes and dreams. It's so dangerous, Heather."

Heather thought of Thraecius' rage and his love for his little sister. Weaknesses the demons probably used against him. Did they offer to help him find his sister? Save her? Avenge her somehow? Did Thraecius even remember his parents now? She thought about her mom and Ross' girlfriend, Jessie. Would the creatures in the Veils use these things against them?

She shuddered. Of course, they would. She and Ross had to be careful and stick together.

"We've got to try, Zakhart," said Heather, glancing at Razasha. "If we can bring Thraecius back here, then we can reach the others. Convince them that this isn't the end. That the Spiral can free us all."

She moved toward Zakhart, laying her hands on his silken sleeves.

"Please, Zakhart. Thraecius deserves a chance to escape the Veils. Will you take us there?"

Zakhart studied her face a moment then Ross. Heather saw his frustration. Like him, she had no desire to enter the Demon Veils. Even the pathway was shrouded in thick, indigo darkness that strangled the woods. In Ross' eyes, she saw that he'd resigned himself to whatever Zakhart advised, but she didn't know if Ross would follow her.

"All right," said Zakhart, "but only if we carry you there. It's the only way to keep the dusk from swallowing up both of you."

Heather turned to Ross. "I'm going. I'll see you back at the clearing."

He shook his head. "Not happening, Heather. We go together or not at all. I won't let you tackle this alone."

She smiled, reaching out to touch his face. Ross closed his eyes a moment, laying his hand on hers. Then he let go, turning toward Zakhart again, a troubled look tightening his features.

"What if Death finds us?" His voice was so quiet, so final, as if he expected to meet Death along the way.

Zakhart's eyes widened. "We'll fly fast and hope we lose her in the marshlands. But if she sets her sights on you, her pursuit is relentless. You'll have to keep moving or face her scythe."

The cold rush of fear trembled through Heather. That scythe meant nothingness. Forever. It hadn't bothered her before. She'd counted on it. But now, that finality terrified her.

"We have to try and reach Thraecius," said Heather. It was as much for her and Ross as it was for Matthew and Ester.

Time had no steady march in this place. It was silent and deceiving. Nothing decayed or aged. Everything was exactly how it had been when Ester and Matthew left ancient Rome. A shadow of real life.

What if she closed her eyes and discovered a whole century had passed? Or two? Here, there was nothing to mark time passing.

Outside this place, time and space rushed on in its dance of entropy and chaos, the world changing by the second as people were born and others aged and died. It scared her how much time had already passed.

Had it been minutes since her death? Months? Or longer? Had she left even the tiniest of marks behind? What would it all look like—feel like—now?

"Heather, you ready?" Ross asked, a hand on her shoulder.

She stared at Ross a moment, the rustle of Zakhart's wings strangely comforting. "How much time do you think has passed since you first found me in the grass?"

His face scrunched into a grimace, brows pressed into hard lines above his eyes.

"How much time since what?"

"Since you died," she said. "Since I died."

He shrugged, staring off into the clearing a moment. "I don't know. Weeks maybe? A year since I died? Why?"

A cold ball of dread knotted her stomach. Over sixty years had already passed since he died.

Would she eventually lose all concept of the world she'd left behind? Had the people she'd known (like Ashley) already forgotten her? Were they even still alive?

"It's been over sixty years, Ross," she said in a hushed voice, gripping his arm.

His eyes widened into a frightened stare as he looked past her now, a hand against his face.

"My God...sixty years? Are you sure? What year did you die?"

"I died in 2022, Ross."

"What? 2022? So much time..." He sighed, rubbing his temple. "I don't know why, but that frightens me."

Zakhart leaned toward her, a hand on her shoulder, kind smile on his face. "Time is not so linear. Time ebbs and flows on currents and eddies, changing its direction and timbre. It's not an unbending, flat line, Heather. It's like a string that twists and bends, curves over itself, even knots in places. And even where it's stretched tight, it can cast ripples, resonating when plucked."

"But won't it eventually end?" Ross asked.

Zakhart shook his head. "It's a cycle, Ross. The breath of life is but a moment, but the force behind it is eternal." He squeezed her shoulder. "The very fact that you stand here now should be more than enough evidence."

He was right. She thought she'd ended everything. Turned off the light and snuffed out that breath of life, that happy little accident inside her. But she'd only destroyed the container. Cast off her human shell. Somehow, her lifeforce went on in this place beyond human reach, beyond human contact.

"I thought I'd ended it," she said, biting her lip. "I thought I could make all of it stop."

Zakhart pulled her into a gentle hug. "None of us can stop eternal forces."

She frowned. "Like death?"

The pale angel nodded, solemnness shadowing his features. "Death is an elemental force forever entwined with life. They can't be separated, but together, they have no beginning and no end."

Heather glanced at Ross who nodded at her. She motioned toward the dark sky. "We're ready when you are."

Zakhart trilled an alto note through the dark forest, reminding Heather of a sparrow's chatter. In moments, Razasha and Halea rose into the air, slipped through the treetops, and back again, landing beside Zakhart. They moved toward Ross as Zakhart scooped Heather into his arms and lifted her into the air, his wings a soft hush against the wind.

Above the treetops, the Between looked small and fragile. Handfuls of warm gold and orange lights dotted the clearing where the great tree's branches reached into the sky. The air smelled clean and fresh, almost a hint of pine trees. She smiled, remembering the scent of pine nettles tanging the crisp, cool Washington State air. Another memory?

Heather closed her eyes as Zakhart carried her above the trees. Behind her, wings beat the air as the other pale angels rose from the clearing, carrying Ross between them. One held his torso and one held his legs as they followed Zakhart across the edge of the grasslands and toward the swampy lands beyond the trees. Ross didn't look very comfortable. She hoped the Veils weren't far.

They flew a long while until the stink of sulfur bubbled up from brown and green muck tangling across the ground. Moss scabbed the rocks and crusted the branches of dead river birch. Their white trunks were broken, scalded, limbs bare, roots strangled by the toxic mud and stench. She traced the wide, ashen path as it wound through the bone-white tree trunks, eventually leading back to the safety of the great tree.

The path clung to the edges of the murky swamplands and slithered around a white, rocky outcropping that jutted up from the ground like a broken bone through skin.

Zakhart flew closer.

The outcropping was a cave. Angry firelight leapt outside the dark entrance, wild shadows twisting across the swamps as a cold wind scoured the marshlands. Heather shivered, folding her arms against her chest as she searched for movement in the air, in the water, and below.

Nothing stirred or scurried across the spongy ground as Zakhart descended toward the ashen path. He landed with the grace of an eagle, setting down without even a stumble. He held her aloft as he took a few steps forward, his gaze flicking over his shoulder, toward the black, marshy soup that gurgled near his feet. He took a step back then moved toward the outcropping of white rock that arched into a cavernous entry. Pitch black. Only then did he set her down.

The air smelled cool here, scent of loamy soil faint against the sharp chill. Heather pressed her arms against her stomach, trying to hold in some warmth. She looked up, watching the other pale angels circling overhead, Ross in their arms. They seemed reluctant to land.

Finally, Zakhart motioned them down. With a gentle sweep of cream-colored wings, both pale angels banked toward the swamp, turned, and soared to a stop on the ashen pathway. Razasha let go of Ross' feet, setting him on the pathway. Only when he seemed to have his balance did Halea release him.

"Thank you," he said and moved toward Heather.

He stood beside her now, his body so close that she felt his warm, anxious breath against her neck. He folded his arms against his chest, his breath fogging the air. Was she imagining that?

She leaned against him, the solid feel of him comforting. He slid an arm around her waist, pulling her close. He was shaking. She reached out and covered his hands with hers, trying to warm his hands.

"I've never traveled this far from the clearing," he said in an uneasy voice. "It's so dark here. And cold."

Zakhart nodded. "The cold is an illusion, Ross. And there are darker places in the Between. You've seen very little of its landscape."

Heather shuddered. Like the poppy fields. She'd only seen them from a grey, murky distance.

Halea and Razasha stepped close to Zakhart, both pale angels looking frightened.

"You don't know anything about the Veils, do you?" Halea asked.

"Only the name," said Ross.

Heather nodded. She stared at Halea. Fear burned bright in the tawny-haired angel's coppery eyes.

"The Veils are sort of a-window into all physical lifetimes. At this window, humans can see the thread of their physical life through the Veils."

"When your life passes before your eyes when you die," said Ross. "Judgment or something? A life review?"

Heather frowned. "Like a replay? Or like a near death experience? Y'know? So, it's like when someone's life passes before their eyes? Guess this is more of an after-death experience."

Zakhart shook his head. "People can step through the Veil of their life and see the events leading up to their death. See what happened afterward, what happened to loved ones, how things turned out, that sort of thing. An objective view of what happened—for better or worse. You've been warned."

Could she really see what happened after her suicide?

She stepped away from Ross, moving toward Zakhart. Ross moved closer, too, curiosity burning in his eyes.

Zakhart unfurled his taupe-colored wings and enfolded Heather and Ross in them.

"I see those looks on your faces," Zakhart said with a wary look. "It's not a comforting trip, I assure you. Seeing what you left behind can be very painful. Remember that. That's why the Veils are the most dangerous place in the Between. It draws people like moths to fire. That's why the demons congregated here. The Veils are a natural lure, drawing people in because they are the last connection to the world they left behind. The demons feed on that, twisting facts and inventing stories. Making it even harder to leave. Don't ever forget that!"

That's how Thraecius got trapped here. They had to be careful.

A grey face peered out at them from the darkness, hard, steely eyes glaring. Tiny horn buds protruded from its wide, angular face as it crossed its arms and stood immobile at the white cave's entrance.

Sizing them up, Heather realized.

Zakhart drew his wings tighter around them. "I don't want to leave you here," he said, hands on hers and Ross' shoulders. He watched the demon with a suspicious gaze. "I'm not use to handing over my humans to demons."

"We don't intend to stay," said Ross through gritted teeth as he watched the demon emerge from the opening.

The creature's body was smooth and leathery except for the shadowy trace of hair around its jaw line. It looked about Heather's height. But the grey skin soon warmed to a terra cotta stain, showing a pattern, a little like scales, even though it looked soft and fleshy. The demon wore a thin, blowsy shirt with ragged sleeves and black pants with worn hems.

It scampered toward them, studying Heather with hard, dark eyes. Finally, it snorted, a laugh scraping past a mouthful of yellow, pointy teeth.

"You look awfully lost, little humans. And where'd you score those whiny little birds at your shoulders?"

Zakhart's lip curled, a scowl on his face. Razasha and Halea glared at the demon, hands on their hips, wings flexing in nervous, angry twitches.

"I know exactly where I am," Heather said. She started to step forward, but Ross grabbed her arm, holding her back.

She glanced at him. His face looked tense, worry in his eyes. He shifted his weight to his right foot as he studied the demon and the massive cave ahead. Heather wondered what he saw beyond the cave's thick, inky blackness.

If they went in there, could they get out again?

The demon smirked. "So, you came looking for us then? Another power seeker. Guess you've figured out who holds power here in the Between."

"The Red City?" Zakhart quipped.

"Death," said Heather, her gaze unblinking at the demon.

The demon let out a hiss and shrank back.

Heather stepped forward and this time, Ross didn't hold her back, instead moving alongside her. His steady presence felt protective, comforting when Zakhart pulled back his protective wings. The chill against her skin deepened, her fear rising. She wouldn't show fear to these demons. She'd let this one think that she was a power seeker like all the rest. For now.

"We want to enter the Veils," said Heather.

"You and so many, many others, little human," said the demon, sidling toward her. "Sooner or later, all of you need that connection back, don't you? How long has it been since you've been home? Heather, isn't it?"

Its feet were long and thin, toes looking shriveled as it walked toward her. She looked up at it as it eagerly reached shriveled fingers toward her face. Heather froze, doing her best not to flinch from its touch. But even as its cold, almost slimy skin brushed across her cheeks, she felt its power.

"I can give you what you want, Heather," the voice echoed in her head, purred in her ears even though the demon made no sound.

"I'll take you to your mother. Or your friends. I have the power. I can travel the Spiral, too. Give me your hand and I can take you to all those places. Here, you can find what you lost again."

Her fingers twitched a moment, her hand almost moving of its own volition, but Ross' firm grip on her wrist softened the voice in her head. She let out a deep sigh and glanced at Ross. His face was taut, lips pressed into a tight grimace, gaze unwavering from the creature's face. He walked in front, keeping her behind him. Protecting her, she realized. Like he'd done since she arrived here.

Here, at the Demon Veils, she didn't mind.

Some of the demon's excitement fled as it cast a long, challenging look at Ross. Finally, its gaze returned to Heather.

"My name is Mulciber. My job is to help the new arrivals. I'll take you where the Veils are, but I can only take you inside one at a time."

Ross' arm slid around Heather's waist, drawing her back against his chest. "No way!" he snarled, his tone sharp, clipped. "We go through together or not at all."

Abruptly, Ross fell quiet, squinting. His head twitched against something Heather couldn't see.

Were they crawling into his head, too? Whatever it was, he was visibly struggling against it. Mulciber had some kind of hold of him.

He let out a groan, his body trembling now.

"Ross, look at me," said Heather. She tugged on his arm. "Ross!"

At last, his gaze snapped toward her and he looked disoriented, blinking as he glanced around. He seemed unsure where he was. Finally, he squeezed her hand.

"I was home," he said with a gasp, turning to Heather. "I was back home in Flora. W-with Jessie. Before—the garage."

He was still shaking. Heather took hold of his hands, gripping them hard until he looked at her again.

"It's not real," she whispered. "Stay with me, okay? Don't let him get inside your head like that."

Nodding, Ross let out a sigh and the glare returned to his face as he studied Mulciber again.

"Don't do that again," Ross said with a growl.

"You invited me in," said Mulciber with a shrug.

Zakhart stepped between Mulciber and Ross, his wings nearly hitting the demon in the face. He turned his back to the demon, shielding them from its unblinking stare.

"You don't have to do this," he whispered, worry burning in his pumpkin-orange eyes.

"Zakhart, if we can't overcome even one minor demon," Heather whispered, shaking her head, "then what chance do we have of getting out of there?"

This brought a look of grim acceptance from Ross who nodded.

"She's right. Be on guard. We have to at least try to help Thraecius. No one else has bothered."

The muscles in Zakhart's jaw tightened as he cast an uncertain glance at the taller female angel.

"What say you, Halea?" Zakhart asked, shielding them with his wings.

"You have to let them try," said Halea. "But remind them who has the power."

Heather cast an uncertain look at Mulciber who leaned patiently against the dark rocks, looking almost bored.

"It's too dangerous," said Zakhart, turning Heather's face back to look at him. "But I can't stop you. Never forget that *you* have the power. Not them. Never them, Heather, Ross. They don't have the power to hold you against your will. Only you can trap yourself behind the Veils. Don't forget that."

She had to remember that if she wanted to help Thraecius.

"Thanks, Zakhart," she said and laid her hand to his face which made the pale angel smile. "We'll call for you and the others when we're done here."

He nodded, a nervous smile on his face. "I'll listen closely for your call." He touched her forehead with his fingers. "Remember, you hold the power."

"I won't forget."

"Neither will I," said Ross.

Mulciber spat on the ground. "Angels make me sick."

When Zakhart let go of her, Heather walked toward Mulciber.

"Take us to the Veils," she said. "Together."

In two long strides, Ross was beside her, a hand on her arm, his body positioned between her and Mulciber.

"Suit yourselves," said Mulciber. "It'll be a tight squeeze, but it's this way."

Mulciber turned toward the rocky outcropping, ducking under a low hanging rock.

Heather and Ross followed. The darkness was so thick she

couldn't see the path, much less Ross behind her, but she felt his warm strength, the press of his arms around her waist. She felt off balance, but knew she couldn't fall and kill herself because she couldn't die twice. Nothing here could kill her—except for Death's scythe.

Fear quivered in her stomach with every step down this sloping path. The wind had fallen silent, the echo of her footsteps sharp against the rocky walls.

She still felt Ross behind her, his arms around her waist. His presence was a lifeline, giving her something to concentrate on, something to keep Mulciber's mental prodding at bay.

Finally, the darkness lightened to a soft golden haze from torches perched on the walls, guttering in the thick silence. As the path leveled off, a steady but distant machine-like thrum reverberated in the silence.

"What's that noise?" she asked.

"It's just the mechanism," said Mulciber as he walked toward a fork in the path.

"The what?" Ross asked.

"It's what keeps the world below here warm," the demon said with a shrug and turned to the right. "This place gets really cold."

As they entered a huge cavern, the air felt balmy, bringing a blush to Heather's cheeks. Ahead, in the guttering torchlight, stood a huge machine that filled the entire room. People in dirty, tattered fabrics that once resembled the strange clothes that she and Ross wore milled through the chamber. Many of them wore filthy rags.

Dozens and dozens of men and women toiled on this machine that belched plumes of thick black smoke toward the rocky ceiling. Soot clung to the rocky walls and coated the floors, the room smelling musty and smoky. Some of the workers huddled over instruments while others turned large flywheels with both hands, teeth gritted and sweat dripping off their faces. Others flipped switches and pumped levers while others shoveled what looked like coal into a fiery vent in the back.

Almost like hell fires, Heather thought, a chill raking her spine. Did these demons expect her to make that connection? Were they counting on it?

An equal number of leathery-skinned demons wandered through the room, some barking orders and shouting at humans and others drifting through the tunnels.

"What is that thing?" Ross demanded, moving toward the dark, greasy machine with its massive steel plates and rivets, gears whirring and spinning, smoke billowing in thick, tangled coils.

"The uh, furnace," Mulciber said, a guttural laugh rumbling through the cavern. "How do you expect demons to survive in this pervasive cold without a furnace?"

"So, you force these people to slave over this machine to heat your caverns?" Heather felt the burn of anger ignite inside.

Mulciber raised a leathery, scaled finger into the air. "We never *force* humans to work here. It's their choice. They're free to do whatever they wish."

Heather felt an ache in her chest at the thought. They'd all been tricked—or allowed themselves to be tricked—into an endless struggle to maintain this furnace. And if she wasn't careful, she might end up next to them.

"What's beyond the furnace?" Ross asked.

"The coal fields," said Mulciber as he leaned against the furnace. He patted a grateful Asian woman on the top of her head. "The Veils. Oh, and our little amphitheater for soul sport. We like to mix it up with the Red City from time to time. Good work, Shuying," he said, turning to the young Asian woman struggling to turn a wheel. "A fine job."

The slight Asian woman grinned at his praise, turning the flywheel faster.

Heather shook her head. Was that poor woman so desperate for praise that she'd toil here for eternity to get it? She seemed to hang on his every word. Three others worked beside her: two Caucasian women, and an Indian man. They stared at Mulciber with reverence, like they were waiting for him to praise their efforts, too. But the big demon, its fleshy skin the color of terra cotta, just walked past, ignoring them.

"Soul sport?" Ross whispered in Heather's ear. "What the hell is that?"

"I'm not sure I want to know," Heather answered under her breath.

She walked toward the Asian woman, studying the exhaustion in her face and the effort that corded her muscles with every turn. She was a few inches shorter than Heather, her body lanky, rich black hair that fell to the middle of her back. The two older women beside her struggled to turn the wheels fast enough. One was short and stocky, the other looked frail and sickly. The man seemed to be lost in his own misery, turning the wheel steadily. Over and over and over. Their silky clothes hung ragged and greasy, blotches of soot clinging to their sweat-covered faces.

"Shuying, you're an excellent worker," said Heather, laying a hand on her shoulder. "The best one I've seen here."

Her words seemed to bend into a common language that all of them understood.

Shuying's face beamed. "Really? You think so?"

The others looked up, staring angrily at Heather who nodded.

"I know so. Look how well you've kept this furnace going for so long. You've earned a rest. All of you, great job! Now, take a break."

"You mean...stop?" she asked, the worry shining in her dark eyes.

The others looked away, heads down, turning their wheels faster. They didn't want to hear anything about stopping.

"It's all right," said Heather. "You've earned it."

Shuying stopped turning the wheel. "Is—it all right?"

Mulciber glared at Heather then Shuying. "Of course, it's all right, Shuying. I'm sure it won't get cold right away."

Shuying glanced from Heather to Mulciber, her eyes widening as the tears welled in her eyes.

"Ignore the demon, Shuying," said Ross, laying a hand on the woman's shoulder. "It's your choice. Let it go."

She stared at Mulciber then Ross.

"They're demons," Ross snapped. "Let 'em freeze!"

Her nervous gaze flicked from Ross to Mulciber and back again until finally, she let go of the wheel.

"Good work!" Heather cheered, mocking Mulciber with her gaze.

Shuying collapsed beside the machine in a knot of tears. Ross and Heather helped her to her feet. The others beside her shuffled away, frantically churning their wheels into motion. Mulciber walked over and patted the man on his shoulder.

"Good work, Dhirahnj," the demon said in a silky voice as he walked past Shuying. "Ladies, you're doing excellent work, too. Keep it up, Doris."

The two women made faces at Shuying as they pumped their wheels faster, the mechanism belching out a thick cloud of black vapor.

"It's not too late," Ross said to the others, but they turned away, ignoring him.

Heather wondered if it was fear or pride that kept them working at this machine. She tried to convince them to leave, too, but they refused to budge.

"I'm frightened," Shuying said, glancing at Mulciber. "I not here long, but I not remember anything but working the mechanism."

"Remember who you used to be," Heather whispered in Shuying's ear. "She's still in there. If you want to save her, come back with us. To the great tree."

"It been too long," she said with a moan. "I don't know my way back anymore." She pressed her hands to her face. "Everything's so fuzzy. So far away."

"Don't worry, we'll show you how to get back," said Heather.

She nodded, smiling. "Thank you. I'd like that."

Mulciber glared at Heather as she moved Shuying away from his angry stare. She'd do what she could to get Shuying out of this place.

"How did you end up here?" Heather asked.

"I-I follow the others. The others who came from the tree."

Ross turned toward her, his eyes wide. "Were you seeking the Spiral?"

Shuying frowned. "The Spiral? No, I don't think so. I don't remember."

"Think back. Was it the Spiral?" Ross asked.

Her gaze fell to the rocky floor, a faraway expression lighting her eyes. Finally, she lifted her head and gave him an uncertain nod. "Yes, maybe that's what the others try to find. But we all end up here somehow. Trying to escape the soulstalkers."

Heather sighed. And they found something so much worse.

"Do you know Thraecius?" Heather asked. "We're trying to find him."

Shuying's face scrunched as she dragged the toe of her boot across the rocky ground. "I seem to remember someone by that name. Tarcus, Tarius,...Tracius. He used to work on mechanism with us, but he went through the Veils and then to the soul sport. I think he now in coal fields."

"So, it's Thraecius you're after," said Mulciber, grinning at Heather. "He won't be as easy as this one." He stuck out his chest. "He was my champion. He earned his heart. There were none better than ol' Thraecius. Now, he oversees the coal fields."

"Earned his heart?" Ross asked. "What does that mean?"

"Be careful of the questions you ask, Ross," said Mulciber, turning around suddenly. He stood uncomfortably close to Ross. "You may not want to hear my answers."

Ross squinted, grimacing. He pressed his fingers to his forehead, tilting his head down as if in pain.

Heather laid her hand against Ross' forearm and gripped his wrist when he groaned. She rubbed her thumb in soothing circles against the back of his hand until the look of pain dissipated.

She let go, turning to face the demon. "What are these coal fields?"

"Heed my warning to Ross, Heather," said Mulciber, smirking at her. "Coal keeps the machines running."

"And you demons amused," she snapped.

Where's your mother, Heather? The taunting voice asked, over and over.

"Stop it," Heather growled, turning away from him.

Why can't you see your mother? Oh, I remember! Because you killed yourself. But it's not too late. I can still take you to her. Follow me. Through the Veils.

Heather squeezed her eyes closed and shook her head, hunching her shoulders as she pressed her hands against her temples. She felt Ross' hand on her back, supporting, comforting.

"Stop it!" She whirled around, baring her teeth at Mulciber. "I'm not afraid of you."

"Oh, but you should be, Heather," he said in a soft voice, an unsettling glint in his steely black eyes. "You absolutely should be."

"Why?" she demanded. "You can't force me to do your bidding, so why should anything you do scare me?"

"Because everything connects to the Spiral, little one," he said in a gravelly voice. "Everyone and everything, including the fallen. And those between."

Mulciber circled them, his steps slow and steady, that grin never leaving his fleshy face. Ross slid his arm protectively around her waist and pulled her closer to him.

"Eósphoro has the Fallen Angel of Death's ear, you know," said the big demon, its fleshy skin flushing a deep russet, accenting the mottled, leathery texture. "And Afeziel? He could bring her here in a —" Mulciber chuckled. "In a heartbeat—if you still had one."

Heather felt the chill rush down her spine, her stomach clenching. What if that was true? Could Mulciber, or those other demons he named, summon Death? She'd never see her mom again.

She cast an uncertain look at Ross who looked worried. But the word fallen nagged at her. There were hundreds of angels of death, dozens of archangels of death, too. What had that demon called this one—Afeziel? She'd ask Zakhart about that name. And the other one. What was it—Eos something?

Mulciber paced around the mechanism, hands folded behind his back as if waiting for her to make some decision—or deal.

With a demon? As if.

He stopped and turned, his large steely eyes enveloping the chamber as he took in every detail and then his intense gaze fell onto her, studying her face, examining every twitch of her mouth, every blink of her eyes, every glance at Ross.

Because it was a lie.

She glared at Mulciber. He was using anything he could to trick her. Control her. Somehow, he had the power to tap into her fears, her weaknesses.

"You'd so like me to believe that, wouldn't you?" said Heather. She pointed left toward the archway that led to the main exit tunnel. "Ross and I walked in through that tunnel and we'll be walking out it again shortly. Got it?"

Mulciber's mouth quirked into a hideous smile. "That path must feel a million miles away right about now."

Heather bit her lip, turning toward Ross. He was crouched on the floor, eyes closed, clutching his head, and chanting something she couldn't hear over and over.

"Ross? What is it?"

He didn't answer as he rocked back and forth, whispers hissing from his lips, but she couldn't hear him above the squeaks and rushes of steam from the mechanism.

"Ross!" She dropped down on her haunches in front of him and took hold of his wrists, shaking him. "Ross, look at me. Ross!"

His eyes snapped open, his lips still moving, still chanting silent words.

"Don't let Mulciber get in your head," she said, gripping his wrists tighter.

He gritted his teeth, his voice audible now. "It's my will, it's my will," he chanted, sweat dripping down his face.

Finally, he shouted out the phrase, his voice sounding like a wounded animal. His muscles corded, lips almost white, arms shaking until finally, he sagged and Heather caught him.

"Ross, are you all right? Ross!"

"I'm okay now," he said in a hoarse whisper, his chest heaving. "I pushed him out."

Heather turned to glare at Mulciber who grinned at her.

"Humans have such trouble with reality," he said with a sneer.

The horn buds above his eyes gave them such a wild expression as he laughed, holding his belly, flushing russet again.

Ross' gaze was murderous as he struggled to his feet with Heather's help.

"Tell me what happened," Heather said in a low voice as she rubbed his shoulder, but his eyes didn't glance in her direction. They stayed focused on Mulciber. Looking murderous.

"Jessie," he hissed. "I saw Jessie at that machine. Heard her voice in my ears, begging me to join her. It took every ounce of my strength not to grab the flywheel that Shuying just abandoned."

Heather laid a hand against his face, pulling him against her, shielding him. He put his arms around her waist, holding onto her. He was unsteady, those burnished gold-hazel eyes looking weak, so she did her best to hold him up and try to keep him on his feet. He was trembling, his breath huffing as he fought to stay upright.

"You were stronger," she told him, brushing his damp bangs out of his sweat-slicked face. "Don't forget that. You were stronger."

Ross nodded, gaze still fixed on Mulciber as he wiped the back of his hand across his mouth. At last, she felt the taut muscles in his arms relax, his breath quieting.

"This time," he said in a soft voice against her ear that only she could hear. "What about next time?"

His question scared her, but she understood. Mulciber hadn't hit her quite as hard as he had Ross, but she knew he could when she least expected it.

"Next time, we'll fight him together," she whispered in his ear.

He nodded, the hint of a smile on his face.

When Ross was steady again, she turned toward Mulciber.

"All right, demon, I'm tired of these games. Show me this power you're hiding. The coal fields. The Veils."

"And the soul sport?" Mulciber asked, raising an eyebrow. He looked her up and down like she was a heifer at the State Fair. "You're small, but you're feisty. You're not from the Red City, but you'd do well." He pointed at Ross' shoulders. "Wiry with nice wide shoulders—so would you, Ross. I do need another champion. Thraecius has gotten soft."

The demon laughed with a snort, his corpulent belly lumpy like a smashed melon.

"Heather, no," Ross said with a growl, gripping her forearms. "Don't trust that thing." He lowered his voice, his mouth brushing against her ear. "Zakhart was right. This is too dangerous."

A lightness touched Mulciber's black eyes and they turned shiny again like steel ball bearings.

"We've got to go through with this," she whispered to him and moved forward.

"Come on, Shuying," said Heather, tugging Ross away from the machine. "After we come back from the Veils, we'll go to the coal fields and you can point out Thraecius to us."

Mulciber broke out into a belly laugh, that fleshy belly undulating like a snake swallowing a mouse. Two other demons added their voices to his when they heard Thraecius' name, their laughter scraping against Heather's nerves.

Heather turned away from them, Ross and Shuying on each side as they followed the path toward the darkness of the coal fields. She didn't know if the demons were still playing games with her. Right now, she had to assume they were lying about everything.

Was Thraecius such a hard case? Would he be impossible to

reach? She hadn't tried very hard on the others at the mechanism, but even they seemed lost to her reasoning. Or quickly pulled back by the demons. Maybe all of that would change if she got through to Thraecius?

For Ester and Matthew, she had to try.

"Thraecius must be some real hard ass," said Ross in a quiet voice. "Don't think I can take him."

"Neither could I," Heather replied with a wink which made Ross chuckle. "But together, we can totally take him."

Ross stared at her a moment, a smile brightening his face. "Deal. We'll have to convince him together then," he said, his hand brushing across her cheek.

Shuying glanced at them, nodding. "If Thraecius is the man I think of, he more demon than Mulciber."

"The Veils are this way," said Mulciber, motioning to a small opening to the far right. He sighed, crossing his scaly arms. "You can search the coal fields for Thraecius afterward."

"Which way?" Heather asked Ross.

Ross sighed, shaking his head. "If we go to the Veils, we stick together, okay? It's the most dangerous place in the Between, Heather. That I know of anyway."

She reached out and took Ross' hand, squeezing. "I want to know what happened...y'know—afterward." Her voice grew small and tight. "After I died. Don't you, Ross?"

Ross rubbed his hand across his face, staring at his feet. Finally, he nodded. "Of course, I do, but it's dangerous, Heather. We can't go back, so it's gonna hurt. A lot. Much more than you realize." He reached out and brushed a lock of hair out of her eyes. "You ready for that so soon? You haven't been here long. It's all gotta be so raw and fresh still."

He was right. It was an unending ache, but she had to know. Did her dad think about her much since she was gone? Had Ash forgiven her? Where had they buried her? She hoped near her mom. But beyond all of those questions, she ached to see something familiar, something tangible that she could touch and feel.

She needed to see that the world still turned on its axis. She needed to know that things continued on, that they made sense when nothing here had made sense for so long. Maybe then she'd know what to do? Where to go? Maybe she'd find some small sliver of hope to hold onto, that told her this place wasn't the end?

Heather nodded. "I need to see it, Ross. To know it's all still there." She laid her hand on his shoulder and he slid his hand over hers, squeezing. "But I can't do it alone. Will you stay with me when I go through the Veils?"

"Of course," he said, his warm tone soothing. "I'm here. And I won't let go."

He leaned toward her and kissed her forehead, his warm mouth sending shivers through her. She closed her eyes, holding onto the sensation.

For the first time since she'd opened her eyes in this place, she wanted to kiss him. Her heart no longer beat, but she still felt love and she felt something deep for Ross. Something she couldn't explain. They'd bonded so quickly. She wanted to lean up and kiss his mouth and throw her arms around him, but she let him go and they stepped forward into the passageway.

Ahead in the shadows, something sparkled. Heather moved toward it, Ross still gripping her hand. Ribbons of light danced above the rumble of the mechanism, swaying in the eddy of air currents that swirled around them as she stepped toward the pale glimmer.

Folds of soft blue light and shadow billowed through the chamber ahead, coils of sparkling gold floating like threads that hung from diaphanous swaths of pale light. So calming. So peaceful.

Voices whispered, laughter carrying on a sweet, pine-scented breeze as the curtains of light rippled. People from her past.

She stepped forward.

Her mom's voice lilted up from the Veils, the sound aching through her. Calling her name. Her eyes burned at the sound that had been only a muffled memory for so long. It seemed like forever since she'd heard her voice.

"Mom?" she called, letting go of Ross' hand.

"Heather, don't let go!"

The gold coils of light brushed across her face, against her hands as she followed the voices. The sounds of a world she thought she'd lost forever.

Heather closed her eyes and stepped into the billowing curtains of light. Immediately, it enveloped her in the soft vanilla spice of her mom's cologne, the nutty, toasted aroma of hazelnut coffee hanging over the briny scent of Seattle's piers. Numbing cold winds stinging her face as she stood at the front of the ferry, fingers frozen against the railing, headed home to Bainbridge Island. She inhaled the warm, doughy scent of grandma's yeast rolls filling the Spokane farmhouse on a brisk Thanksgiving Day. The memories rolled over her every time one of those golden threads touched her face.

But one strand glittered and pulsed bright with life, like the heartbeat she no longer felt. And frequently imagined.

She reached out to it, fingers brushing across the coil of energy. Was the Spiral like this somehow? She closed her eyes, Ross' desperate voice fading, and gripped the gold thread with both hands.

The air sparkled as the gold thread of energy wrapped around her hands, twisting around her arms as it stretched and draped itself around her torso, snaking down her legs to her feet. Pulling her into the Veils.

eight

· · ·

THE BETWEEN FADED, the misty edges of her vision growing bright and familiar. She held her breath, eyes fluttering.

Sunlight!

Glittering across Elliott Bay, fog burning away as morning brightened into a delicate but crisp, blue sky. She let out a breath. The emerald city was waking up.

She couldn't halt the tears as she fell to her knees, clutching green grass in her fists and brushing cold sand through her fingers. The salty tang of sea water scrubbed the cool air, call of sea gulls mingling with the steady hush of waves lapping against the familiar, rocky Bainbridge Island beach.

She was home! She was alive. It had all been a horrible, ecstasy-filled trip.

Heather laughed as the sun warmed her face, the sand cold and soothing against her palms. Relief rushed over her as she twirled around and around on the beach.

It was just a bad trip!

She hadn't overdosed. Just rolled too much Molly, that's all. She hadn't taken enough and she'd never been so relieved in her entire life.

She turned her face to the sun again, the warmth drenching her skin. Wind brushed across her cheeks in numbing caresses so clean and pure as it dried her tears. The sun was the brightest she could remember in Seattle. She laid her hand against her chest, desperate to feel the subtle quiver of her heart beating against her ribs. Nothing stirred against her fingers. She sucked in a breath and turned away from the bay.

Seeing the dark shape on the beach.

No. Her stomach twisted into a knot. No!

She balled her hands into fists and beat the ground. This wasn't happening! She was alive! She was still alive.

She ran toward the drenched body lying in the surf, white hoodie soaked and grey, brown hair tangled with sea grass and sand, flashes of burgundy and copper highlights glinting in the sun. Green eyes open, empty, staring up at the sky, dull against her alabaster-pale skin. So still. So deathly still. And cold, a chill so deep that no blood could ever warm it again.

She hung over her body and cried. Not because people had hurt her. Not because she'd been bullied. Not because she'd lost her mom.

Because she'd mattered.

Because she had worth and importance like every living creature. And she'd forgotten it. There was no one else like her in the world. She had double-jointed elbows and could recite the Star-Spangled Banner backward. She loved banana milkshakes and had streaked her hair burgundy and copper because she liked how it all sparkled when the sun hit it. She could talk like a chipmunk and she hated raspberries. Like everyone else, she'd been important in her own way, but she'd listened—and agreed—when someone told her she was worthless.

She'd listened when the world told her that she didn't matter. That she meant nothing. That the world would be better off without her. She was the one person she should have loved without question, but she'd listened to all those horrible things instead.

And believed them.

What would Ash think now? Would Dad even feel sad? Would he even find out? He couldn't just send a card and a check this time. Not that it was anywhere near Christmas or her birthday anyway.

As the sun rose over the beach, the coroner and the police arrived, scouring the beach as they snapped pictures, marked the area with bright yellow tape, and bagged up her things.

She could only stare as they covered her body with a sheet, put bags on her hands, and loaded her body into the back of an ambulance, siren and lights off as it drove away slowly.

An early morning crowd had gathered. They'd be back to their own lives soon enough, unaffected by her quiet little death as the world forgot about her and her short, invisible life. Like it had just been a couple of sticky notes on a refrigerator somewhere that had fallen off and slid underneath.

Forgotten.

By afternoon, the beach was quiet again. Heather sat on the shore, watching the skyline lights wink on, one-by-one, harbor lights bright against Elliott Bay's cold water. The bay gleamed as it caught hold of the sunset and held onto it, bruising the sky with magentas and oranges until the moon rose to cover them.

Only then did Heather feel the gold thread coil around her body again, tugging her away from the beach. She gripped it tightly, letting it carry her into the night.

When the sun rose again, she was in the Orca Café where she'd spent so much of her time, especially after Mom died. Jimmy stood at the counter, eyes rimmed red as he spoke to a police officer, newspaper beside him.

"Jimmy!" she cried, running toward the tall man, short spiky brown hair gelled in place.

She tried to hug him, but her arms passed right through him.

Jimmy ran his hand through his short, stiff hair, Charles the bear sitting behind him on a shelf, a note attached that read, "For Emily".

Heather winced, moving behind the counter to touch the white, sparkly bear. Her hand passed through him, but just seeing the little, sparkly bear again made her smile.

She stared at the newspaper on the counter, its headline read: *Local woman found dead after posting suicide note online.* She scanned the article as it talked about a toxicology report and the cause of death was yet to be determined. Funeral services were pending said the last line.

"Kid's been all alone since her mother died," Jimmy continued, hands shaking. "Dad's in Boston. Remarried. New family. Doesn't seem real interested in Heather, to hear her tell it."

"We contacted Mr. Billot this morning. He's on his way to Seattle. He sounded pretty broken up."

Jimmy nodded, his gaze falling onto Charles the bear. He reached over and stroked the white bear. "Damn well should be," Jimmy snapped. "This shouldn't have happened. She was so young."

"Sir, what time did you see Miss Billot yesterday?" the officer asked. He was young with ash blond hair, kind blue eyes, and a slim build, navy jacket and pants, clipboard in hand as he took notes.

"Here's a copy of the receipt," he said, his voice tight as he slid the full sheet of paper across the counter to the officer. "God, if only I'd known what she was planning," Jimmy cried, his voice breaking again. "I feel so terrible. I thought something was wrong yesterday. I asked if she was all right, but I should have pressed her more! Should have kept talking until she opened up."

Stunned, Heather stared at Jimmy. She had no idea he'd felt that way about her. She'd had a good friend and didn't even know it.

"It's not your fault, Mr. Girard," said the officer, looking up from his clipboard.

Jimmy shook his head, a hand over his eyes now. "Here she was, pouring her heart out in a suicide note right behind me, and I didn't even know it!" He wiped tears out of his eyes with thumb and forefinger. "I loved that kid. Used to give her free mochas and butterscotch cookies every time she came in. Let her work here during holidays. She kept the place clean and the register to the penny." He sighed, tears thick in his eyes. "If she'd just talked to me, told me what was happening! I'd have done anything for her!" He sucked in a breath. "Anything."

"Did she tell you where she was going after she left the café yesterday?"

Jimmy shook his head. "No, she was real quiet yesterday. Then she gave me her bear." His eyes reddened, the realization hitting him now. "God, I'm so dumb! She loved that bear more than anything. Her mother gave it to her. I should have known she'd never part with that bear."

"She gave you a prized possession?" the officer asked, eyes wide.

"Yeah, asked me to give it to my daughter because she didn't need it anymore." Jimmy closed his eyes, gritting his teeth. "Why didn't I say something?"

Heather felt bad now. She hadn't wanted to make Jimmy feel guilty. She'd just wanted a good home for Charles. She reached out and tried to pat Jimmy on the shoulder, but her hand went right through him.

"Any idea where she hung out online? Favorite sites?"

Jimmy shook his head. "Most of the time, she Instagram where most of her friends hang out. And some site called TickTick or something like that. She was a good kid. Didn't get in trouble."

"Names of friends she had? What about drugs?" the officer asked.

He shrugged. "She was twenty, Officer. My guess is she tried some things like all the other kids."

"She mention anything?" the officer asked, unblinking.

Jimmy sighed. "Guess it doesn't matter now, but she talked about a friend named Molly a lot. I've got a young daughter, so I keep up. But she had other friends. A girl named Ashley came in with her sometimes. I've heard her mention a Marta and a Carly, too."

The officer flipped through the pages on his clipboard, nodding. "Last names?"

"No idea," Jimmy said, shaking his head. "They all went to high school together. On Bainbridge Island, I think. That's all I know."

"All right, thanks for your time, Mr. Girard. If you think of anything else, please give me a call." The officer pulled a card out of his jacket pocket and handed it to Jimmy. "I'm sorry for your loss."

"Thank you," said Jimmy, shaking the officer's hand. "At least she's not in pain anymore. Hope she's in a better place now."

Heather wandered over to the table where she'd always sat, the one by the window with a great view of the bay and the ferry terminal. Two women sat there, phones sitting on the table. She reached toward one of the touchscreens and it flickered, allowing her to touch the energy that ran through it, connecting her to all the heartaches and joys she'd cast out there on her own phone. All of it spilled out around her, pages and paragraphs and texts and voices. She found Ash's response to her last post.

She'd been begging Heather to call and tell her where she was, begging Heather not to do this. Frantic updates on their blogs as Marta and Carly and others went out looking for her. And then someone posted a link to the newspaper article.

Ash's Facebook post broke her heart.

September 10, 2022

HEARTBROKEN. You were the best friend I ever had, Heather. We've been friends since second grade. Now, how am I going to live my life without you? Why couldn't you see how much I cared about you? I loved you. You were more than a friend, more than a sister. You were everything to me.

Now, I can never again share every good and bad thing that happens in my life with you. You'll never laugh and cry with me again. You'll never meet my next boyfriend. You'll never meet my future husband. You'll never help me plan my wedding or walk down the aisle as my maid of honor. You'll never throw me a baby shower or see my first grandchild. You'll never sit on the deck, drinking wine coolers and talking about our greatest hopes and fears again.

Losing you was my greatest fear, Heather. And I'm so angry at you for taking that lifetime of friendship away from me. There will always be an empty photo frame on my wall where your latest picture should have been.

God, I miss you, Heather. Love you forever.

Some people posted ugly, hateful things on her wall, but they left Heather unaffected now. Some posted confusion and others just seemed stunned, but most of the posts showed Heather how many friends she'd had, people she'd never even realized that had cared about her. Even Marta and Carly.

What had she done?

Her chest ached, the absence of a heartbeat disturbing as she backed out of the café. A cold chill brushed her neck, the memory of the Between seeping back through the Veils, reminding her of what she'd already lost.

And how final it was.

Again, the gold cord tangled around her, tugging her away again. Away from Jimmy and Charles the bear. Into the cold, pervasive greyness that had already soaked into her bones and pooled in her thoughts, making her feel so heavy and lost. But she didn't want to let go of the cord, didn't want to leave the sunlight and the thrum of life behind for that bleak, desolate world between sleep and death. She couldn't go back to that emptiness.

Heather clung to the cord and it pulled her into the growing darkness as the molten sunset cooled against the cold Puget Sound.

When the sun rose again, Heather was on the deck of the Bainbridge Island house where she grew up. Japanese Maples cast frilly shadows across the hardwood deck, grill sizzling with fresh Copper River salmon. The smoky, sweet scent of maple syrup mixed with garlic, dill, and salmonberries.

Mom was at the grill, glass of merlot glimmering as the sinking sun caught its garnet shades and cast them across the lacy leaf shadows. She wore a thick grey sweater with floppy sleeves and her favorite jeans, curly hair loosely tied back with a purple headband. Her lilting voice echoed across the deck as she sang some stupid eighties song.

Heather was overcome.

She wrapped her arms around her middle, shivering at the sight of her mom, in remission, healthy and real, standing in front of her. Smiling and dancing around the grill.

At the time, Heather had felt embarrassed, saying, "Mom, stop! You're too old to dance."

Mom had just laughed at her, scrunching her nose, and belting out the chorus as Heather put her hands over her ears and giggled.

Ash was there with her own mom, Marta and Carly, and their parents, too. She watched her seventeen-year-old-self laughing and drinking wine coolers with Ash, Marta, and Carly, and she wished she could stay in this moment forever. Feel her mom's arms around her one more time as she listened to Ash's boyfriend troubles and Marta and Carly argue over who had the best taste in music.

Because in that moment, everything had been perfect, whole—just about everything she'd ever wanted out of life right there. Only an arm's length away.

She wanted to freeze that moment and press it into her brain with all its senses and emotions so she could experience it any time she needed it. Why couldn't she have recognized that? Cherished it while it was happening?

"I'm so sorry, Mom," said Heather, shaking. "I was seventeen. I thought we had forever." She winced, the tears burning her eyes. "I didn't know it was only a year."

She walked over to where her mom danced and laughed, sipping merlot as she marinated the salmon, eyes not yet hollowed, face still full of life and strength, body still fighting. But the cancer was already starting its final assault, a sneak attack that none of them saw coming. On this June night, they thought they'd won. They thought they'd taken back the world, celebrated a win, and laughed in cancer's face.

Fuck cancer.

Heather stood beside her mom who swayed back and forth across the deck, waltzing as she belted out the song in hoarse, alto notes. With tears clouding her eyes, Heather reached out and tried to touch her mom's arm and waist. She held out her arms and twirled and turned with her. Heather danced with her mom and sang along to *Dance with Somebody*. She moved as close to her mom as she could, smelling her soft, familiar vanilla body spray, faint smell of lavender laundry soap on her clothes.

Heather closed her eyes, laying her head against her mom's shoulder, Mom's favorite mint and rosemary shampoo tingling against her nose.

She leaned against her mom's ear. "Mom," she whispered. "I miss you so much. I'll never stop missing you."

A strange look touched her mom's face. As if she'd somehow heard Heather's voice.

Her mom stopped dancing and glanced around the deck until her gaze fell on Heather's seventeen-year-old-self and her friends. Then she turned and looked right at Heather standing in front of her.

Mom smiled, reaching out as if stroking Heather's face.

"Time is a funny thing," her mom whispered. "It's all connected. We're all connected. Even in death."

She took a long sip of merlot as Heather closed her eyes and took another deep breath of the memory. Holding onto that summer night, that moment when just for a little while, everything in the world was all right.

One last time.

But as hard as she tried to hold onto it, it was already fading, fading into the dark like a vivid sunset as the golden thread tightened again, pulling her toward something else.

Dull, olive green walls and beige, vinyl floors. Metal table and two chairs. A round, brown clock hung on the wall. Eight thirty-nine A.M., a heavy, black hand ticking away the time with loud clicks. The room smelled like antiseptic and oranges. The police officer from the café sat in one of the chairs. Across from him sat a tired face she hadn't seen for three years.

Thick, dark hair cut short. Expensive blue suit and shiny black shoes. He always smelled like leather, even when she was little. Even now, she smelled traces of it as he sat there unshaven, moss-green eyes watery and sunk into his cheeks, thin mouth quivering.

"Suicide?" he sputtered finally.

The officer slid a manila folder across the table, but he shoved it back.

"She left a note online, Mr. Billot. We're still waiting for the toxicology reports, but we found more than enough MDMA in her backpack to overdose."

He was shaking now, hands pressed against his face.

"When was the last time you talked to your daughter, Mr. Billot?"

He hung his head, a long, heavy sigh filling the room. A sound weighed down by a decade of regret and not enough time and not enough words to make any of it right anymore. He'd immersed himself in his new life in Boston, in his new wife and young children, always planning to make time for her. When he could take some time off, he'd fly her out. After the car payments and the mortgage and the orthodontist bills. After the spring break trip to the Cayman's and that leadership conference in Tampa.

Heather had waited patiently, not giving up on him. But as the years slipped by, the calls turned into twice a year, along with the cards. Dad had always thought that showing love meant writing a check.

If only he'd understood that she'd rather spend time with him than spend his money.

"I'd been meaning to call," he said finally in a shaky voice.

"When did you last talk to her?" the officer repeated.

"February, I think," he said, his voice quivering. "She'd sent me a poem she—uh wrote for me. Asked me when she could um, see me again. I'd planned to call her this...this Friday. I was going to fly out and see her next week." His face screwed up. "But not here—in the morgue."

He broke down, hand over his face as he sobbed.

Heather heard the regret, felt it like a sick weight in her stomach. Her whole life, he'd been a step behind her. A few more minutes, sweetheart. Next time, little girl. I'll see you later. I'll catch that next time. Let's reschedule that for next week.

Always too late.

The gold thread twisted around her hands, jerking her out of the room, into the shift of another memory.

nine

. . .

THROUGH THE HAZE of the Veils, Heather felt hands grab hold of hers, squeezing, caressing, pulling.

Shimmering, translucent curtains of light fluttered around her like clouds, like mist. She couldn't see anything past the haze. Couldn't concentrate on anything but the past. And the pain. The cavity in her chest where her heart once beat and raced and danced, pumping blood and oxygen along with emotions and dreams, was still. Silent. Those emotions and events passed now.

She let the curtains of light enfold her, the golden cord wrapping around her, entombing her in the moments she'd once cherished. Connecting her to the people she didn't want to live without, she realized.

Through the expanse, she felt a strong grip on her hands. The surge of warmth that bled through the cold, vapory Veils obscuring her vision.

Heather concentrated on her hands and the bloom of heat against her fingers, the softness of skin against her palm and wrists. The voice against her ear, calling her name.

Over and over, the strange yet familiar voice filled her head, growing louder as her name echoed through the mist.

"Heather?" the anxious voice persisted, sharp in her ear now. Desperate. "Heather, come back!"

Something about the urgent male voice made her recoil from the swaths of light and memory, from the only life and world she'd ever known. But she couldn't speak. She couldn't focus on the voice.

"Heather, please!"

The voice ached through her, hands cradled in a warm embrace. A kiss so soft against the back of her hand. Brushing across her lips.

"I need you."

She smashed her eyes closed, concentrating on the voice, the presence cradling her hands.

"Ross?" she whispered, terrified now.

She couldn't let go. She couldn't untangle the thread or the Veils. And they were growing so cold now. Dead. Cloying. She was shivering, teeth chattering.

"Ross...help me."

Heat rushed over her, a force pressing against her lips, wrapping around her, pulling her back from the Veils, from the cold memories drifting away as the fog receded.

At last, Heather opened her eyes. Ross had his arms around her, dragging her out of the chamber, out of the Veils, away from everything she loved but could no longer touch again.

She wilted in his arms, head on his shoulder, silent tears rushing down her face as he carried her into the rocky corridor and collapsed against the wall with her.

It had been worse than a dream. Worse than pretending to eat and sleep in the great tree. Worse than thinking she was just on holiday. It was like watching the world through a sealed window that could never be opened. So close, so real, but impossible to reach. To return to.

Ross cradled Heather in his arms, smiling at her. He brushed a lock of copper and burgundy hair out of her eyes.

"You okay?" he asked, a hand against her cheek.

She stared at him, grateful to feel his warm touch, grateful to hear his voice. She'd never felt so empty before.

She nodded. "Because of you I am," she said. She threw her arms around him, holding onto him with every bit of strength she had left. "Please, don't disappear like everything else from my life."

He held her closer, stroking her hair. "I'm not going anywhere," he whispered as she kissed him, pressing little feather kisses down the side of his face until she found his warm mouth.

Never had she craved the feel of another human being against her skin as she did right now.

He kissed back with an urgency that startled her, his fingers tangling in her hair, trying to pull her even closer. She melted into him, the huff of his breath, the whisper of her name on his lips, the heat of her hands sliding under his shirt. His hands fumbled through the silky fabrics. She gasped, the warmth of him touching her breasts, sliding down her stomach. She pressed him against the rocky wall, her breath rasping as she sipped his mouth in white-hot gulps.

"Not here," he whispered against her ear. "It's...not safe."

She nodded, not wanting to let the heat go or the moment. But the thought of those leering demons feeding on their thoughts and emotions made her sick inside. Sighing, she laid her head against his chest, her body still against his, knowing he wanted her, too, but Ross was right. It was too dangerous.

When her shaking had stopped, Ross pressed his forehead to hers and caressed her cheek. He took her hands in his again and helped her to her feet, not letting go.

"What did you see in there?" Ross asked finally, his voice a ragged whisper.

Heather shook her head. "The parts of my life that I cherished. It was so beautiful, but it hurt so much not to be there anymore. To see all the things I could have fixed, things I couldn't see before, things I couldn't take back. It hurt so bad, Ross. I wish I could go back and change it. I hurt so many people." She squeezed his hands. "I wish I'd mattered more to myself. Talked to someone who could have helped me. Stopped me."

He held her close again. "Maybe figuring that out was the whole point, Heather?"

Heather pulled away. "When it's too late? What's the point of that now? All it does is taunt me."

Ross shrugged. "Maybe that's the reason for the Between? Figuring that out. Wanting to live again. If the Spiral is life, why would anyone who wanted to stay dead be searching for it?"

For a moment, she couldn't breathe.

This whole time, she'd been searching for this Spiral like it was some exit door she could just open and run through without even caring where it led. She'd overdosed on Molly because she didn't want to feel anything ever again. But she'd felt more here—with Ross and Lamarr and Shuying—than she had in the last three years of her life. Shouldn't she want to lie down in the poppy fields? Just go to sleep, like she'd planned before.

But those fields terrified her. The only thing that felt right at all (besides Ross) was finding the Spiral because maybe, just maybe it would let her live again? Now, she was willing to risk everything for that chance. Maybe Ross was right? Maybe that was the point? She was fighting for herself now—for the first time in a very long time. If ever.

"You're right, Ross," she said and took his hand in hers, holding him close again.

He smiled, sliding an arm around her waist. "For the first time in my life. And death."

"Let's get Shuying and try to find Thraecius," said Heather, motioning toward the passageway that led back to the mechanism. "Convince him to follow us back to the tree."

Ross nodded and they made their way back.

Shuying sat on the floor by the passageway entrance, huddled against the rock wall, eyes smashed closed, hands over her ears as demons strutted past. Dozens of people toiled at the mechanism.

Heather and Ross tried to get them to stop working, but most refused to listen. The ones who did listen seemed uncertain, pausing at their tasks, but not stopping.

"Why can't we help them?" Heather cried.

"Let's find Thraecius first," Ross whispered. "If we convince him to stop working for the demons, then the others might follow."

"Let's go."

Heather tapped Shuying on the shoulder. Startled, she scrambled to her feet, watching Heather and Ross fearfully, her gaze drifting from the mechanism to the other passageway.

"How did you end your life?" Heather asked.

Shuying sighed, arms wrapping around her body as she shifted her weight from one foot to the other.

"I was factory worker in China. Build touchscreen phones, tablets, whatever the new model, my factory churn them out. Things that cost me a year's pay to buy. We work seven days a week with no days off. So very exhausting. We barely sleep or eat."

"That's awful," Heather replied.

Ross frowned. "Touchscreen phone? Tablet? What's that?"

Heather kept forgetting that Ross died in 1961. He'd never seen these devices. That Shuying helped build. He'd never even seen a portable phone. Much less a cell phone.

"It's a telephone that runs on a battery and fits in your pocket," said Heather.

"Touchscreen let you connect to wireless and internet, to all kinds of stores and services online," said Shuying.

"Wireless? From your telephone? And it's small enough to fit in your pocket with no wires?" Ross smiled. "Wow, the world's changed so much since I was there."

Heather laughed. He couldn't quite see what Shuying meant, but a cold chill brushed her spine. Would that be her soon? New people that found their way to the great tree would soon tell her about a world she didn't recognize either. She felt so sad now. She could have been there. Could have seen it, felt it, experienced all of it, but she chose to leave it all behind.

She sighed. For this?

Shuying nodded, looking past them now. "So much demand. Nobody happy with anything old anymore, even if it work just fine. Have to have the newest thing."

"Bragging rights," said Ross.

"Youngest and prettiest partner," said Shuying. "Everything shiny and no scratches or dents. No grey hair. No wrinkles or creases. Not bony, not plump—just perfect. Why? Nothing, no one in this world perfect. They all go have plastic surgery to make them perfect, but if they have ugly babies, their husbands divorce. Can't be old, can't be average or no one want you. Like these devices. One scratch and they scrap, force us to remake. I work night and day on that line. My back hurt, I work. I sick, I work. My sister die, I work. One night, in 2009, I was too tired to even eat. Or sleep. They tell us to increase production or no pay. I jump off dormitory roof so I not have to work anymore."

Heather put her arms around Shuying who cried in her arms. 2009. She winced. Over a decade had passed since Shuying died.

"I was ashamed. I quit. And now, I here. I hate myself."

"Shuying, no," said Heather, letting her go. "You didn't know any other way to stop the pain. None of us did. But there's something called the Spiral out there that will change everything. It's life! And it's our last chance."

Shuying wiped tears off her face. "You mean a way out of here?"

Ross nodded. "We're trying to find it. Join us."

At last, a smile touched her heart-shaped face. She nodded. "Yes. I'd like that."

Ross motioned her toward the passageway and the three of them slipped into the dim-lit passage. They veered left, following a long, dark tunnel toward the distant clang of metal against rock.

As they drew nearer to the dim-lit cavern ahead, a sharp, snapping sound echoed through the expanse. Ahead, stalactites hung in jagged spikes across the cavern's ceiling as the steady clink of pickaxes filled the silence. Workers clustered around the black walls, swinging pickaxes against glistening, ebony rock while others filled carts with broken fragments of shiny rock.

Heather frowned. It didn't look like coal.

The snapping sound grew louder until she saw a man ahead, standing on a flattened rock, towering over the others. He swung a large whip at the nearest group of people, his chiseled face twisted and angry.

"Get back to work!" he shouted, his deep voice thundering through the cavern.

Tall and muscular, he wore only a pair of torn blue pants, no shirt. His shaggy, black hair hung a little long, pale blue eyes wild in the thin light from torches guttering on the walls. His handsome face was chiseled, fine lines and graceful curves like a Michelangelo statue. The muscles of his broad shoulders flexed as he drew back the whip and popped it across a slight man's shoulders. The smaller man cried out and stumbled, scattering hunks of shiny black rock all over the rough ground.

"Pick that up!" The man with the whip growled. "Now!"

"Let me guess," said Heather, pointing at the man with the whip. "That's Thraecius, right?"

Shuying nodded. "Yes, that is him."

Ross groaned. "Great. Nobody bothered to mention he was a freakin' gladiator."

"Was kind of an important detail to leave out," said Heather, stepping closer to Ross.

Thraecius' body was slicked with sweat, face taut, every muscle chiseled and defined like an athlete or a boxer. But rage clenched every muscle in his face, tightening his jaw and hardening those vivid blue eyes into stone. His forehead scrunched into tight lines, lips taut and angry straight.

Anger permeated Thraecius. It consumed him. Somehow, they'd

have to soothe that rage to find the man beneath it. From the looks of him, there wasn't much compassion left. Only pain.

A lot of pain. She'd focus on that.

Heather took a step forward, but Ross grabbed her arm, pulling her back.

"Are you crazy? Let me face him."

She patted his hand, shaking her head. "He'll see you as more of a threat than me. I'll go."

"What if he hurts you?" Ross' eyes were wide with concern. "I can't let that happen, Heather. You mean too much to me."

She smiled, reaching up to touch his face, staring into his bright hazel-gold eyes, so full of life and passion. He was beautiful with his sandy-haired guy-next-door looks. The kind of guy who'd help you move, wrap your sprained ankle, watch your cat, and let you cry on his shoulder after your boyfriend dumped you. The kind of guy who'd always been watching your back and loving you for a long time until you finally realized what a treasure he was and you suddenly just knew you loved him. And always had. Knew he was the only thing in your life that wasn't complete shit, the one thing you finally realized you couldn't do without.

"What can he do?" Heather asked with a shrug. "I'm already dead, remember?"

"But you still feel pain." Ross sighed and ran his hand through his hair. "All right. Maybe you're right? Maybe he won't hit a woman? But if he tries, I'll be an arm's length from you. Got it? Then we'll get our faces punched in together."

"Got it," she laughed and Ross let go of her arm.

Shuying fidgeted beside Ross. "Be careful. He always full with that kind of rage. Like wounded lion. I see a few like him at the factory in China. Most want to die, but not brave enough to do it themselves. But a few attack supervisor until security haul them off."

"Maybe he's got a good reason?" Ross said, his gaze not leaving Heather as she approached the Roman. "Don't forget what Ester told us."

"Thraecius," Heather called as she moved with steady steps toward the brawny Roman.

The whip swung around, lashing the air in front of her. She cringed, but kept walking.

"You! Get back to work! Now!"

He was ready to snap. She could see it. Every part of his body was like an over-wound spring, ready to pop. She winced. She'd have to wind him that last turn to make it happen.

"I don't work for you or anyone else here," said Heather, holding her arm in front of her face as she walked toward him.

Thraecius bared his teeth like a wild animal, fury burning in his eyes.

"What did you say to me?"

He jumped off the rock, taking a step toward her. Snap! The whip cracked near her face, but she kept her pace steady, stomach in knots.

"I'm not your servant, Thraecius. None of these people are. I've just come to talk to you."

His eyes narrowed, arm cocked, ready to swing the whip at her. She stiffened, knowing she was in range now.

"I have nothing to say to anyone. You understand that?"

"Of course, you do," Heather said. "I know there's still a strong voice inside you, one that needs to speak your pain."

The whip snapped across her forearm, the pain like razor blades. Startled, she yelped, grinding her teeth together as an angry welt rose.

"Now, shut up and get back to work before I flay the flesh from your back!"

His eyes were wild, like a cornered animal, teeth bright white and bared in the dim lighting.

"Hypocrite! You'd beat me? You didn't let them beat Juliana like this, did you, Thraecius?"

His eyes widened, lips parting in a momentary gasp of pain. "Back to work!" He snarled a feral growl, but moisture glistened in his eyes.

Snap! The whip lashed across her leg and she swallowed the cry of pain.

"Heather!" Ross called, his voice edged with pain.

"Stay back," she called to him and turned back to Thraecius.

The Roman climbed up onto his rock again, lashing that whip at every worker within range, over and over, his voice raging through the cavern.

Heather rushed toward Thraecius. She scrambled up the rocks and grabbed the whip, jerking it out of his hands. Stunned, he froze a moment.

"You will listen to me, Thraecius! We're talking about your dead sister, Juliana! Fed to the lions, remember?"

Fury twisted his face and his whole body spasmed, rage a black wave rushing over him, owning him. He lunged at her.

Heather tried, but she couldn't hold onto the whip. He ripped it out of her hands and reared back, whip raised over his head to strike her point blank.

"Heather!"

Ross ran toward her.

His footsteps pounded against the rocks, the cavern falling silent as the workers froze and stared as Heather took a breath, closing her eyes, and bracing for the slash of that whip against her flesh.

ten

· · ·

THE WHIP WHISTLED through the air and snapped against flesh.

Ross cried out in pain.

Heather opened her eyes. Ross was in front of her now, his body between her and the whip. It struck him in the chest, slicing through the loose fabric of his shirt. He rubbed the slash furiously with his hand.

"Damn that hurts," he replied.

"Leave!" Thraecius shouted. "Now! While you still can!"

All along the rocky walls, workers cowered, arms over their heads. Others scurried as far back from Thraecius as they could scatter. The gladiator drew back the whip again.

"What about Juliana, Thraecius?" Heather demanded, stepping in front of Ross as she motioned at the cowering workers. "You're shaming her memory here."

Thraecius turned and rushed toward her, arm raised, whip poised.

"Look at what you've become! Thraecius...you're just like the brutal soldiers that killed her. You're no different than they were!"

She cringed, waiting for the whip to strike.

The Roman wilted, the whip falling out of his hands. "No! That's not true!" He sank to his knees against the rocky floor. "No," he moaned, holding his face in his hands.

His muscles went slack, all the fight leaving him. His chest heaved, his sweaty face contorted with the agony of memories. She could almost see him replaying the scenes of his life in his mind. He began to tremble, looking small and vulnerable now.

"You know nothing of Juliana," he said with a snarl, most of the anger gone, replaced with despair.

"Only that her death was senseless and cruel," said Heather, taking a step toward him. "The people responsible will pay for what they did to her."

"Pay?" He laughed, his voice rising through the cavern like a mad man. It was a bitter sound that made her skin crawl. "They were promoted! Caesar revered them!"

Heather moved beside him and reaching out with the softest touch she could manage, she touched Thraecius' cheek. He didn't flinch away. Instead, his gaze softened, eyes closing a moment, as if it had been a lifetime since he'd felt a compassionate gesture. He stared at her now.

"Caesar lauded them," Thraecius continued, his face contorting, an ache in his voice. "She was sport that day. A good time had by thousands of my countrymen. It filled the entire arena." He bit his lip, his gaze broken and hurting. He bowed his head. "I couldn't stop it. Couldn't save her." He balled his hands into fists, beating them against the rocks. "But I took as many of them with me as I could." He gritted his teeth, "including the man who drew first blood."

"First blood?" Heather asked.

"They cut her," he said with a moan, anger trembling through him. "So the blood scent would draw the lions."

Heather shuddered. Overwhelmed by the cruelty and the horror.

"I returned the favor though." Thraecius grinned, slicing his index finger across his neck. "I slit that centurion's throat with his own sword and every soldier who'd worked the pits that day. Spilled their blood in the dirt—just like they spilled Juliana's."

A sob shuddered through him, his eyes glistening with tears. "Juliana!"

His desperate shout echoed through the chamber, mixing with sobs as he wept bitterly.

"She was seventeen," he moaned. "In the prime of her life. So beautiful. So pure and kind. I worshipped her. I'd have done anything for her." Tears dripped down his dirt-smudged face. "Three times, I tried to take her place that morning, but they wouldn't let me." He covered his face, jolting. "I'll never erase the sound of her screams. Never!"

Heather bent down and laid her hands over his, taking them away from his face.

"Thraecius, she's no longer in pain. And that loving spirit that you loved so much, it hasn't died." Heather motioned to the rocky ceiling. "She's out there somewhere beyond this awful place. Waiting for the rest of her family to join her."

He bowed his head, but he didn't try to pull away.

"Heather's right, Thraecius," said Ross, dropping down beside the angry man. "We're just like you. When we took our own lives, we put incredible distance between ourselves and the people we love. Yet all we were trying to do was get back to them. Any way we could."

Thraecius stared at Ross for several painful moments and then his gaze fell onto Heather.

"An insurmountable distance now." His voice was so hollow and final. "I knew that when I fell on the centurion's sword." Thraecius unfolded his tall frame, lifting his chin in grim acceptance. "I'm prepared to follow the path I undertook. I know what I've done and I take full responsibility for it."

"Thraecius, no—" Heather turned his face toward her. "It's only the end if you stop trying. There's still a way to move on from the Between."

He shook his head. "There's no way out," he said, glancing at Ross. "Believe me, I've tried. I've been here a very long time. I've traveled up and down every path through the grasses, past the soulstalkers, into the poppy fields. To the gates of the Red City. Into the Demon Veils. There's no way out."

"Not if you've already given up," said Heather.

"But why give up here?" Ross asked, shaking his head. "Why, of all places, the Demon Veils?"

Thraecius bowed his head. "I got tired. Sometimes—in the quiet —I go to the Veils to...to visit her. Remember her." He sighed. "Doesn't matter. I belong here—with the demons."

"No, you don't," said Heather. "You look at me, Thraecius."

His surprised gaze snapped to her face and he squinted at her.

"When you disconnect completely, you've lost." She gripped his shoulders. "The first disconnect was your physical body. The second disconnect was your mind. And the third disconnect? It's your soul— your essence. When that happens, it's over. No more possibilities. No way to be reunited with those you care about. Don't you understand?"

His jaw sharpened, the muscles twitching as he shook his head.

"Your parents followed you into the Between and you cut yourself off from them. And everyone."

The anger sparked in his eyes again. He gritted his teeth and pulled away from her.

"My parents." He nearly spat. "It's their fault Juliana's dead! Them and their stupid conversion—it cost Juliana her life." He kicked at the ground. "Calling themselves Ester and Matthew, flaunting it to all of Rome. I want nothing to do with them. Nothing!"

Heather rose on her knees. "You're wrong, Thraecius. Caesar's to blame—and the men who did his bidding. Your parents had a right to choose how they wanted to live their lives."

Thraecius looked drained now. He dropped on his knees to the rocky ground.

"But they knew when they took those names that Caesar would

retaliate. They knew that, yet they risked their children's lives on some flimsy faith. Turning away from the gods was a death sentence in Rome."

"Look around you." She held out her arms. Even this rocky cavern with its black rock and the ashen paths outside that led into grasslands and forest was a thing of amazement. "We each took our lives, expecting an end, not a transition. Seems to me that the fact we still have some sort of life affirms there's something beyond death."

She hadn't realized that until now. Hadn't even considered the fact that this place confirmed that something went on after death. Maybe it was consciousness? Maybe even a soul? She wasn't sure what, but something went on.

Ross slid his hand across her shoulder, giving it a gentle caress.

Finally, Thraecius lifted his head. A faint smile played on his face. "Maybe that's so."

"Maybe you should tell your parents that? I know they'd love to see you again. Especially your mother."

Thraecius looked away, deep in thought.

"I don't think I could find my way back there," he said in a quiet voice as he rose to his feet. "Not sure I want to go back." The whip lay near his feet and he nudged it away.

"We can take you there," said Ross, reaching out to touch Thraecius' shoulder. "Talk to them and decide for yourself. If you disagree, you know the way here. You said so."

"All right," said Thraecius glancing around the cavern as if surprised by its darkness and chill. "For Juliana, I'll do it."

"Follow us out," said Heather. "We're leaving. Now."

She motioned at Shuying who hurried toward her and the four of them moved toward the cavern's entrance.

"The rest of you, if you're tired of this back-breaking work, come back to the great tree with us," said Ross. "You don't have to keep suffering like this!"

Lines of workers threw down their pickaxes and stumbled into the tunnel behind them. Heather and Ross led the way through the confusing passages, past the Veils, and the mechanism until they reached the final passage that led outside.

Halfway through, Mulciber and four other demons gathered. He gaped at Heather as Thraecius followed behind her, Shuying and Ross behind Thraecius, and a steady line of freed workers behind them.

"No way! Not Thraecius!" Mulciber glared at Heather.

Other demons crowded into the passage, their foul breath hot against her face and arms. She concentrated on the path ahead, ignoring their proximity—and intimidation—as she motioned everyone forward.

She remembered Zakhart's warning, that her free will protected her from the demons. They couldn't hold her against her will, but they could deceive her, especially in Thraecius' confused, weakened state. She feared that they'd get to him again. Turn him against his own mind and draw him back into the Veils forever.

"No matter what happens, Thraecius, concentrate on Juliana. She wouldn't want you trapped in this place. She wants you with her and if you stay here, you'll be forever apart."

Thraecius nodded, swallowing hard, and kept walking. "I won't let them trap me again," he said in a soft voice.

Heather glanced back to make sure Ross and Shuying were right behind her. Two demons were at her back now.

"Ross?" she called.

No answer.

"Ross!" she shouted, whirling around. She stopped in the middle of the path as the line of workers traipsed past, following Thraecius outside.

Two demons blocked her path. Their cold, sticky skin pressed against her forearms as she shoved past them to get to Ross who was on his knees clutching his head. Shuying tried to pull Ross to his feet, but he didn't seem to know she was there.

"Ross!"

Heather grabbed him by the shoulders. She jerked him to his feet, shaking him hard, but he stared past her with empty, listless eyes.

"Listen to me! Whatever it is, it's not real! It's not real!"

He didn't react.

She wrapped her arms around him, terrified now. She was losing him.

Shaking him hard, she shouted in his ear. When he still didn't respond, she pressed her mouth to his and kissed him as hard and deep as she'd ever kissed anyone. He didn't respond.

Desperate, she slapped his face.

At last, the recognition returned to his eyes as he pressed his hand to his stinging cheek.

"I'm sorry," said Heather, biting her lip. "But you're in danger. I can't lose you, Ross."

He nodded, muttering thanks and grabbed hold of her hand. With Shuying in tow, they ran down the pathway until they caught up with Thraecius and the others. The Roman stared uneasily at Ross.

"He all right?" Thraecius asked.

Ross nodded and they fled, running hard toward the opening ahead, the ground uneven against their feet. Heather stumbled, fell, and picked herself up, Ross' hand firm against hers again.

Mulciber's whispers echoed in her head.

"Your mother's calling, Heather. You left her behind. She's working the mechanism now. Come and see."

"No!" she shouted, squeezing her eyes closed. "No!"

The horrible possibility blazed through her brain, but she shoved it away, concentrating on the incline that led out again.

"Zakhart, we need you," she whispered, her voice growing louder as the thick blackness softened to a deep grey.

A flutter of wings flashed past the opening in the rocks as she stepped out into marshlands. Sparrow's wings, she thought with a smile.

Zakhart hadn't left them. He'd waited.

"We're here!" she called, waving at him.

Zakhart landed in front of her, smiling.

"You waited for us," said Heather, gripping his sleeve.

He nodded as Halea and the other pale angel, Razasha, landed behind him.

"I couldn't leave you in there." He reached out and smoothed the hair out of Heather's eyes. "Halea's called for more pale angels. They'll be here in a moment to lead the others to the clearing. They'll be protected all the way to the great tree, so don't worry, Heather."

Thraecius stiffened. "This one isn't like the soulstalkers."

"No, they're pale angels. They brought us here."

"I hope Death doesn't catch our scent in the marshes," said Ross, craning his neck to look around the swampy grasses.

Zakhart cast an uneasy gaze toward the horizon. "We shouldn't linger. The longer you're all out here, especially so many, the easier it is for Death to hunt you."

A shadow fell across Zakhart's face and he glanced into the sky as Razasha and several pale angels fluttered overhead. They landed on the loamy soil beside him. Razasha's eyes were a coppery gold like the long tresses of sunlit wheaten hair that coiled about her shoulders. Diaphanous, ivory silks swaddled her slender frame, her wings a soft creamy tan. She spoke in soprano notes to the other angels, the sounds becoming a melody and they responded in a chorus.

Razasha extended her hand to Thraecius who stared at her in awe, a look of reverence in his eyes as he took her hand. With a whisper of wings, Razasha lifted him into the air. Halea scooped Ross into her arms and carried him into the air, Shuying following in the arms of another pale angel.

"Ready, Heather?" Zakhart asked, holding out his hands.

She nodded and took his hand. He lifted her into the air, away from the chill of the marshes, up above the treetops where the sky stretched endless and grey. The air smelled clean above the smell of loamy soil and gurgle of swampy water. The air felt warm against her skin as Zakhart flicked his great wings through the greyness and carried her above the treetops. Across the sea of grass and shifting shadows of the soulstalkers.

The wind burned across her face, so sharp above the trees with nothing to block it. Zakhart held her close to his chest as he sailed over the thin, ghostly river birch bowing in the breeze. Ahead, Halea and Razasha landed in the clearing, setting Ross and the others on their feet. Ross brushed off his clothes and looked toward the sky for Heather. Zakhart seemed to take his time, but finally, he joined the flock of pale angels in the clearing.

Where the paths diverged toward their strange destinies. Where one path led straight to Death's lair. A ruddy clay that led to the Red City. And one led...out.

To where, she wondered. Would it take them to the Spiral?

Ross moved toward her, his eyes filled with pain.

"Thank you for what you did back there, Heather," he said in a soft voice that only she could hear.

"Thank you for pulling me out of the Veils, Ross."

He nodded. "I was really in trouble back there. You have no idea."

Heather slid her arms around Ross' neck and pulled him into a tight hug. "Are you all right now?"

When he didn't answer, Heather's stomach twisted into a knot. She pulled back from him, gripping his shoulders as she studied his face and tried to read what emotions swirled in his kind, beautiful hazel eyes. But couldn't.

A flicker of despair hung there, but she didn't know how deep that emotion ran in him. Or what images Mulciber had pressed into his mind. She knew they were images of Jessie, but Heather had no idea how deeply he'd been affected.

What had he seen back there? Had he somehow touched the Veils like she had?

"Ross," she said, her gaze fixed on his eyes. "You need to tell me what you saw back there. Please. Did you touch the Veils?"

He offered her a smile and motioned toward Thraecius. "It's not important right now. Let's get Thraecius back to his folks first and the others settled. Then we'll talk."

She nodded. "I won't let this go, Ross." She leaned up and brushed a soft kiss against his mouth. "Or what happened between us back there."

She couldn't. Ross meant so much to her and right now, she couldn't imagine him not being here beside her. She depended on him.

And something more.

Something that tugged at her chest, an emotion she couldn't quite identify. What she knew for certain was she didn't want to be away from him. Or without him.

"That's right," he said, winking. "Lots to talk about. As soon as Thraecius and the others are settled. All right?"

"Okay," she said, returning his smile.

Heather slid her arm around his waist, holding him close as they approached Thraecius and Shuying. He felt so good—safe—in her arms.

"It's coming back to me now," said Thraecius, glancing around the clearing. "I'm remembering this place more and more."

"Me, too," said Shuying, offering Thraecius a shy smile. "I prefer it to demons. Why did I walk away from it?"

They waited until the pale angels had returned with the last of the workers. When the group gathered around Heather and Ross, Ross motioned them forward.

"Let's get back before the soulstalkers get us," he said, motioning Thraecius and Shuying and the others toward the glimmer of amber lights deep in the forest.

"Thanks for everything," Heather called to the flock of pale angels as they took flight.

Ross and the others called out their thanks, too.

"Be safe," Zakhart called as he lifted into the air, rising on an updraft beside Razasha. Halea and the other pale angels were already hazy specs on the horizon. Zakhart and Razasha lingered along the path to the great tree, protecting the rest of the rescues.

Heather walked beside Ross, holding his hand on the path that led away from the clearing and twisted toward the smoke people's great tree. What would Avana think when she saw Thraecius return to the tree? And all these other people? Heather hoped it would humble that arrogant bitch and show her that these human exiles were worth the effort.

Everyone fell silent as they approached the tree's warm lights and familiar shelter. Heather opened the door and motioned Thraecius inside and then Ross followed by Shuying and some of the others. The rest from the Demon Veils were still filing down the path toward the great tree. They'd be here shortly, pale angels still protecting them.

Ross paused in the door's threshold and reached out a hand to Heather's face. He touched her cheek and smiled, starting to speak, but something made him stop. Instead, he just squeezed her hand and stepped inside.

Inside the great tree, Avana gasped, her vaporous form solidifying as she thrust a hand to her mouth.

"Thraecius? You return from the Demon Veils? How is it possible?"

Thraecius shrugged his thick shoulders and nodded at Heather and Ross. "Blame the girl and her boyfriend. She got through to me somehow."

"Boyfriend?" Avana sputtered, her gaze flicking from Ross to Heather.

Heather grinned and hugged Ross. "Problem, Avana?"

"Are you talking about our Ross, Thraecius?" Avana asked, shaking her head.

The Roman nodded. "A very brave man, facing those demons. And me."

Avana stared at Ross now, looking surprised and impressed for the first time.

Thraecius turned away, gazing toward the sectional in front of the fireplace. Where Ester and Matthew sat as they did every evening, watching the flicker of the fire in the hearth, pretending to eat roasted fowl and sip mulled wine. Heather expected the rich smell of spices and simmering meat, but only faded images and misty impressions of food and drink hung in the air. Ester pressed a wine glass to her lips, dull burgundy liquid sloshing.

Thraecius' eyes turned glassy. He bit his lip and moved toward the sofa. He knelt, hesitating a moment before he reached for Ester's hand.

"Mother? It's me—Thraecius." He thumped his hand against his chest, pants dusty and ragged.

Ester stared at the man kneeling before her as if she didn't recognize him. Several moments passed as Ester just stared at him. Finally, the recognition touched her eyes.

Ester gasped, her mouth gaping. "Thraecius? My son?"

He nodded. "I've returned from the Veils, Mother."

"You're safe!" she cried, letting go of the wine glass. It dissipated in a puff of smoke. She threw her arms around him, pressing his face against her shoulder. "Oh, Matthew, our son is safe!"

"Thraecius!" Matthew rose from the sofa as Thraecius turned to face his father. Matthew's bottom lip trembled until finally, he clasped Thraecius to his chest.

They were together again, but Heather felt little comfort. All of them were still dead and still trapped in this limbo with no way out. They'd all escaped the Demon Veils, but the Spiral was still a lifetime away.

If they ever found it.

Shuying dropped down on the floor beside the fireplace and held her hands out, trying to warm them against cold flames. She seemed content, but that same disturbed undercurrent ran through her dark eyes, like the one that haunted Ross. Heather wondered if that same expression stared out from her own eyes.

Ross leaned against the wall and stared out the window at the growing darkness, arms folded against his chest. He looked lost, troubled.

Something horrible had stared back at him behind those Veils and even now, it stayed with him. She'd been through something similar. Even when she closed her eyes, it remained. Something neither of them had expected. She wanted to tell him what she'd seen and she needed to get him to talk about what happened to him back there.

The door opened, small groups of people who'd followed Thraecius to the Veils stumbling inside. Avana's spirit form flitted through the room, mingling with others of her smoke people until finally, she coalesced beside Shuying at the fireplace. The spirit woman stepped over Shuying like a piece of furniture and stopped in front of Heather, her gaze unblinking.

"What is it?" Heather asked.

"You did something amazing out there, Heather," said Avana, her gaze flicking from Shuying to Thraecius and finally Ross. Disdain hardened her eyes. "It was just you, wasn't it? Not Ross."

Heather glared at Avana, hands on her hips. "You leave him alone! If it hadn't been for Ross, I'd have been carried off to the poppy fields. Thraecius and Shuying and the others would still be trapped in the Veils. He pulled me out of those Veils when I couldn't do it myself. Ross got me moving, got me caring. So don't you dare treat him like he doesn't matter. Because he does! Especially to me."

She looked away. Why'd Avana say that out loud? Had Ross heard it?

Ross meant so much to her. No, it was more than that and until now, she hadn't even recognized it. She'd felt a connection with him she hadn't felt for anyone before. But why now? Why here?

"Ross?" she called, turning away from Avana. She walked toward him and leaned against the wall.

He didn't even look at her. He stared past her. He seemed so far away as he stared out into the dark woods surrounding them. His cold distance frightened her.

What had Mulciber done to him?

She grabbed his arm. "Ross, look at me."

It took a moment or two before Ross turned toward her, a blankness in his eyes like Ester used to have. That same detached, checked out look. Empty. Lost in what had been left behind.

"We need to talk, Ross. Tell me what happened in that passageway! What did you see? What did the demons do to you?"

He sighed. "It doesn't matter anymore, Heather." He sounded tired. Hopeless. A tone she'd never heard in his voice before. "I know it was my fault. Like everything else. Let it go, okay?"

"I won't," she said, her voice rising. "Not when I see you like this. What was your fault, Ross? What did you see?" She gripped his arms. "Please—talk to me. You're scaring me."

"Not now," he muttered, pinching the bridge of his nose with thumb and forefinger. "I can't think about this right now. I'm tired. I need to sleep." He turned away from her, moving toward the right-hand staircase.

"How can you be tired?" Heather replied, only half kidding as she took a step toward him. "You're dead, remember?"

"I said I'm tired," he snapped, not turning around. "Later, okay? I just need some time alone."

There was a strange tone in his voice. Anguish? Guilt? He was blaming himself for something. But what? What had he seen in the Veils?

Ross walked away, climbing the stairs and disappearing into the upper levels. He'd go up to the top floor like he did when he was avoiding Avana. As soon as Shuying and Thraecius were settled, she'd go and find him.

Outside, the thick greyness had lightened against the windows when Thraecius finally rose from the couch, Ester and Matthew beside him. The three of them climbed the left-hand staircase to the tree's next level. It was the first time she'd ever seen Ester and Matthew go upstairs. Now that the three of them had reconnected, maybe they'd want to help the others, too? Maybe this change would lead all of them to the Spiral?

Heather steered Shuying and some of the other frightened workers upstairs to choose spaces for themselves. Shuying created a small room just one floor up.

"I feel safe here," said Shuying. "Not too high, but close to a door."

The walls looked like polished maple. In the corner, a small fireplace cast thin light through the room in amber flickers. A twin-sized bed stood in the corner beside a sink. A thick, reed mat covered the floor, pale blue rice paper screens separating the bed from the room. Red silk fabric decorated with silver cranes and pink lotus blossoms draped the walls. The calming notes of a flute punctuated the trickle of running water from a little fountain by the bed. Shuying smiled as she sat down on the bed and stretched out under a soft pink blanket.

Heather stayed until Shuying turned on her side and closed her eyes.

Like the others, Shuying still needed to pretend she was alive. Heather understood. She had her own little sanctuary on the top floor.

She left Shuying to her illusion and went to find Ross, hurrying up the endless flight of stairs, through the warm, amber glow of lanterns and fireplaces until she reached the top.

Ross' chamber was empty.

"Ross? Where are you?" she called, rushing down the stairs.

She went up the other side of the tree, feet pounding up the left-hand staircase as she called for him.

No response.

Terrified now, she rushed back to the first floor, finding Avana alone in the usually crowded space. Everyone else had gone upstairs. The smoke woman was in solid form, sitting on the couch where

Ester and Matthew used to sit all the time. Smiling, Avana glanced around as if she preferred the emptiness to the crowd of shellshocked humans. Heather didn't know which was worse.

"Where is everyone?" Heather asked.

"Off deluding themselves, I suppose," Avana said, rolling her eyes. "My tree is overflowing with lost souls! Tons of them crammed in, pretending they're still alive while they give up on everything again. Revolting."

Swirls of smoke coiled through the empty room as more smoke people entered the room. They wandered through the great tree all the time in their smoky forms, so Heather didn't notice them like she did tonight. The mist was thick, trails of smoke twisting and braiding up and down the staircases, winding through the space in gentle, smoky curves. Heather wasn't used to seeing so many of them. Or seeing this room so empty. With only smoke people for company, Heather felt hollow and lost inside.

"Why can't you help them?" Heather asked.

Avana's eyes turned hard. "It's not up to me to help them. They're lucky I allow them refuge under this roof. If I wanted to be cruel, I'd lead them to the soulstalkers and be done with it. Or the poppy fields—they're a painless end. It would be kinder than a long, slow eternal death in here."

Avana looked away and Heather saw a flicker of humanity in those almost animal eyes. Somewhere deep down, Avana felt sorry for the lost souls, but most of the time, the smoke woman hid it well. She'd shed the majority of her humanity a lifetime ago.

"Where's Ross?" Heather asked, hands on her hips. "Did he come this way?"

Avana smiled as she pointed toward the door. Like she was gloating. "He went out," she said as she propped her chin in her hand.

"Went out? Out there? With soulstalkers prowling?" Her breath caught. "But it's too dangerous alone—he said so himself."

Avana shrugged, a pleased expression shining on her dove-grey face. "All he said was something about poppies," she said with a chuckle.

Heather gasped, chills slicing through her like a knife blade. The poppy fields! He'd gone alone. To try and rescue Jessie.

Her fingers went cold as she whirled around and darted toward the door.

"Where are you going?" Avana demanded, jumping up from the sofa.

She surged toward Heather, her form changing to smoke in an instant. "It's not safe out there. You know that!" Avana grabbed hold of the door, preventing Heather from opening it more than a crack.

"I've got to stop him! Find him before the soulstalkers get him."

"Maybe you shouldn't keep trying to rescue him, Heather," said Avana. "Wouldn't it be kinder to just let him go?"

"No!" she shouted, yanking the door out of Avana's grasp as fear pulsed through her. "Not Ross."

"He's too filled with guilt to let you save him," Avana replied. "Why is he worth risking everything for?"

Heather pressed her hand against her chest, trying to hold back the crushing ache. "Because! Even when I'd given up on me, he didn't. He kept me going. Kept me fighting. He cared about me." Her voice strangled in her throat, her eyes stinging with hot tears. "He loved me."

She knew why she needed to save him.

Heather ran into the indigo darkness, lantern light trailing after her, Avana's voice sharp in the breeze.

A wild screech pierced the quiet, chilling her blood.

Then another.

Shadows darted across the grass. Blades rustled.

Another inhuman shriek. A cry of pain. Human.

"Ross!" she shouted, recognizing his familiar voice.

Wings beat overhead. She looked up. Two soulstalkers flew past, carrying Ross between them.

"Nooo! NO!"

Tears flooded her cheeks as she dropped to her knees in the ashen soil, her heart breaking at the blur of soulstalkers on the horizon, carrying Ross toward the distant poppy fields.

eleven

. . .

"ZAKHART!" Heather shouted into the wind. "Please! Help me!"

She couldn't wait. There wasn't time.

She ran down the path away from the great tree, feet pounding across the ashen soil toward the forest clearing, side aching, wind rising at her shoulders.

The excited shrieks and trills of soulstalkers carried like blue jays chattering at sparrows. They reminded Heather of vultures.

Would they tear Ross apart and drop his body into the poppy fields? To sleep forever.

She winced, the ache burning all the way down to her stomach as she ran, shouting at the sky.

"Zakhart!"

If her shouts brought soulstalkers, she no longer cared. She'd tear apart their wings until she left a trail of feathers from here to the great tree.

Ahead, in the clearing, lay the seven paths. Heather veered toward the far-left path. The one that led toward the sea of tall grass and the poppy fields.

"Zakhart, please! Help me!"

As the grasses rose around her, hiss of long, whiplike blades against her calves, Heather felt the pale angel's presence beside her. She glanced up, relieved by the soothing orange of Zakhart's eyes.

"Soulstalkers have taken Ross!" she cried, winded as she ran through the grasslands. Zakhart flew beside her. "I saw them carry him off—but I couldn't stop them."

"Oh, no!" Zakhart lamented, wringing his hands as he hovered beside her. "This is terrible! When did it happen?"

"Just now! Please, you've got to help me save him! Before it's too late."

He landed in front of her, blocking her path. She skidded to a stop.

Zakhart reached out and touched her face in a comforting gesture, gripping her shoulders, that look in his eyes. Like the one they gave her that night in the ICU when her mom died. And the one the lawyer gave her when they sold the house out from under her.

No! She wouldn't make time for one more being to give up on her. Not with Ross' existence hanging by a thread.

"Heather," he said in a sharp voice.

"No, Zakhart," she moaned, face contorting as she shook her head. "No."

"It's too late," the pale angel said with a sigh. "He's probably already under the poppies' spell."

Heather's eyes widened as she stared into Zakhart's large, unblinking eyes. She couldn't believe that. She shook her head, hair whipping across her cheeks and sticking to her lips.

No. She wouldn't.

"It can't be too late," she said, her voice aching.

Zakhart nodded. "I'm so sorry."

He squeezed her shoulder, but she shrugged it off, stepping away from him. She refused for it to be too late. To let Ross be lost forever.

"Fine. I'll go by myself then."

She swerved around him, bolting down the trail, moving deeper into the tall grasses.

"Heather, no!"

Zakhart shot past her, his wings beating hard as he dropped down in front of her, forcing her to stop again.

"It's too dangerous! You can't help him now. Save yourself."

Heather glared at the pale angel, arms crossed. "Not without Ross! And I won't give up on him, understand? So, either help me or leave!"

Zakhart grabbed by her shoulders again, shaking her hard.

"Heather, listen! He's given up. Back at the Veils, I heard him say that what happened to Jessie was his fault. There's nothing you can do now."

Zakhart was wrong. She wouldn't let Ross give up on himself.

She pulled away from the pale angel again, storming down the path toward the grey hills that rose ahead.

Beyond those hills loomed the poppy fields.

Ahead, in the thick tangles of grass were dozens of large, basket-like structures woven from grass and twigs. The basket-like things nestled in the tall grasses like birds' nests, dozens and dozens perched in the tall, reedy meadows.

Soulstalker roosts. Their hovels were everywhere in the sea of grasses, standing between her and the poppy fields.

Feathers rustled. Grass swished.

She had to get past them to reach Ross.

The path widened, curving past clusters of those grass and twig roosts. Heather crept quietly until Zakhart tackled her to the ground. She fell into the sea of grass.

"Sssshh," Zakhart hissed, a hand over her mouth, his other arm around her waist, holding her silent and immobile.

She looked up, intending to shout at the pale angel, but a sharp, black shadow cut across the grass.

A scythe.

Heather froze, trembling.

Grass crunched, footsteps methodical in the sudden stillness.

Zakhart kept his hand tight against her mouth as the thick

shadow passed over them.

Had Death seen her?

She held her breath, waiting for the shadow to pass completely over and disappear.

Several long minutes crawled past as Heather lay in the grass with Zakhart, both afraid to move.

It seemed forever before a calm wind whispered across the meadow, scattering the smell of dirty rain across the hills and grasslands. Only when the tension in Zakhart's arms and wings dissipated did he let her up.

Heather pulled herself up on her knees, brushing grass and twigs off her clothes. It felt strange not to feel her heart pound like a drum in her chest. All she felt was a tight clenching and the anguished ache of time running out for Ross.

Zakhart sat up in the grass beside her, his chest heaving. He looked exhausted now.

"Thank you," said Heather in a hushed voice, folding her arms against her stomach. "I-I didn't see her."

Zakhart nodded. "I didn't until nearly the last moment. She hadn't been there long, but I shielded your body from her detection. That was too close, Heather. Now, let me take you back to the great tree."

Heather shook her head. "I told you, Zakhart, I'm not leaving him to their mercy. Please, will you fly me to the poppy fields? It's his only chance."

Zakhart cringed. "You're not going to let this go, are you?"

She shook her head.

"I can take you there," he said, sighing, "but I've already warned you that it's too late."

Pain shot through her chest and she winced at his declaration. The finality of it. Like all the sand had run out of the hourglass. Like someone had flashed game over across the sky and she was just supposed to accept it and forget him.

"No," she moaned. "I can't be too late."

"I don't know what lies those demons branded into his head," said Zakhart, his pumpkin-orange eyes sparking with anger. "But Ross is overwhelmed with guilt. He blames himself for what happened to Jessie. He doesn't think he deserves to be saved. He's given up."

"I tried to get him to talk to me, Zakhart, believe me, I did. He was so strong when I couldn't escape the Veils. I'd still be there if he hadn't pulled me out. I don't know what those demons did to him, but he was so troubled on the way back." She sighed. "He's fought so hard for so long. He wouldn't let me give up. I won't let him either."

Zakhart studied her face a moment. "Did he say anything about the Veils?" he asked. "Anything?" He glanced skyward then stretched his wings as he rose to his feet. "Let's get out of the grasses. Too many creatures can hide here."

Heather nodded and Zakhart lifted her into his arms, rising into the encroaching darkness.

"I know it's about Jessie," Heather continued. "I think Mulciber's still torturing Ross with images of Jessie dying in those poppy fields. Feeding on his guilt. Pushing him toward giving up, too." A warm glimmer of hope shuddered through her and she smiled. "Or—what if he let the soulstalkers capture him. So he could try and rescue her? That's it, Zakhart! It's a rescue!"

She wanted to believe that. She had to believe it, to keep her going. To try and save him.

"I hope you're right," Zakhart replied as he floated above the rolling meadows, Heather in his arms. "If he hasn't given up, then there might be a chance, Heather. There's only one way to find out then."

Heather threw her arms around his neck. "Thank you, Zakhart! I knew you wouldn't let him perish out here!"

"According to Archangel Turiel, saving humans is a weakness of mine," he said with a sigh, flying higher above the grasslands. He pointed toward a ridge in the distance. "Beyond these hills are the poppy fields. We'll have to avoid the sand runners when we get there or you'll slumber forever in those fields, too."

"Sand runners?" Heather frowned.

Zakhart nodded. "They're dusk creatures. Shadowy forms that prowl on all fours, like panthers. Assassin demons like to take their forms when they hunt humans."

"Panthers? As in a big cat?" Heather asked, wide-eyed.

"They patrol the fields, protecting the poppies and scattering the poppy dust across the fields." Worry flickered in Zakhart's eyes. These creatures made him almost as uneasy as the soulstalkers.

"Why do they scatter poppy dust?" Heather asked with a frown.

Zakhart's eyes narrowed to slits. "They sprinkle it across the sleepers, keeping them asleep. Every evening at dusk, the poppies release more deadly pollen for the sand runners to collect. The longer someone stays in those fields, the deeper they fall under the dust's spell as *they* slowly turn to dust. Including their souls."

Heather winced. Was there a way to wake up the sleepers? Before Ross reached a point of no return?

"If we carry him out of there, away from the poppy dust, will he wake up?"

Her heart twisted into a knot when Zakhart shook his head.

"He'll never awaken without intervention. Without help, his soul will turn to dust."

Heather tried to blot that image from her mind. She refused to believe that Ross was lost forever.

"Is there any way to break the unending sleep?" she asked.

Zakhart held up a finger. "There's a rare heartlily that only blooms in total darkness. Its petals absorb the poppy dust. Only if his soul hasn't turned to powder though."

"We have to try, Zakhart!" said Heather. "Take me to where they bloom."

He banked right, wings stretched wide as he turned toward a small, clear stream bubbling through the darkening fields. The pale angel sat Heather down beside the stream and pointed toward the distant burble of water that disappeared into almost total darkness.

"I've seen one or two heartlilies bloom here—along the stream.

We'll try to gather a bloom or two if we can." He sighed. "But Heather, you need to be prepared for the fact that Ross might be too far gone to save."

Heather clutched his arms. "Not until I know it's hopeless, Zakhart…I won't quit on him. Please. Help me!"

He sighed as he took Heather by the shoulders and fixed her with his piercing, pumpkin-orange gaze. "I'll try," he said in a quiet voice. "It's all I can promise, Heather."

"All right," she answered finally, nodding. At least it was something. A chance to try. "Just tell me what to do."

"Follow the stream toward the darkness. If a lily has bloomed, you'll see its pale orange glow."

She slogged through the chilly water toward the curtain of darkness. Her feet grew numb in the cold stream, making her stumble several times, but she followed the clear water's rush toward the darkness ahead. As she drew closer to the thick swirl of darkness, a smear of orange luminescence pierced the black shadows.

A heartlily!

She rushed forward. Shadows snaked through the flowing water. Fish? Eels?

Sucking in a breath, she stepped into the swath of darkness and hurried toward the faint orange gleam ahead.

On the bank's edge, the orange blossom shone bright, illuminating the curve of the stream and the uneven ground. Heather reached toward the glowing orange bloom.

Something tore into her hand and she gasped, jerking it back.

Even through her partially numb state, Heather felt the raw pain vibrate through her hand.

"Something bit me!" she cried, staring up at Zakhart as she clutched her hand to her chest. "Was it the lily?"

Zakhart shook his head. "No, it was some sort of dusk creature. But I've never seen it before. So many unfamiliar creatures prowl this place. They even frighten me sometimes."

He reached into the water. A twisting, eel-like shadow undulated toward his outstretched fingers, snapping. He pulled his hand back.

"That was close," he said with a hiss.

Heather tried again to retrieve a blossom, but the shadow creature in the water was faster. She drew back her stinging hand a second time.

"Zakhart, try and distract it!"

Nodding, the pale angel floated near the stream, bobbing above the swift-flowing water as he stuck his hand into its coldness. The shadow slithered toward his hand as he pulled it along with the current, away from the blossom.

Heather snatched at the blossom, plucking it from the cold water a moment before another shadow creature lunged at her hand.

"I got one!" she shouted, holding up the fluted, glowing flower.

"We'll need one more," said Zakhart. He pointed to the edge of the water. "Climb onto the bank or they'll start attacking your legs."

Something tore into her calf. Heather cried out, lurching out of the water and onto solid ground barely visible in the cloying darkness.

Zakhart disappeared into the writhing blackness as Heather looked downstream. Seeing another orange bloom. She listened for his wings as she walked across the bank and knelt near another blossom.

"Ouch!" Zakhart shouted, drawing his hand out of the water. "I was too slow."

"Are you all right?" Heather called out, unable to see the pale angel. She could only hear his wings flutter in the dark, still air, barely audible above the flow of the stream.

"I'm fine," he muttered. "So, these creatures are following us. And they're gathering quickly around us, ready to swarm. You'll have to be fast, Heather."

She dropped down on the bank, extending her hands toward the blossom that grew just off the shore in the stream. She waited to hear the beat of Zakhart's wings as he led the creatures away. As the sound traveled farther, she poised her hands over the top of the blossom. And counted.

One. Two. Three.

She plunged her hands into the cold water and grabbed the blossom.

As she pulled, shadows swirled around her fingers. Needles pounded into her hands as she struggled to free the blossom. Gritting her teeth against the intense pain, she pulled hard.

Snap!

The blossom and accompanying leaves tore out of the water as she fell backward.

Got it!

Her hands ached and burned, but she had two blooms now. Enough to revive Ross, she hoped.

"I've got two, Zakhart!"

The flutter of wings grew louder until he emerged into the darkness swirling around her, hovering at her shoulder. She grinned, holding out the blossoms.

"Here, I'll take them," said Zakhart, extending his hands. "When any light hits them, they'll open and their power will be lost." He patted his side with one hand. "I'll wrap them and keep them safe in my satchel."

Nodding, Heather handed off the long, tube-like blooms to him and he slid them into a grey silk satchel.

Zakhart smiled, extending his hand to Heather. "Ready to find the poppy fields?"

She nodded and took hold of his hand. "As fast as we can. Ross is depending on us."

The pale angel lifted Heather into his arms and rose into the stormy blackness surrounding the stream. He lurched forward, following its curve until he came out into the dusk.

Ahead, the hills rose above the sea of grasses. Zakhart flew toward the hill and Heather gripped his robes as he fluttered high into the air, a look of intense focus on his face.

"Why so intense?" Heather asked.

His gaze softened as he looked into her eyes. "There's not much time."

Only then did Heather feel Zakhart's hopelessness. It nearly overpowered her.

She slid her arms around his neck and squeezed her eyes closed, trying to hide the tears sliding down her face. Zakhart squeezed her arm.

"All we can do is try, Heather," he said in a soothing tone as the hillside rose ahead. "Don't lose hope now that you've convinced me to try."

"I won't if you won't, Zakhart."

The pale angel pulled in a sharp breath.

Heather swallowed the sob that bubbled up. She wouldn't give in to the despair. To the same dark emptiness that had led her to choke down all that Molly and end her life.

No, she'd get to Ross in time. It wasn't too late yet. It couldn't be.

She held onto that one thought as Zakhart sailed over the hillside, flying low. An ocean of grey and black poppies swayed in the breeze. They stood at least eight feet tall.

Heather shuddered as they got closer. Beneath the huge poppies' ragged leaves and grey blooms lay pasty white bodies. People. Some curled into balls among the charcoal grey leaves, others stretched out on their backs, some on their sides.

It looked like a graveyard.

Shadowy black panther-like forms stalked along the furrowed ground, sprinkling handfuls of pollen across plants and bodies like sand with their massive paws.

As Zakhart flew closer, Heather saw that the chalky, dusty bodies were slowly losing form, looking more like weathered statues with sand-blasted faces and disintegrating bodies.

"Oh, no," she said with a gasp and turned her head.

"Don't turn away now, Heather," said Zakhart, his voice barely above a whisper. "You must look at their faces and locate Ross while I keep an eye on the sand runners."

"I can't," she moaned, her voice cracking. "What if he's like the others now?"

"What if he's not?"

Zakhart was right. She had to look. For Ross, she had to.

Heather willed herself to turn and face the field of poppies and their rows of human captives. So many of them were lost now, wearing away. Others looked whitewashed—like statues. As if they'd just stretched out among the poppies for a nap. Guilt stabbed at her. She couldn't rescue them all. Only Ross. She only had two blooms.

Zakhart flew up and down the fields, dodging sand runners as he swooped low over every chalky figure nestled among the poppies. Heather saw hundreds of faces, but none of them was Ross.

"Keep looking, Heather," Zakhart urged.

"This is impossible!" she cried. "There's too many and too much ground to cover."

A smile lit his face. "Then I'll call for help."

He sang a clear tenor note that carried across the dark sky in crystal lamentation, causing the sand runners to stop prowling and look to the sky.

The flutter of wings filled the air. Heather turned toward the distant forest as the air darkened with wings. Her eyes filled with tears and she was overcome by the sight of dozens of pale angels rushing to Zakhart's call.

"Hang on, Ross," she whispered. "We'll find you."

The pale angels gathered around Zakhart like a flock of mourning doves, hovering above the poppy fields, awaiting his instruction.

Three more hauntingly clear notes filled the stillness, rising on the breeze. The angels dispersed across the almost endless fields of poppies.

"There," said Zakhart, grinning at Heather now, those pumpkin-orange eyes bright. "With their help, Ross still has a chance."

Heather stared at him, unable to speak for a moment, so moved by the pale angels' help.

"Why?" she asked finally, her throat tight. "Why do *we* deserve your help over the others here?" She pointed toward the statue-like people disintegrating into the soil and poppy leaves.

"Because you asked," he said, laying a hand to her cheek. "If only they'd just asked, reached out in some way, we could have helped them, too. But they've walled themselves off so completely that nothing penetrates now. Do you understand? They could have helped themselves by just asking, but they chose not to ask. We must respect their wishes."

She nodded, understanding now. Understanding everything.

If she'd just held on longer, reached out to someone in her darkest moments of grief, maybe she'd have gotten through another day, another hour? But she'd walled herself off until the distance was so great that no one could cross it. Not even her. But here, in the Between, she saw that now, clearly, as she looked into the faces of the desolate, the despairing, and the lost souls.

She didn't feel quite so lost now. But she needed that connection and that meant reaching out to Ross. She'd risk endless slumber. Ross meant too much to her to abandon him now. No, it was more than that.

"Ross!" she called.

Zakhart clamped a hand over her mouth, his eyes wide.

"Sssh, Heather! Quiet or you'll bring Death and every soulstalker into this field after you. Do you understand?"

When she nodded, he pulled away his hand.

"Sorry," she said in a whisper. "What about those notes you hit?"

He smiled. "They're in a pitch that only my brethren can hear. Well, the sand runners hear them, but all they see are wings. To them, we're no different than the soulstalkers."

She started to ask him how he knew that for sure, but the grin that rolled across his face struck her silent.

"Razasha's found him, Heather," he said.

Heather threw her arms around Zakhart's neck, hugging him. "At last!" She couldn't halt the tears of relief. "Please, take me to him."

Zakhart nodded, holding her tight as he sailed at top speed across the poppies, veering in a wide circle, and banking a sharp right. He landed in a thick overgrowth of massive grey poppies and set Heather down among the ragged leaves.

Ross lay on his back, legs and arms splayed like a ragdoll tossed outside to rot in the field. She fell down beside him and gripped his milk-white hand, his face chalky, lips grey.

"Ross, I'm here—it's not too late! Do you hear me?"

He didn't move, not even a flutter of eyelids or a twitch of his mouth.

"Ross," she whispered, bending toward him to press her mouth against his ear. "It's Heather. I'm here. We're carrying you out of this place."

She glanced to her right. A statue-like woman lay near him in the grass, curled into a fetal position. She had long hair down her back, long legs folded against her chest. Her facial features had worn away, arms and legs slowly turning to dust. Sickness balled in Heather's stomach as she stared at the woman.

Jessie. Ross' girlfriend. It had to be her.

Ross must have tried to rescue her and got caught by the sand runners. Seeing Jessie's disintegrating form like this must have killed him. Her heart ached for him.

When he found her like this, he'd probably laid down here beside her. Giving up.

Zakhart motioned Razasha toward Ross and the flaxen-haired angel landed on his other side.

"Hurry," Zakhart whispered, glancing up. "Sand runners are approaching."

Foliage swished in the hush of dusk, the pounding of footfalls filling the silence.

Heather froze.

Razasha scooped up Ross' inert form, lifting him into her arms, and rising into the air.

Zakhart reached out for Heather and she grabbed hold of his hands. As he lifted her from the ground, the singsong of metal split the silence. A sharp-edged shadow slashed across the poppies!

Death's scythe!

Heather fought back a shout as dozens of grey poppy heads flew into the air, cut clean by Death's scythe.

A blood-curdling scream tore across the field, plants and blooms shredded beneath a sparkling curved blade.

Footfalls hammered the heavy black soil.

Sand runners pounced. They shuffled across the flattened grass where Jessie lay. Sniffing the ground, perking up shadow ears.

Searching for Ross. Heather winced.

But Zakhart flew higher above the fields, the other pale angels flocking around him. Ahead, she saw Ross in Razasha's arms.

The frantic beat of Zakhart's heart and the panic in his eyes unnerved her.

"She's on your trail now," Zakhart said in a frightened voice, worry shining in his pumpkin-orange eyes. "She'll soon come for you at the great tree. It won't shield you for long. You can't stay there now, Heather."

Heather felt the weight of his words settle like stone against her chest. "Where will I go?"

The sound of her mother's voice echoed across the landscape, the single word clear and bright. *Live.*

"My mother's voice!" Heather cried, staring at Zakhart.

In the distance, the thrum of chimes, of energy danced against her ears, a force tugging at her.

"The Spiral. You feel it, don't you?"

Heather nodded. For the first time, she felt something pulling her.

"It's your only chance," said Zakhart. "His only chance."

"As soon as Ross is on his feet," said Heather, her voice barely above a whisper. "We'll leave the great tree."

"Promise me you will, Heather."

She nodded. "You have my word, Zakhart."

Zakhart nodded, his expression grim as he sailed over the grasses, flying low with the other pale angels clustered around him. Shielding her and Ross from Death's scythe.

Screeches pierced the darkening sky as soulstalkers soared out of the grasses toward them.

Pale angels lunged at them, wings beating against the wild-faced creatures, knocking them away from Ross and Razasha. She flew on while Halea kept her safe. The other pale angels clustered around Zakhart, fending off a wave of soulstalkers.

But there were too many!

"Go!" Halea shouted, smashing her wings against a soulstalker that lunged for Heather. "Quickly!"

Zakhart tore away from the melee, the wind squeezing tears out of Heather's eyes as she spun with him through dizzying darkness toward the clearing. Right behind Razasha.

Ahead, in the thickening dusk, Razasha set down by the great tree and waited for Zakhart to reach her. His landing was abrupt. He set Heather beside him and fumbled open the door. Heather lunged inside, Razasha and Zakhart right behind her. Carrying Ross.

Avana's mouth fell open and she turned translucent, becoming more vapor than corporeal. Several smoke people floated like ghosts down the stairs, coiling around the people who stared in awe at the pale angels.

"Pale angels?" Avana cried in a high-pitched voice barely above a whisper. "You've brought angels?"

Throughout the room, heads turned, eyes widened as everything fell still. Others crowded onto the stairways, watching the pale angels in silence. The soft crackle of the fireplace was the only sound in the room.

For the first time that she'd been in this shelter, Heather had everyone's attention.

"This way," Heather said, motioning Razasha toward the empty couch by the fireplace.

"What's happened?" Thraecius called from the left-hand stairway. "Heather?"

Razasha laid Ross' inert form on the burgundy couch and Heather dropped down beside him. Thraecius and Shuying crept down the stairs, gathering around him. Ester and Matthew were soon behind them as well as Barb and Lamarr and lots of others. They whispered and chattered, staring at the angels and then Ross.

Heather turned toward the tall, dark-haired Roman. Thraecius' eyes were intense, a mixture of hope and fear in his eyes. Ester held onto his arm, Matthew beside him.

"What happened to Ross?" Shuying asked, motioning toward him. "We can't die twice! Can we?"

Zakhart moved to the arm of the couch and laid his hands on either side of Ross' face. Heather's heart fell when Ross' eyes didn't open.

"It's his soul that's injured," said Zakhart in a hushed voice. "It's...dying."

Heather winced. She had to hurry, before it was too late.

"How?" Shuying asked, pressing her hand against her mouth.

"He went into the poppy fields," said Heather.

Gasps and mutters hissed through the room. Lamarr and Barb shuffled back like his condition was contagious. Javier looked horrified, backing away to stand behind Ester and Matthew.

Heather laid her hand against Ross' shoulder, his body so deathly still. Like he was frozen in time. This was worse than death.

How could they ever bring him back from this state?

"With Zakhart and Razasha's help, we found him and carried him out."

Avana's smoky form coiled around Heather and drifted across Ross' body, a long trail of smoke wrapping around the couch.

"He'll never awaken again, you fools," she said, weaving her way through the crowd and back toward Ross. "Bringing him back here has probably drawn Death right to this door. She'll slay the lot of you now! At last, it'll be quiet again. No more lost souls to bother with."

Shuying looked horrified, her hand still covering her mouth. Thraecius bowed his head as Ester clung to him. The others whispered in frightened voices now.

"Is that true?" Lamarr asked, kneeling beside her. "What Avana says? Is it too late? Will Death come for all of us now?"

Heather reached out and touched Lamarr's lanky shoulder. "I don't know if she's right about Death, but there's a chance to save Ross. We've got heartlilies from the dark stream near the clearing."

Heather motioned toward Zakhart.

The pale angel reached into the silk pouch at his side and plucked out a wrapped bundle. He carefully unfolded the grey silk, revealing two, fluted blossoms that glowed soft orange, pulsing with eerie light.

"It's my only chance to bring him back," Heather replied, taking the blooms from Zakhart's hand.

"Why, oh, why, little Heather?" Avana demanded, her smoky form trailing up to the ceiling. "Why would you bring that little coward back from the poppy fields?"

She materialized in solid form beside Heather, her acidic words and that condescending stare too much.

"Coward?" Heather shouted, seething with rage.

She swung her fist at Avana, knocking the smoke woman across the room. She rolled head over feet until she turned to smoke. Her smoky form scattered into ringlets and dispersed throughout the room.

Heather glared at Avana as the woman struggled to pull her wispy form back together. It took a moment or two before she took solid form again. She looked humbled and a little shaken, but she was quiet now.

"Ross fought three soulstalkers to reach the poppy fields," Heather said. "A place none of the rest of us dared to go. He didn't go there to give up or quit. He was trying to rescue his girlfriend. And it was one of the bravest things I've ever seen."

"Not to mention standing up to Mulciber and those demons back in the Veils," said Thraecius, eyes narrowing. "And he stood up to me. You're crazy, Avana. You know nothing about human bravery."

"My son's right," said Matthew, his brow furrowing as he watched Avana skirt around Heather, keeping her distance. "It was a very brave thing to do."

Heather cast one last scowl at Avana and knelt beside the couch. She brushed back an ashen lock of Ross' sandy hair and laid her hand against his cold brow. Like river rock.

"What do we do?" she asked, glancing at Zakhart. His worried expression frightened her even more.

He pointed at Ross. "Place one of the blooms on his forehead."

Heather took a blossom and laid it across Ross' forehead.

"Put the next one over his heart. Where it should be."

She nodded, laying the second blossom on the left side of his chest.

"What next?"

Razasha touched Heather's shoulder and Heather studied the pale angel with her wheaten hair like starshine, eyes like an autumn sunset.

"You fought so bravely for him, Heather. You must hold deep affection for this man."

She'd fallen in love with this kind-hearted boy-next-door who'd protected her, supported her, and fought for her from the first moment she'd woken up in the Between. Heather blushed, nodding.

She loved him. She couldn't deny it.

"The heartlilies' closed buds will open and bloom as they absorb the poppy dust," Razasha explained. "At full bloom, they will begin to die and turn grey as the dust overwhelms them. Before they lose that last glimmer of light—of life—you must crush the blossoms on head and heart. At the same time."

"It only works if the heartlilies are crushed by someone with a bond to him," Zakhart added.

Zakhart studied her face, his pumpkin-orange eyes lightening. "It's got to be you then," he said, smiling. "I've seen that love in your eyes—in your heart—for a long time, but I don't think you saw it until just now."

She nodded. "I love him," she whispered so only Zakhart heard her. "I know that now."

"Hurry then," he said, motioning toward Ross.

With her left hand, Heather reached toward Ross' brow. With her right hand, she reached toward his heart, her hands hovering over the blossoms. The heartlilies' petals opened wide, their orange glow bright as the blooms pulsed with light. She watched as the blooms absorbed the poppy's poison from Ross' body.

The glow became uneven in the blooms, each one turning bright a moment then dimming and then flushing with bright orange light again. Already, the edges of the petals were curling up, turning dark like they'd been burned as the heartlilies' vibrant color began to wash away.

As the moments ticked past, the silky petals grew brittle, looking dry, washed out, the bright glow fading quickly now.

"Crush them before the last glimmer of light dies, Heather," said Zakhart. "Crush the shadows before the last light fades."

Heather watched the glow fade, the heartlilies turning grey, wilting against the poppy dust's onslaught. The light was dying fast.

Heather held her breath and counted to three. With a quick exhale, she smashed both blooms at the same time.

Clouds of orange dust exploded from the heartlilies, blanketing Ross—and Heather—in sparkly orange powder. It cast a glittery haze throughout the room.

The glimmering dust clung to Razasha's wings and coated Zakhart's robes. The pale angels brushed it away, but Heather didn't move. She kept her hands pressed against Ross' forehead and chest, watching his face for a sign of movement, listening for a breath of life, hoping for a shiver of movement.

"Ross? Can you hear me? You're safe now. You're away from the poppy fields. The endless sleep is gone. Please, Ross—come back to me. I need you."

Her chest ached as she whispered his name again.

He had to come back. He had to. She couldn't do this without him.

"Ross...open your eyes. Come back now—please."

No flutter of eyelids, no rise of breath. He was as stone cold as the statues left among the poppies. Like his Jessie.

Heather bowed her head, unable to halt her tears. She was too late. Just too late.

"Don't give up yet, Heather," Razasha said to her in dulcet tones. "Keep trying."

"Ross, I need you to help me find the Spiral. Help me find it, Ross. Please! I can't do this without you."

Her arms ached and her eyes burned, but she didn't dare move, afraid it would break whatever tiny connection that remained.

"Ross, please!"

A shudder vibrated through his chest.

"Ross? Return to me. Please!" She laid her hand on his and squeezed, his papery flesh feeling almost spongy now. Was she imagining that?

Eyelids twitched. A flutter of breath.

"Ross!"

He gasped. His eyes snapped open, wide and full of fear as he jolted up from the couch.

Heather flung her arms around him as the blossoms crumbled to dust and fell to the floor. He clung to her, his chest heaving as he glanced around the room with a wild-eyed stare. Already, his brittle, ashen skin was brightening as the substance returned to him. Like he'd been dehydrated and soaked in water.

"Where—where am I?" he asked in a scratchy voice, staring at Thraecius who grinned at him.

"Back at the great tree," said Heather. "We carried you out of the poppy fields."

Ross held onto her shoulders as he studied her face, a look of awe in his hazel-gold eyes.

"You carried me out?"

Tears stung her eyes as she nodded. "Zakhart told me about the heartlily blossoms that could counteract the poppies." She smiled. "Looks like it worked."

"Why?" he cried, shaking his head. "Why would you go in there after me?"

Heather bit her lip, her stomach twisting into a knot. "Because I love you."

"Oh, God, Heather," he said, his voice cracking.

He wrapped his arms around her, holding her tight against his chest. He was shaking.

She laid her head against his shoulder, holding him closer, the tension uncoiling from her limbs like untangling headphone cables. His arms felt so familiar, like she'd always belonged there. Warmth filled her chest, the rush of feeling swirling around her like a warm ocean swell.

She loved him. It was the first real emotion she'd felt since her mom died.

"I love you, too," he whispered against her ear. "Don't know what I'd do without you."

Zakhart poked her shoulder. She looked up at him, her head still on Ross' shoulder.

"What's the matter?" she asked.

"Death," he said. "Big scary scythe. Hunting you and all that."

Ross tensed against her, arms tightening, holding her closer.

"She's coming for you, Heather," said Zakhart as the others stepped back from her. "And Ross, now that he's escaped the poppy fields. You've both got to leave here. Set out for the Spiral. Now. She'll quickly see through the great tree's protection, through the spirit masks."

Ross stared at her with horror in his eyes. "Death?" He shook his head. "Why now? Why?" He squeezed his eyes closed, pulling away now. He scrambled to his feet, a little unsteady. "This is all my fault."

"Ross, no," Heather replied. She got to her feet and grabbed his arm, tilting his face toward her. "Listen. It's not your fault. We've got to find the Spiral this time." She glanced at Thraecius and the others gathered in the room. "We have to."

"She's right," said Thraecius, fixing Ross with his gaze. "Because of you and Heather, I'm free of the demons and I have a chance to go on. See Juliana again. So do my parents and Shuying—and so many others. We're all coming with you. Together, we'll make it."

A smile touched Ross' face. He nodded.

"Thraecius is right," said Ross. "We've done our best to reconnect people, bring them back to life, give them hope. We did what Zakhart told us to do. Now, it's time to leave."

Heather understood what reconnecting meant now. What Zakhart had asked of her. Reconnecting meant wanting to live again. And she did. Beside Ross.

"When do we leave?" Matthew asked, grinning as he stepped forward to stand beside his son.

"Now," said Ross, getting to his feet. "The farther ahead of Death we get, the safer it'll be for everyone. Including the great tree."

"You know the path," said Zakhart. "I've done all I can to prepare you." He took hold of Heather's hands and kissed them. "I want to see you and Ross and the others beyond this place, little human. I fully expect to see you again on other planes. Understand?"

She nodded then leaned toward his face, kissing his cheek. The pale angel blushed.

"Thank you for everything, Zakhart," she said and glanced over at Razasha. "You, too, Razasha. Thank you."

"Take care and be swift," Razasha said and slipped outside.

Zakhart waved at Heather, his pumpkin-orange eyes glistening as he followed Razasha outside.

Her heart ached when the door closed. Something told her that she wouldn't see Zakhart again for a very long time. At least she hoped she wouldn't see him again here. It made her sad, but relieved at the same time.

Ross moved toward the fireplace. "Everyone brave enough to look for the Spiral and leave this place, gather around," he said.

Heather stood beside him, her heart breaking when only Shuying and the three Romans stepped forward.

"Lamarr?" she called. "Javier? Barb? Don't you want to leave this place?"

Lamarr looked terrified. He drifted toward the stairs, shaking his head. "Sorry, Heather—I'm...not ready yet."

"Barb!" she called.

"Not me. Sorry. Some day. Just...not today."

"Javier?" she said, but he shook his head and shrank backward toward the stairs. Away from the fireplace.

Ross slid his arm around Heather's waist, pulling her close.

"All right, guess we're it," he said. "Let's get going and head for the Spiral."

"How will we find it?" Shuying asked.

"We don't even know the path," said Thraecius as Ester and Matthew edged closer to their son.

"But we *do* know the path," said Ross. "I feel its hum out there."

"So do I," said Heather. "Do you feel it?"

Thraecius nodded, his parents whispering a quick yes. Shuying nodded, too.

"Heather and I will lead us to it. Are you ready?"

"Yes," Shuying said, starting toward the door.

Ester and Matthew gave him a sharp tilt of their heads.

Thraecius motioned Ross forward. "Lead the way, Ross," he said. "I'd like nothing better than to leave this place behind forever."

Glancing at Heather, Ross reached down and took her hand. "You still with me?" he asked.

She wrapped her fingers in his and squeezed. "All the way," she answered. "I followed you to the poppy fields and the Demon Veils. I'll follow you anywhere."

"It's my turn to follow you now," he said with a smile.

Ross opened the door. Heather and the others followed him out of the great tree and into the growing darkness.

In the distance, shrieks and calls echoed against the cool breeze that shivered through the tall grasses. The Between creatures were suddenly restless in the endless dusk. Heather felt a chill rake her spine. She understood why.

Death prowled close.

She could be anywhere, so they had to leave. Now. Get clear of this place before the sky lightened. Before Death arrived.

They had to go now.

A flock of pale angels took flight, circling the clearing several times before they fluttered across the sea of grass.

Heather smiled. They were diverting the soulstalkers' attention, leading them deep into the grasslands. Away from the great tree.

And Death.

Zakhart was giving them the best chance he could. A head start. It was all he could do and she was so grateful.

"What's all that noise?" Thraecius demanded.

"Soulstalkers," said Heather, the sounds unnerving her. "Hunting us."

"Forget them," said Ross. "Concentrate on the Spiral. Looks like the pale angels are distracting them for us. Stay close and head into the woods. And stay away from the meadows right now."

Nodding, Thraecius grabbed Shuying's hand and pulled her toward the clearing behind Ester and Matthew.

Heather felt Ross' uneasiness as he pulled her into a steady jog toward the clearing, where all the pathways twisted into the forest.

"Death...she's out there," Heather whispered to Ross as they rushed toward the clearing.

"I know," he said, his voice tight. "I feel her, too. There isn't much time. We have to move fast."

Heather knew they couldn't turn back. If they did, they risked a death so final that it terrified her now. Now, that she wanted to go on, to exist beyond her pain, beyond this place. With Ross beside her.

Did they have one last chance to get past their suicides? One last chance to get things right?

twelve

. . .

A SCRATCHY WOMAN'S caustic voice echoed above the treetops in a horrible singsong that made Heather's skin crawl.

"Hea-ther? Roh-oss? Heather and Ross...come out, come out. Your future is at my blade."

Ross lurched forward, yanking Heather closer as they broke into a run.

"Hurry!" he shouted.

Heather picked up speed, keeping pace with Ross as the clearing fanned out through the forest ahead.

Shuying and the three Romans pressed close, fear sharp on their faces. The air smelled sweet, cloying with gardenias, as Ross rushed ahead, Heather beside him. He ran toward the middle path, one of three paths that they hadn't yet followed.

Sharp laughter crackled through the leaves as a breeze swirled past.

"Heather! Ross! There's nowhere to hide! Give up and I'll make your ends quick."

"Are you sure that's the right path?" Ester asked, breathless as she glanced over her shoulder, both hands gripping Matthew's sleeve.

"One leads straight to Death's lair," Thraecius added, his eyes shining with fear. "You know that, don't you?"

"Of course, I know that," Ross answered. "Keep moving!"

Ross didn't miss a step, feet pounding down the centermost trail, kicking up puffs of ashen soil in dusk's feeble light. His face was a mask of concentration and fear, but suddenly, a smile rolled across his face.

Heather nudged him. "You feel the Spiral, don't you?" she said as his pace slowed a little.

He grinned, nodding at her. "I do."

When the others hesitated at the clearing, Ross stopped, turning back toward them.

"It's this way!" he called to them.

"Are you sure?" Thraecius asked, panic at the edge of his voice.

"I've never been more certain of anything in my life," Ross replied and motioned them onward. "It's this way."

Thraecius made the first move down the path, Ester and Shuying following, Matthew only a step behind.

Ross squeezed Heather's hand, tugging her into a slow jog.

"All this time, I was looking for it with my eyes," said Ross, "listening for it with my ears, always expecting something tangible."

He cast a quick look of relief at her as the path wound toward a paler grey sky, a stream running parallel to the path as it left the woods behind. In the distance, white-capped mountains poked through the grey haze. The scent of dirty rain and heavy gardenias fell away, the air smelling clean like fresh-washed linen.

"So did I," said Heather.

"It's deeper than that, Heather," he said, his face bright and so attractive. "Close your eyes and you'll feel it in the distance. A vibration way down deep. You'll feel its spin."

"But I'll fall," said Heather, watching the flat ground stretch toward the mountains. She could see for miles now.

Would it be enough to see Death before she overtook them? Could Death feel the Spiral, too?

His grip on her hand tightened again. "No, it's okay. You won't fall. But if you don't feel it, you won't find it."

Nodding, Heather watched the ashen soil grow harder, warmer at her feet as she kept up a steady pace. When she was satisfied that she wouldn't trip on a rock, she closed her eyes, trusting Ross' navigation.

At first, she only felt her own hurried breath aching through her chest and the vibration of footfalls pounding the ground. From Thraecius and the others, from Ross beside her—and the tremor of a vibration that rippled through her feet.

Was that it? Was that what Ross meant?

She fought the urge to open her eyes, concentrating on her own breathing until the vibrations magnified, fluttering through her entire body. Its cadence was steady, comforting, like the rise and fall of breath, the beating of many hearts—the moan of something ancient and powerful. It electrified the air around her, turning her arms to gooseflesh.

Ahead, in the palest grey sky, near the mountains, lay the Spiral. She felt its energy, its power, and the call of her last chance to live life again.

A chance for all of them.

She opened her eyes, grinning at Ross. "I feel it ahead," she said.

He smiled. "I'm not surprised."

Heather glanced behind her. Thraecius was pulling Shuying along. Shuying looked exhausted. Ester and Matthew had fallen back a few paces. They were letting illusions slow them down now. They didn't have physical bodies. Exhaustion was an illusion.

"Ross, we've got to slow down," she said, tugging on his sleeve. "We're losing the others."

Ross slowed to a walk until Thraecius and Shuying were behind him again. They waited a few moments for Ester and Matthew to catch up. Heather glanced at the stream and the path that wound around its bank. In the distance, a thick cloud of smoke roiled out of the forest, surging along the trail.

Heather gasped. "It's her," she cried, pointing at the smoke.

"Go! Now!" Ross shouted and pulled Heather into a run.

Ester collapsed against Matthew. "You go on," she said, out of breath, motioning them on. She closed her eyes. "It's too far."

Heather let go of Ross' hand, rushing back. She shook Ester.

"It's forever!" she shouted. "You know that, don't you? It's the death of your soul. You'll never see Juliana again."

Ester's eyes welled with tears as she cast an uncertain glance at Matthew. "But I'm so tired," she said with a sob.

"Shake it off," Heather urged. "It's an illusion to slow you down."

Thraecius' jaw clenched as he grabbed hold of Ester's arm and pulled her up from the ground. He yanked her onto the trail beside him.

"I won't let you quit now, Mother," he snapped.

Matthew didn't say a word as Shuying wrapped her arm in his and tugged him into a run alongside her. Heather bolted down the path, doing her best to push the others along. The distance between them and the mountains seemed so far. But they had to stay ahead of Death and her scythe.

Just long enough to reach the Spiral. They were so close!

The run across the barren land seemed endless and Heather's legs felt like concrete with every step, her momentum slowing. She ignored the persistent ache in her side as she pressed against Ester's back, pushing her along. The old woman begged them to let her rest, but Heather shut out her pleas. She'd rest forever if Death caught up to them.

Heather didn't understand why her muscles hurt, why her lungs ached from the exertion. She'd left those things behind when she'd taken her own life. She wasn't projecting that illusion. She knew better.

She glanced over her shoulder at the distant black cloud on the plains. Surging toward them.

They were all past these physical weaknesses, but Death had to be casting this illusion. Making them think they were frail and human again. To slow them down.

Heather shut out the pain, trying to convince her mind that these physical things weren't happening.

"Ester, the pain and exhaustion aren't real," said Heather. "They're Death's illusions. She wants us to give up. Don't you dare give in now. We're so close."

The realization seemed to reach through the older woman's exhaustion. Ester struggled a moment or two then straightened her body, fighting back.

Shuying picked up her pace, Matthew rushing ahead. Even Thraecius straightened his tall frame, the intensity in his eyes softening. Heather ran behind Ester, staying with her as the older woman's strides lengthened, a mask of concentration hardening her features.

They ran farther across the plains, the mountains feeling only a little closer now.

Heather shoved away the tendrils of pain that snaked into her calves and concentrated on the vibrations of the Spiral ahead.

"The Spiral," said Ester with a gasp. "I feel it. I really feel it!"

"We're so close," said Ross, his voice carrying. "It can't be much farther."

Heather glanced back again. The black cloud had gotten closer.

"Faster, Ross!" Heather shouted through gritted teeth.

With a sigh, Ross pushed harder, his legs pumping faster. The others matched his strides.

The stream that had followed them the entire way meandered off to the right until they finally left it behind. Its gentle burble dissipated, replaced by strong winds whipping across the craggy landscape. Dust whirled across the desolate plains in little funnels that spun into the air and disappeared into the dust.

Heather sputtered, inhaling a breath of gritty air. When she emerged from the dust, the mountains seemed much closer.

They were almost to the Spiral!

Beyond the dirt and dust, velvety green grass blanketed the foot of the mountains, looking vibrant and bright, like a summer green lawn after a rain. The air smelled clean and cool, the steady spin of the Spiral a soft whisper around them, audible now.

They ran harder, murmurs of excitement spilling out.

"I hear it, do you?" Shuying called out, holding onto Matthew's arm.

Matthew nodded and glanced back at his wife. When she met his gaze, he motioned her toward him. She ran harder, catching up to him and taking hold of his other arm.

In what seemed like forever, Heather felt the soft thump of her feet against the thick grass as the mountains rose high in front of them.

A snowy path wound between the mountains and Heather knew it led to the Spiral. It was just beyond these stony spires and snow-capped peaks.

"This way," Ross motioned, rushing onto the path.

"Ross, wait!" Heather called, falling behind.

Thraecius and the others followed as the path made a sharp incline and wound through thick evergreens. Heather lost sight of Ross twice, but she pushed harder until she caught up to him. The path made a sudden sharp twist and fanned out into a large clearing. Ross halted in mid-stride.

Ahead, the steady hum of white light churned in a clockwise motion into a towering bright pillar that rose between the trees.

"The Spiral," Ross said with a gasp as Heather stopped beside him.

Heather could only stare at it. The river of life.

Where human beings started and ended lives, moving past the Between with its smoke people and shadow creatures. The current was swift, the energy unlike anything she'd ever felt before. She wanted to touch it, to melt into it, and follow it away from this place forever.

"What do we do?" Shuying asked, uncertainty bright in her dark eyes.

"Return to it," was all that Ross could say and Heather knew that was the right answer somehow.

"Heather . . . Ross . . . come out, come out wherever you are?"

Ross grabbed Thraecius, pushing him forward. "Hurry, get everyone into the Spiral!"

With a grave expression, Thraecius nodded and grabbed hold of his mother.

"We've got to go. Now!"

Ester nodded, hurrying with him toward the Spiral's thrumming light. Shuying and Matthew were right behind them. Thraecius hesitated a moment, reaching out a shaking hand to the fluid energy spinning in front of him.

"Now!" Heather shouted.

Thraecius waved at them then stepped into the current. His form vaporized, rushing into the Spiral, mixing with the pale white light.

Ester gripped Matthew's hand. Closing their eyes, they stepped into the Spiral together. Their forms intertwined into deep gold light and vanished.

"Thank you," Shuying called to Heather and Ross and walked into the Spiral.

"Come on!"

Heather grabbed Ross' hand in hers and they ran toward the Spiral.

A blade flashed and slammed into the ground! Blocking their way.

Death stood on the path, a gaunt scarecrow-like woman in soot grey rags and wild, dreadlocked white hair. She looked almost skeletal, a thin covering of ashen skin clinging to her tall frame. She held a massive scythe over her head, gold blade glinting with the Spiral's light.

"What? Were you expecting me to carry a tuba?" Her laugh was caustic.

Blinded, Heather stumbled as Ross backed away, his hand locked around her wrist.

"Come to me, now, my children," she said, her voice a raspy singsong, the twinkle in her dark eyes deadly, bone-white lips stretched across pointy teeth.

Ross turned and ran, pulling Heather along with him.

The scythe crashed down, nearly severing Ross' head from his shoulders.

He stumbled, Heather falling into the dirt beside him.

Death sprang forward. "Say nevermore, my children," she said with a grin, eyes hollowed, cheekbones protruding from her long, thin face. "Always wanted to say that. You escaped me once, but not a second time. This time, you're mine."

Death raised the scythe above them in her bony fingers.

Heather rose on her knees as the scythe's shadow passed across their faces.

Death swung the scythe over her shoulders in a wide arc.

Ross closed his eyes, bracing for the impact. "Sorry, Heather. You meant more to me than my own life."

Heather felt his words ache through her chest. "I love you forever, Ross Shepherd."

No, she wouldn't let this happen. They were too close. Too close to leaving this place forever.

Heather lurched forward and slammed into Death, knocking the scythe from her hands. She reached down to snatch the scythe from the dirt.

"Don't touch it!" Ross shouted, grabbing her arm, pulling her backward. "It can still destroy you!"

Ross pulled Heather into a heated run around the fallen scythe as Death struggled to her feet.

"Damned humans! Come back here!" Death's gravelly voice sang out to them, calling to them as she lunged for the scythe.

Heather and Ross rushed headlong toward the Spiral, the cold chill of Death a sharp breath against her neck. So close behind them.

She glanced down at her sleeve as they leaped toward the Spiral. Poppy petals. Tucked into the folds of her sleeve.

In an icy instant, Heather felt the Spiral's energy envelope her as Ross leaped into the Spiral.

She felt him beside her, his energy against her own. She felt the momentary beating of his heart against hers, each fighting to gain rhythm in this grey wasteland.

But Death was still a sharp presence nearby. She felt the struggle, the clash of light and dark. A scream.

"Ross!"

Heather dissolved into the Spiral, rushing through the current. She felt the sudden calm, the presence of others as she surged ahead through the river of energy.

But not Ross.

She struggled in the maelstrom, trying to find Ross' presence beside her, feel the press of his soul against hers. She called out to him, her form surging through the coursing energy. But she couldn't feel his lifeforce nearby, couldn't sense his consciousness.

Weariness pressed against her soul, defying any physical form. She wanted to not think and not feel for a while, to not reflect on two worlds she'd left behind now. Places she'd barely begun to understand. Things she'd felt but couldn't pursue. The heavy loss. She felt it instantly.

She and Ross had been separated.

Was he lost to her now? The man she loved with all her heart?

In that last instant, when Ross thought they'd lost everything, his words had made all of it worthwhile.

You meant more to me than my own life.

She'd felt that same rush of emotion. She'd wanted to say those same words back to him. But she didn't get that chance. She told him that she loved him, but there had been so much she'd wanted to say to him. Maybe if she'd felt even half that much for another person in her physical life, she wouldn't have ended hers after her mom died?

If she could have just made that connection to another person... stayed with Ross somehow...if...

Even now, he'd made a difference to her heart. His words still mattered to her. And she still felt the distant connection. It hadn't broken. Even though her heart was breaking—again—whatever happened now, she knew she'd fight to hold onto him. Life's heartbreaks never seemed to end. But she knew that she'd meant something to one soul besides her mother.

Heather sank deeper into the warm currents of the Spiral, floating along as a strange sort of slumber overcame her. One last time, she cast Ross' name out as a ripple in the flow that rolled through the Spiral.

"I love you forever, Ross Shepherd," she whispered. "With everything I have."

With a final, deep breath, Heather let go.

thirteen

· · ·

SATURDAY, *June 8, 2052*
Bainbridge Island High School Graduation

HANNAH GIRARD-DAVIES, DRESSED IN A ROYAL BLUE graduation gown, gold tassel turned across her mortar board, waited for her parents and grandfather outside the Bainbridge High School auditorium. With a whisper of bangs on her forehead, her long, brown hair was pulled back in a single barrette. Green to match her eyes. She balanced the strap of her purple backpack on her left shoulder as she hugged her friends and said her goodbyes.

The air was sweet with fresh mown grass and tanged with a faint hint of salt water from the Puget Sound. She felt at peace, yet something made her restless, something down deep that she couldn't identify. A restlessness she'd felt her entire short life. It was summer and she was free until she started classes at the University of Washington in the fall. Studying Environmental Restoration Science, but she hadn't made any firm decisions. There was plenty of time to decide.

She had her whole life ahead of her. Yet...something was missing. Something so important, so critical, but just out of her reach. She'd felt this feeling her entire life, but right now, it was so strong. Aching. Urgent. Like she'd left a candle burning near the bedroom drapes. Left the stove on or something.

What was the matter with her?

Shouting out a three-count, the Class of 2052, three hundred and twenty-three seniors tossed their mortar boards into the crisp summer-blue sky and cheered, the ceremony and the hat toss streamed online. As each family stepped out of the gymnasium, their mobile devices buzzed as the school pushed senior pictures, graduation images, and videos of the event to their screens. It sounded like a swarm of bees around her, Hannah thought with a chuckle.

She waited on the sidewalk until her parents and grandpa filed out of the gym. Mom saw her there and rushed to her, throwing her arms around her. Hannah hugged her back, the moment suddenly fragile.

"You did it, kiddo! We're so proud of you!" said her mom, letting her go.

Mom had that familiar, warm vanilla and coffee smell, from the coffeehouse she ran for Grandpa Jimmy. The Orca Café. She'd smelled that scent her entire life. And cherished it. Mom looked slim and young in her purple sweater, grey pants, and flats.

"Thanks, Mom," Hannah replied as her dad held her in a long embrace.

Dad stood beside Mom, a hand on her back. He wore a tan suit jacket, white dress shirt, brown pants, and loafers. His thick brown hair feathered in the wind, green eyes smiling as he wrapped his arms around Hannah and twirled her around.

Hannah wrinkled her nose at the fake ocean smell from his latest aftershave, this one just as stinky as the last one. But Mom liked it, so Hannah kept her mouth (and nose) shut about it. His stubbled jaw rasped against her chin as he kissed her cheek. At five-foot-seven,

Hannah was almost as tall as his five-foot-nine height. He got grumpy when Mom wore high heels that made her taller than him.

"Congratulations, baby girl," said Dad, his voice cracking. "I'm so proud of you I could bust."

"Thanks, Dad," she replied as he let go.

"Are you feeling all right, Hannah?" her mom asked, studying her eyes. "You're not having chest pain, are you?"

"You've got your medication, right?" her dad added, looking concerned. "You know the doctor said to keep it close."

"No, I'm not having chest pain, Mom," Hannah said, patting her jeans pocket through her graduation gown. "And yes, Dad, I have my medication."

Grandpa Jimmy slid his arm around her shoulders and hugged her. He wore jeans, tan Birkenstocks with blue socks, and a black sweatshirt emblazoned with the bright white Orca Café logo: an orca leaping out of a coffee mug. Grandpa had a gentle way about him with his soft voice, kind smile, and wide, square hands. He'd always been there for her, always listened. His hair had gotten thinner, his face a little rounder and lined. It was the first time she'd noticed the years, the wear of life on her family. It made her sad.

"They just worry about you, kiddo. Most kids haven't had two open heart surgeries by eighteen, so they're a little protective. I know that's never held you back though. And I also know that you're going places, kiddo!"

Grandpa Jimmy handed her a lavender envelope.

Hannah grinned and tore open the envelope. A card with sparkly, purple dragonflies glistened as she read the sweet verse about a grandfather's pride in his granddaughter, his wish for her dreams to come true, and his assurance that his love never ended. She had a few dreams: learn to play guitar, get her degree, and find the love of her life. Only one required that burning flame of obsession. Maybe that was the problem? Suddenly, all those dreams seemed so unimportant, like she needed to put them all in a box and close the lid for a while.

When she opened the card, she found a stack of one-hundred-dollar bills that covered the Happy Graduation verse.

Hannah gasped, nearly dropping the card. "A thousand dollars? Grandpa Jimmy!"

"For one of them immersion slates or something," he said, his smile widening. He nudged Hannah's mom. "Right, Emily? To help with your classes. Back in my day, slate was something you put on your floors, not something that did holographic modeling and dimensional rendering. Bet first person shooter games will be awesome on it!"

"Thanks, Grandpa."

She hugged him hard. He'd always been there for her. Even when Mom and Dad separated, he'd done his best to get them back together. For now, her folks were getting along. They seemed happy to see each other for the first time in a year. She didn't know how long it would last, but for now, there was a little peace in the family.

And a strange growing distance. Distance she didn't understand.

"Hannah, you'd better put that away before you lose it," said her mom.

The name Hannah had never felt quite right to her.

She let go of Grandpa Jimmy and unzipped her backpack, stowing her card and money in a zippered pocket beside Charles the white, sparkly bear (sort of grey now), her favorite stuffed animal. Grandpa Jimmy gave him to Mom when she was little. When her parents were fighting and Dad moved out for a while, Mom had given her Charles the bear. He'd been with her for a long time now and she cherished him.

Her mom peeked inside Hannah's backpack. "You brought Charles?" she asked, grinning

Hannah nodded, taking out the little white bear. She cuddled him against her face which brought a smile from Grandpa Jimmy.

"You still have that little bear I gave you, Emily?" he asked. "You were just a kid!"

"Sure do. I loved that bear, Dad," said Hannah's mom. "He seemed so lost and sad when you gave him to me. When Hannah started feeling—a little lost—I gave the bear to her."

Grandpa Jimmy had a faraway look on his face, his dark blue eyes a little misty. "One of my favorite customers gave me that bear, Emily." He sighed, bowing his head. "To give to you. She was such a sweet kid, so lost—troubled."

Hannah's eyes teared up. She didn't even know why. And she didn't understand that strong sense of loss that hollowed her heart any more than she understood the connection that burned between her and this story. She wanted to drop to her knees and cry her eyes out every time Grandpa Jimmy told that story, but something kept it wrapped tight inside her heart.

She hugged the little bear closer, not sure where this sudden sharp pain in her chest had come from. Her hand jerked toward her pocket, fumbling for the little bottle of nitroglycerin, but after a moment, she stopped, pulling her hand back. This pain wasn't like the angina she'd had all her life. This was a dull, hollow pain like hunger pangs from an empty stomach.

Her mom nodded. "I remember how sad you were later, Dad, after you'd given me the bear. A few weeks after that, you told me how special Charles was, how he'd meant so much to a young woman who'd died."

A lump rose in Hannah's throat.

"What? The woman who had this bear died?" She'd never heard this part of the story.

The pain in her chest intensified, like a tennis ball bouncing frantically through a closed space. Her heartbeat fluttered and she couldn't breathe for a moment, a tear slipping down her face.

Grandpa Jimmy nodded. "Yeah, I never told you that part, did I, kiddo?"

Hannah shook her head.

"Her name was Heather Billot. So young and alone."

Heather? She closed her eyes, that name so familiar, so raw against her ears.

He smiled, staring past her. "Some nights when it was slow, she and I'd talk. She always had something supportive to say, telling me to hang in there with the bills, telling me how great the café was. She was so passionate about some things. Books she'd read, movies that frightened her, news headlines that bothered her. I never dreamed that line of despair was so wide. Or that she'd cross it."

"What happened?" Hannah asked.

He bit his lip, letting out a long sigh. "Killed herself a few hours after giving me that bear. I'll never stop wondering if I could have helped her." He stared into the distance for several moments. "They found her on a Bainbridge Island beach, just south of the ferry terminal. All alone. No one there to—" His voice broke. "To even hold her hand. Never got over that—that...note."

Hannah took hold of Grandpa Jimmy's hand and squeezed it.

"What note, Grandpa?" she asked.

He pulled in a breath, pausing until he could talk again. "She left a-a suicide note. An online post. Posted it in the café with me standin' right there ringing up her coffee. Wish I'd known what she was planning. Wish I'd said something, done something."

She sucked in a breath as the air rushed out of her lungs. Like she knew about those events, could almost see them unfold in the back of her mind, feel them against her fingertips. Bitter taste of raspberries mixing with sand and sea water. Heat and thirst roiling through her body. Exhaustion mingling with sleep, the world darkening.

How could she know about any of this?

"You did help her, Grandpa, more than you know," said Hannah, not sure why she'd said that, but it brought a smile and a hug from Grandpa Jimmy.

Someone called her name and she turned around. Rebecca Ross from track. Tall and thin, sandy hair tied away from her face, gold-hazel eyes bright as she reached out and hugged Hannah.

"Hannah! Sign my yearbook?"

"Aren't you coming to the party?" Hannah asked.

Rebecca shook her head, eyes downcast. "No, I'm throwing a party for some close friends tomorrow. I'd love it if you'd come, too. Four o'clock at Finney's Restaurant."

Hannah took the tablet and signed the inside cover page with a stylus. "I'll try to be there."

"Thanks," said Rebecca, wiping away tears.

"What's wrong?" Hannah asked.

"Sorry," she said, forcing a smile. "This day is kind of bittersweet for me."

"How come?" Hannah asked, handing the tablet back.

"My twin should have been here today, graduating with me. Rick. Remember him?"

Hannah shook her head, frowning.

"Sorry," Rebecca replied, rubbing her eyes. "Everybody just called him Ross."

Hearing that name was a gut punch. Hannah clutched her stomach, wilting as her knees turned weak. Her heart shuddered then raced and for a moment, she couldn't breathe.

Ross! That name was so familiar. So dear to her. The sound of it made her heart ache.

"Ross?" she replied, squinting.

Rebecca nodded. "He died in a car accident last year. We'd just moved here from Flora, Indiana. Someplace I'm sure you've never heard of before. He survived a terrible crash four years ago in Indiana only to die in one here. It's so unfair. God, I miss him, Hannah."

Flora? Indiana? Where had she heard of that town before?

"So do I," she said, not sure why she'd said that.

Somehow, his absence made her heart hurt worse than it ever had before. It made everything feel so fuzzy and out of place.

And made everything about her life uncomfortable.

For an instant, a white spiral of light gleamed in Rebecca's eyes.

The world contracted, as if a lifetime had just passed. Hannah stumbled backward.

"I've got to go now."

"Maybe we'll have some classes together in the fall at Udub," Rebecca called. "Hope to see you at the party tomorrow."

Hannah waved and hurried back to her grandpa, pretending everything was okay, that she was fine. She pulled Charles the bear out of her backpack and hugged him against her face. But she wasn't fine. Everything was swirling out of control. And she couldn't stop it.

What was happening?

Just minutes ago, everything was fine. Normal. Comfortable. Now, she could barely breathe and someone named Ross was heavy on her mind. On her heart.

She couldn't remember why though. And she needed to. Desperately.

Hannah glanced at the sky as a flock of birds took flight. Maybe it was the sun peeking through the clouds or the reflection of glass against water, but as the birds winged past, Hannah saw an almost human form among them, with pale sparrow-tan wings.

And pumpkin-orange eyes.

She squinted, but the form disappeared into the clouds.

Had she really just seen a-a man with wings?

"I'm going to the school's graduation party," Hannah told her folks, patting her backpack. "Gonna get my yearbook signed and hang out. I'll be home later, all right?"

"Have fun, Hannah," her mom called. "Enjoy this moment. It's one of those important times in your life, so savor it."

"See you Saturday at the café, Hannah," Grandpa Jimmy replied, waving goodbye as he and the rest of her family headed toward the school parking lot.

Tomorrow she was scheduled to work at the coffeehouse with her grandpa. A job she loved. Free mochas helped, too.

Never had a Saturday felt so far away.

She gripped Charles the bear tighter as a cold wave brushed across her heart, a feeling of dread so profound that she ran across the parking lot to her family. She hugged Grandpa Jimmy first, then her mom, and finally her dad.

"Hannah?" Mom asked, studying her face. "What's wrong?"

Hannah pasted a smile on her face. "Nothing," she replied. She glanced from Grandpa Jimmy to her dad and back to her mom who looked concerned. "But if there were...I just wanted to tell you how much I love you. All of you."

One more time, she hugged her mom and then rushed toward the graduation party in the gym, blue gown fluttering against the summer-blue sky.

She stopped at the gym door and turned to watch her family drive away. They almost seemed to move in slow motion, her heart aching with every turn until the red sedan pulled onto the highway and disappeared in traffic.

"Don't be afraid," a voice whispered in her ear.

She turned as an arm wrapped around her waist, hand covering her mouth as someone pulled her behind the shadowed line of trees beside the school.

Large, pumpkin-orange eyes stared at her, soft creamy tan wings unfurling to their full length. The man smiled at her, ivory silk robes flowing around him. His face was so familiar.

An angel?

He pulled his hand away from her mouth and she relaxed a moment. With a gentle turn of his wrist, he pressed his hand against her forehead. Releasing a hailstorm of memories tumbling through her head. Including names. So many names!

Zakhart! The pale angel.

"Zakhart?" she asked. "Is it really you?"

He nodded and she threw her arms around him, clinging to him. The pale angel enfolded her in his arms, his wings bending into protective curves around her body.

"I couldn't remember you," she sobbed, laying her face against his silky ivory robes.

Zakhart held her tightly. "I know," he said in soothing tones, stroking her hair. "You weren't supposed to remember. Not yet. Not here. But something's gone wrong. Heather."

Her head snapped up. *Heather.* The world contracted again. *She was Heather. Heather Billot.*

Everything surged back in an aching burst of emotions and pain. She clutched Charles the bear against her chest, the death of her mom slamming into her body like hurricane-force winds.

The suicide flooded back.

Horrible moments of despair that she couldn't shake, the deep, dark well of pain that she escaped, all of it surged back like a ruptured dam. All of it spiraling through her at Zakhart's touch.

"I'm Heather?"

Zakhart nodded. "Yes," he replied, his voice soft now, barely above a whisper. "And you were supposed to have someone else with you."

"Ross!" She grabbed Zakhart's arms. "Zakhart, what happened to Ross?"

Her whole life, her heart had been injured, weakened. She gasped. Broken. From losses so profound that Zakhart had to block them out so she could go on living. A new life.

The pale angel bowed his head. "Death was faster than we realized. She grabbed you inside the Spiral, but Ross pushed himself between you and Death. She took him instead."

"No," she moaned. "Ross...he was right beside me!" She sank to her knees. "We'd gotten out! We were both safe. Now...he's...he's dead!"

Zakhart caught her, holding her up. "No," he said. "Not yet, anyway."

She gripped Zakhart, hope rising inside her like a plume of warm air. "Where is he? Take me to him! Please!"

"That's part of the problem, Heather. I can't."

Heather frowned. "Why not?" she demanded.

"Razasha and I were close enough to snatch Ross out of Death's hands. But moments after we carried him to safety, the—the whole between...just changed."

"Changed?" Her eyes widened.

Zakhart nodded. "Yes, changed. Something's gone terribly wrong, Heather. We couldn't stop it. We had to run. There was no choice. Ross was lost in the chaos. But I have to go back and do something. If we don't, the between will disappear and so will that last chance for all lost souls. For anyone who chose to end their lives."

"Disappear? The between can disappear?" Heather stared at him in shock.

This couldn't be happening. It was all just a bad dream that she'd wake up from at any moment.

"It can," Zakhart replied. "And worse. If those shadow creatures organize and gain enough ground, they'll spill into the Spiral."

"What happens then?" Heather asked, frightened now.

The pale angel bowed his head. "They can enter the physical world at any point. And take souls from the living, Heather. Take them at will."

"Anyone's soul?"

Zakhart nodded.

She frowned, thousands of thoughts swirling through her head. "Can I still save Ross?"

He'd sacrificed himself to save her, pushing her deeper into the Spiral, away from Death so she could escape. She remembered Rebecca Ross' story, about her brother dying in a car crash. Ross should have been here. Beside her. She imagined hundreds of tortures and terrible things that might be happening to him right now. It made her heart ache and her head rage.

Zakhart nodded. "Things in the between are broken, but they're not lost, Heather. Not yet, at least. Yes, I think you can save him. But it's going to take more than just you, Heather."

"I'm listening," she said, crossing her arms. "Tell me what to do."

Zakhart's gaze fell to the grass, his wings twitching as they folded flat against his back. Finally, he sighed and looked up at her, taking her by the shoulders. His pumpkin-orange eyes darkened, a fire burning in them now.

"The shadow creatures outnumber the lost souls by three to one now. And their numbers are growing. Making it impossible for any lost souls to reach the Spiral. Breaking the balance in the between. That balance has to be restored."

Heather's eyes narrowed. She studied the pale angel who looked nervous and distracted now, wings twitching, gaze shifting away from her.

"What aren't you telling me, Zakhart?"

He sighed. "You have no idea. I'll tell you everything when there's time, but right now. We've got to stop the flood of shadow creatures, stop them from organizing into an unstoppable force."

"Organizing?" she cried. "They're organizing?"

She squeezed her eyes shut, wincing as the answer slammed into her brain. The demons. Before, they pretended to be a place of refuge. Now, they were probably offering their services to all the scattered soulstalkers and dusk creatures throughout the between, bringing them together in the Veils. She gasped. Into an army.

"That's what we have to discover, Heather," Zakhart replied. "Who's organizing them and why?"

"To stop them, we'll have to raise our own army, Zakhart," she replied.

The pale angel smiled. "Exactly. Pale angels, lost souls, and neutrals. We'll have to train ourselves to fight them as one group against this shadow army."

Learn to fight? Heather had never fought anyone before. She'd never even taken a self-defense class or shot a gun before. *How would she learn to fight these creatures?* It seemed impossible, but for Ross, she'd do it.

"There's strength in numbers, Heather," he said, extending his hand to her. "Are you with me?"

She smiled, shaking his hand. "I'm with you. But...how can I go back? Can you take me there somehow?"

He let out a groan, his gaze falling away from her face. He turned away.

"What is it?" she asked, a hand on his sleeve.

"There's only one way in for a human."

The air fled from her lungs, her heart racing.

"Take my own life?" she whispered.

Zakhart winced, nodding.

"It's the only way, Heather. I'm so sorry. I know what I'm asking you to do and I feel horrible for even suggesting it. But you were the only one who could bring all those souls and personalities together. You're our only hope."

Heather motioned toward the parking lot. "What happens to my new family? This is so cruel." She hugged Charles the bear to her chest. What happened to him now? She felt sick inside.

She moved toward the brick wall, pressing her forehead against the cool bricks and closing her eyes. This was unthinkable! She couldn't fathom even attempting that kind of end again. She hadn't felt that bottomless, choking despair this time and hoped she never had to go through that pain again.

Zakhart slid his arm around her shoulders, pulling her close.

"If there was any other way I could do this, Heather, I'd change it in an instant. Believe me, I would. You have my word that I will surround your family and friends with comfort. And I'll keep guardians close and on alert. It's all I can do though."

Heather nodded. She had to give this promising life up. Her eyes welled in tears. Another life wasted. She knew her parents wouldn't survive this. Their marriage would disintegrate now. They'd only kept it together for her anyway.

"Could I ever come back here?" she asked.

Zakhart shook his head. "Don't think so. Once that door closes on a life, it doesn't open again."

She winced, bowing her head. This wasn't her life to keep anyway. She was only here because Ross wasn't. She wasn't supposed to be here. She loved her parents and Grandpa Jimmy. *Maybe she'd get to see them again somehow?*

Charles had seen better days, too. His fur was grey, ears resewn, the two, red hearts that dangled around his neck restuffed. She kissed Charles the bear on top of the head.

"I've got to leave you again, little guy." She sighed and glanced up at the clear blue sky, already missing its vibrant color. "Goodbye again, Bainbridge Island."

She sucked in a breath, pulling the graduation gown over her head. She dropped it on the ground and turned toward Zakhart.

"Okay, how do we do this?"

He held out his arms and she fell into them, her entire body trembling now.

Zakhart lifted her out of the trees, carrying her in his arms across the brilliant gun-metal waters of Elliott Bay, the sun drenching the sun-starved landscape. The air was clean and crisp, cool against her face, stirring up dusty memories from so long ago now, but so important to Heather. Her mom's smile. Her full, flowering laugh that had always filled a room with light. Her deep, quiet insights that had always turned the world at an angle Heather hadn't seen before.

"God, I miss you, Mom," she whispered into the wind.

And Ross' vivid, gold-hazel eyes, bright with a distant hope when everyone else had given up. The warmth of his arms settling around her like a blanket hot from the dryer. The protective stance he took as he walked beside her, ready to defend her from the slightest danger.

She laid her hand against her chest, feeling the unsteady rhythm of blood coursing through her chest, churning up her emotions, percolating the rhythm through her entire body. She'd miss the beat of her heart again with its surge of life and promise of something beyond this fragile place.

For Ross, she'd find another way to create that rhythm of being alive. Until they could go through the Spiral again. Together.

Zakhart landed in the middle of a crowded Seattle sidewalk that ran in front of the ferry terminal. He let Heather go. She turned to stare at the dizzying traffic along Alaskan Way, cars and busses flashing past the tangles of tourists and panhandlers and commuters.

Her stomach lurched. She knew what she had to do.

Glancing left, she saw a little girl, six or seven, sitting on a bench beside her mother. The girl wore lavender pants and a white sweater, her brown hair tied back in a purple bow. Her eyes were rimmed red, tears still clinging to long lashes.

Heather wandered toward the little girl.

"I know you miss Daddy, Michelle," said her mother, an arm around the little girl's shoulders. "Just remember how much he loved you. He'd be here if he could."

"I'm trying, Mommy," said the little girl named Michelle. "Sometimes it's just too hard."

"I know." Her mom kissed her on top of the head and pulled her into a quick hug. "Someday, it won't hurt quite so much. He'd have been here today for your tests, honey, if he could. Know that, okay?"

The little girl nodded. "I know, but I'll never stop missing him."

Heather knelt in front of the little girl and her mother sat up straight, a wary look on her face.

"Can I help you?" the woman asked.

"Hi," said Heather, smiling, and extending Charles toward the little girl. "I'm trying to find a home for one of my best buddies. And you look like you might need a new friend right now."

Eyes grew wide and a grin curved across the little girl's face as she stared at Heather's greying sparkly bear. "Can I, Mommy?"

Her mom scrutinized the small, stuffed bear and finally nodded. "All right. Thank you, yes. That's very sweet."

Heather gently placed Charles in Michelle's lap. The little girl scooped him up and clasped him to her chest.

For a moment, the greying bear sparkled and turned pearly white, grime and Frankenstein stitching disappearing into a hazy glow. Heather blinked. Charles looked brand new again. She glanced over at Zakhart who looked away.

"His name's Charles the bear," said Heather, standing up. "Please take good care of him. And he'll take good care of you."

"Thank you," said Michelle, smiling now, the tears drying as she cradled the bear. "He's so beautiful!"

Heather patted her on the head and walked away, unable to stand losing her little bear for a second time.

She walked with slow, deliberate steps toward the busy street, feeling Zakhart walking beside her now, his hand cradling hers.

"I'll make this as easy as I can, Heather, I promise," he whispered.

She nodded, reaching the curb. Her heart hammered against her chest and throbbed into her ears, fingers turning cold as fear washed over her. She balanced on the curb's edge, watching the traffic.

"I'm scared, Zakhart," she muttered.

To her left, the air shimmered and Razasha appeared beside her. Smiling, she reached out and took hold of Heather's left hand, squeezing it tight.

"I know," he said, his voice sad. "I'll be with you the entire time, Heather."

Nodding, Heather swallowed hard and glanced to her right. Zakhart gripped her right hand in his, his face a taut mask of emotion.

Cars and trucks rushed past. Sidewalks flooded with people. Horns honking. Ferry horn blasting in a single long note.

Behind her, someone coughed. A gull laughed, its shadow flitting overhead.

The city bus lurched toward the intersection, surging to the next bus stop beside the ferry terminal. Heather's heart bounced into her throat, pounding a frantic I-don't-want-to-die-again staccato through her entire body. She stiffened, closing her eyes.

I'll do this for you, Ross. Because I love you.

Taking a deep breath, Heather set herself and stepped in front of the bus.

The End of Between, Book 1: The Spiral Series

The story continues in…
Reprise, Book 2: The Spiral Series
(Preorder now! Releases 7/30/23!)

A love in danger. A painful return to a dark past. A broken heart. She'll give up everything to fix it.

NOVELS BY LISA SILVERTHORNE

Standalones:

ISABEL'S TEARS

LANDFALL

PACIFIC BLUE TATTOO

A Game of Lost Souls series:

THE CINDERELLA HOUR

THE PRINCE CHARMING HOUR

THE EVER AFTER HOUR

THE FALLEN HEARTS SEASON

THE RISING SPIRITS SEASON

THE ETERNAL SOULS SEASON

THE ROYAL WEDDING HOUR

THE HEAVENLY HONEYMOON HOUR

THE DIVINE NEWLYWEDS SHOW

THE CELESTIAL COUPLES SHOW

The Spiral series:

BETWEEN

REPRISE

(*releases 7/30/23*)

SHORT STORY COLLECTIONS

THE SOUND OF ANGELS

THE MAGIC OF ORDINARY THINGS

SCIENCE FICTION WRITING AS L.S. SILVERTHORNE

Standalones:

REDISCOVERY

Experiencing True Purple series:

RECOMBINANT, Book 1

HELIX, Book 2

FORTHCOMING

A Game of Lost Souls series:

The Enochian Apocalypse Show, Book Eleven

The Angelic Anniversary Hour, Book Twelve

The Spiral series:

Avenge, Book 3

Ruin, Book 4

Descent, Book 5

The Resurrectionist Papers:

A ROMANTIC FANTASY MYSTERY SERIES

Grave Reckoning, Book 1

Corpses Delicti, Book 2

Stiffed Again, Book 3

SCIENCE FICTION WRITING AS L.S. SILVERTHORNE

Experiencing True Purple series:

Splice, Book 3 (coming in 2023!)

Cipher, Book 4

Renascence, Book 5

LISA SILVERTHORNE
ISABEL'S TEARS
Magical sea glass.
A century-old abandoned inn.
Two drowned lovers.
Murdered, says the bride's ghost.

LISA SILVERTHORNE
EVER AFTERS ON WINGS

about the author

LISA SILVERTHORNE has published over 20 novels and 150 short stories and novelettes in many genres. She is the author of **A Game of Lost Souls** series, **Experiencing True Purple** series, the new **Spiral** series, and the upcoming **The Resurrectionist Papers**. She lives in Las Vegas, Nevada.

Before you go, you are invited to please leave a **review of this book**!

Reviews are a wonderful way to help an author. They are also an exciting opportunity to share your honest thoughts with other readers, so **please post yours,** in as many places as possible!

* 9 7 8 1 9 5 5 1 9 7 3 8 0 *